PRAISE FOR
The House on Biscayne Bay

"Chanel Cleeton goes Gothic with her latest, and it's a smashing success! *The House on Biscayne Bay* is a splashy, atmospheric thrill ride!"

—Kate Quinn, *New York Times*
bestselling author of *The Diamond Eye*

"*The House on Biscayne Bay* has it all—glitz, glamor, and a mesmerizing murder. This haunting tale is gorgeously written and will keep you riveted until the end. Such a fabulous read!"

—Madeline Martin, *New York Times*
bestselling author of *The Librarian Spy*

"Chanel Cleeton never disappoints. Her books bring history to life with gorgeous prose, nuanced heroines, and enough scandal, mystery, and glamour to keep readers turning the pages. *The House on Biscayne Bay* is a haunting, atmospheric novel about buried secrets and forbidden love. I couldn't put it down."

—Cristina Alger, *New York Times*
bestselling author of *Girls Like Us*

"A mysterious but very glamorous mansion, sensational secrets, and a story spanning several decades are the ideal cocktail, and they're mixed to perfection here by a brilliant storyteller. I guarantee you'll race through the pages of this thrilling, Gothic tale, while at the same time wanting to linger a little longer amongst the beautiful but haunted people gathered together at the house on Biscayne Bay."

—Natasha Lester, *New York Times*
bestselling author of *The Paris Orphan*

"*The House on Biscayne Bay* shows a new facet of Chanel Cleeton's talent, and I'm utterly enthralled—between the hair-raising character that is the house, the expertly crafted murder mystery, a dash of romance, and quick pace, I couldn't put it down for a moment. Brilliantly done!"

—Evie Dunmore, *USA Today*
bestselling author of *Portrait of a Scotsman*

"Lush, evocative, and shimmering with Gothic eeriness, *The House on Biscayne Bay* is a riveting page-turner with two dynamic women at its core. Chanel Cleeton's marvelous writing drew me in from the first page and kept me riveted to the last. Unputdownable!"

—Mimi Matthews, *USA Today*
bestselling author of *The Belle of Belgrave Square*

"I devoured this lush, propulsive, and twisty Gothic in one sitting. *The House on Biscayne Bay* is an atmospheric and haunting tale with deliciously tense scenes and superbly delivered surprises. With Chanel Cleeton's expertly rendered historical detail and evocative imagery, this haunting and atmospheric novel is the perfect read."

—Adriana Herrera, *USA Today*
bestselling author of *An Island Princess Starts a Scandal*

PRAISE FOR THE NOVELS OF
CHANEL CLEETON

"A beautiful novel that's full of forbidden passions, family secrets, and a lot of courage and sacrifice."

—Reese Witherspoon

"A sweeping love story and tale of courage and familial and patriotic legacy that spans generations."

—*Entertainment Weekly*

"*Next Year in Havana* reminds us that while love is complicated and occasionally heartbreaking, it's always worth the risk."

—NPR

"A thrilling story about love, loss, and what we will do to go home again. Utterly unputdownable."

—PopSugar

"A remarkable writer."   —*The Washington Post*

"You won't be able to put this one down."   —*Cosmopolitan*

BERKLEY TITLES BY CHANEL CLEETON

Next Year in Havana

When We Left Cuba

The Last Train to Key West

The Most Beautiful Girl in Cuba

Our Last Days in Barcelona

The Cuban Heiress

The House on Biscayne Bay

THE HOUSE ON
BISCAYNE BAY

CHANEL CLEETON

BERKLEY

New York

BERKLEY
An imprint of Penguin Random House LLC
penguinrandomhouse.com

Copyright © 2024 by Chanel Cleeton
Readers Guide copyright © 2024 by Chanel Cleeton
Penguin Random House supports copyright. Copyright fuels creativity, encourages
diverse voices, promotes free speech, and creates a vibrant culture. Thank you for
buying an authorized edition of this book and for complying with copyright laws by
not reproducing, scanning, or distributing any part of it in any form without permission.
You are supporting writers and allowing Penguin Random House
to continue to publish books for every reader.

BERKLEY is a registered trademark and the B colophon
is a trademark of Penguin Random House LLC.

Library of Congress Cataloging-in-Publication Data

Names: Cleeton, Chanel, author.
Title: The house on Biscayne Bay / Chanel Cleeton.
Description: New York: Berkley, 2024.
Identifiers: LCCN 2023034732 (print) | LCCN 2023034733 (ebook) |
ISBN 9780593440513 (paperback) | ISBN 9780593440506 (hardcover) |
ISBN 9780593440520 (ebook)
Subjects: LCGFT: Novels.
Classification: LCC PS3603.L455445 H68 2024 (print) |
LCC PS3603.L455445 (ebook) | DDC 813/.6—dc23/eng/20230828
LC record available at https://lccn.loc.gov/2023034732
LC ebook record available at https://lccn.loc.gov/2023034733

First Edition: April 2024

Printed in the United States of America
1st Printing

Book design by Katy Riegel

To Miami . . .

for everything

THE HOUSE ON
BISCAYNE
BAY

CHAPTER ONE

Anna

I cannot for the life of me imagine why anyone would want to live in Florida.

The house looms before me, a pale stone behemoth jettisoning from the swampy earth. It casts a long shadow, towering three stories high with a parapet on top as though it's readying itself to guard against intruders. Its palatial size and exterior appear to have been plucked from some European city and dropped on this godforsaken plot of land in Miami. There are arches and flourishes all around the building, the fanciful embellishments reminiscent of a wedding cake's intricate design. Enormous glass-paned windows dominate the facade, equally impressive doors leading out to a front patio set atop a stone staircase made of the palest coral that matches the house's exterior walls.

The grass sways a few feet away conjuring images of snakes slithering through the tall blades. What sort of reptiles do they have in Florida? Large ones capable of felling a full-grown person? This feels like the end of civilization as we know it—a far cry from Manhattan and the sensibilities we have grown accustomed to.

The house is nearing completion, the progress an undeniable sign of just how long my husband has been keeping this secret.

Robert took me to Italy for our honeymoon years ago, and it appears he gathered a great deal of his inspiration from the grand houses we saw on our trip there.

There weren't alligators in Italy, though.

And it wasn't this hot.

A thin line of sweat trickles between my shoulder blades, my already dampened gown sticking to my skin as I trudge away from my husband's roadster toward our future home. As a little girl sitting in the pews of St. Patrick's Cathedral in New York City, I often thought about the fires of hell as I prayed for my immortal soul. I envisioned the devil's playground to have a climate like this one, but in all my wild imaginings, Lucifer didn't have lizards.

Men mill about the property, working on the construction Robert has planned. It looks to be rough work, heavy pieces of stone being carried from one side of the house to another, the radiant sun beating down on the men. It must be hell doing such strenuous physical labor in this stifling heat.

A few cast curious glances our way, no doubt wanting to get a measure of the new owners; some low chuckles drift toward us, and my cheeks burn as I realize they're likely laughing at *me* and how out of place I look in such a rugged environment. When Robert told me he was taking me for a trip to Miami for my birthday, I fancied a romantic weekend at one of the luxurious resorts that have cropped up along Florida's east coast. I thought the surprise he mentioned would be an elegant necklace or perhaps a pair of earrings. After all, forty feels like a momentous occasion that should be marked, albeit with something smaller than real estate.

"What do you think, Anna?" my husband asks, spreading his arms out expansively as though he could encompass the whole of the property in his reach, seemingly oblivious to my obvious discomfort. "Isn't it amazing? There's no other house for as far as the eye can see and then some."

I'm saved from a response by an insect swarming perilously close to my face.

It hovers in midair, likely calculating its plan of attack, before it finally retreats with an irate buzz as though recognizing me as an interloper and reluctantly ceding its territory.

I wish I could hie off with it.

There are those who hate city life, the houses close together, the streets teeming with people, the noise, and the bustle, but I've grown accustomed to it, find familiarity in the sounds that play in the background of my days.

The silence here is deafening.

"Anna?" Robert asks again.

I take a deep breath, lifting my skirt out of the swampy muck.

"I would like to see the rest of it," I announce, biting back a string of blistering curses.

"You should see the best part," Robert announces, pointing past the house to the view of Biscayne Bay. "You can't put a price on this location."

I could, and my price would have one zero attached to it

whereas I fear Robert's has quite a few dangling behind an astonishing number.

I trudge past the house, and I walk toward the water's edge, careful to keep a healthy distance between me and the bay. I've always had an uneasy relationship with the ocean. It's lovely to look at, but never having learned to swim, I am terrified by the crashing waves.

The closer we get to the bay, the breeze grows, offering a respite from the heat.

The water is undeniably stunning, sparkling beneath the sunlight, nothing but horizon before us. For an instant, a breath, I can understand what drew Robert to the property. I imagine there's a great deal you would put up with for a vista such as this one.

I glance down at the rocky seawall, a nearly six-foot drop between the land and the water. The turquoise sea crashes against the coral, forming white foamy caps. It's an abrupt change from land to ocean; should we put up a railing or something for safety?

Robert laughs when I posit the question. "And ruin the view? Besides, to do it the length of the property would cost an absolute fortune. We'd be better off just heaving our money into Biscayne Bay."

It feels like we're already doing that.

"What about hurricanes?" I ask, turning back to face Robert lingering behind me.

"The architect working on the house has built it to withstand hurricanes."

Is such a thing possible? It seems hubristic to assume that anything man makes can meet Mother Nature's fury.

I turn and peer over the edge of the seawall. Fish flit back and forth beneath the water, their bright colors like vibrant jewels flashing in the sunlight.

You don't see that in New York, I suppose.

I lean forward—

A bloodcurdling shriek peals through the air.

My shoes slip on the wet ground below, my legs shaking, my body lurching forward—

A hand settles on my waist, fingers curving around my dress, settling just above my hip bones, tugging me backward away from the sea.

I jump, startled by the motion, my heart thumping wildly as I struggle to get my rattled nerves under control.

"Wh—what was that?"

"Peacock," Robert answers, his voice in my ear, his breath hot against my neck. His fingers dig into the soft flesh at my waist. "They're loud birds and they're all over the property."

I swallow, the rush of fear leaving a bitter, acidic taste in my throat. "It sounded human."

He chuckles, his fingers stroking over my waist as though soothing a skittish animal. "I had the same thought the first time I heard them. You get used to it."

Somehow, I doubt that.

I turn to move out of his grasp, but Robert doesn't let me go.

"Be careful. We've already had a worker fall into the water during the construction."

I swallow, the sea no longer looking so pretty or the fish so enticing. "What happened to him?"

"He drowned or so I'm told."

"How horrible. Poor man."

I glance back at the house, trying to imagine living here knowing that I'm only hundreds of yards away from where a man lost his life.

"It's not very deep, but if you're too short to stand and you can't swim, it doesn't really matter, does it?" Robert muses.

I want to go back to New York.

Oh, it's beautiful on the bay to be sure, the way deadly things can be beautiful. The water is a lovely sparkling shade of blue, the sun shines brightly, and the trees and palms are a vibrant green. If you cast your gaze in the right direction, it is possible to see nothing but unending sea. It's a beautiful place, which is likely what leads so many to their folly in the first place—they believe they can make it theirs when it's obvious Miami is its own entity, stubborn and unwilling to bend to another's conception of what it could be.

I imagine there is a type of person who would thrive here, one who can see the beauty that lingers amid the danger, who can put down roots in this perilous place where the ever-present risk of a hurricane threatens to upend them, but that person is certainly not me. I don't belong here.

"It's surely a grand piece of property," I say, choosing my words carefully, because undeniably, it is that, with this panoramic view of Biscayne Bay, and given the state of near-finished construction and Robert's nature, what choice do I have? His mind is clearly already made up. "And a far too generous birthday gift."

I wrap my arms around Robert and press my lips to his. His

whiskers are coarse against my skin as our mouths meet, twenty-two years of marriage in the gesture. I like to think that I know Robert better than anyone, that as a wife I can predict his moves before he makes them, but here he has caught me entirely unawares.

If my husband can hide a plan as enormous as this one, what other secrets does he have up his sleeve?

Robert releases me, his hands lingering on my waist for a moment before setting me aside. I duck my head, embarrassment filling me as I remember the workers lingering around the property privy to this emotional display.

Love and frustration wind their way inside me like twin snakes. If twenty-two years of marriage have taught me anything, it's to choose my battles. I wish he'd asked what I thought before he bought the damned place, but the genius of all of this is that in bestowing the property to me as a birthday gift, he neatly backed me into a corner. To refuse or complain would make me appear ungrateful. If he had consulted me, I would have told him that I have no desire to live among bugs the size of small dogs, the lace fan I brought woefully inadequate to combat the heat and humidity. If he had consulted me, I might have been able to head this impending disaster off at the pass as I have so many of Robert's other more questionable ideas.

"We'll have the largest estate anyone in South Florida has ever seen," Robert announces.

What will it matter if no one ever wants to visit us here? And truthfully, I can't imagine why anyone would. The ocean is beautiful, yes, and the sun is shining brightly even if it is abominably strong, but we have sun and sea in Newport, and our bugs are a more respectable size. This place looks as though it would just as soon kill you as welcome you, and I half expect to see an overgrown alligator tottering by. For all intents and purposes, this might as well be the end of the world, and if it must be Florida—*why must it be Florida?*—I for one would vastly prefer to head north a bit and brave the wilds of Mr. Flagler's Palm Beach over Miami.

Part of marrying a man who builds things, who invests in the future, who sees opportunity where others view obstacles is that your life becomes a lesson in going along with plans you don't quite agree with yourself, in keeping quiet when faced with something that could be either a fantastic stroke of genius or utter folly.

Robert is a talented businessman whose hunches nearly always pay off, but this vision of his seems far too ambitious.

"It's a bit remote," I say hesitantly. "Although, I'm sure the warm climate will be welcome when winter comes," I add when he frowns.

We're both getting older—Robert twenty years my senior—so perhaps the more temperate weather will be a welcome change. With every year, it feels as though my body becomes more vulnerable, more susceptible to the strange aches and pains that come with time, the blistering cold certainly no friend of mine.

Robert smiles. "That it will. Mark my words—in a few years, everyone will want to come to Florida, and we'll have the most magnificent mansion in all of Miami, perhaps even the entire state."

Considering Whitehall, the impressive estate that Henry Flagler built in Palm Beach prior to his death, it's a lofty goal.

Robert's enthusiasm is nearly infectious, his charm such that I can almost believe him that anything is possible, that if anyone can transform this wild landscape into a manicured estate, it's him.

Robert's gaze drifts beyond me to some point off in the horizon. "Here he is now, the man who is going to bring this vision to life. The architect."

I turn, and Robert gestures toward a man standing over a makeshift table off in the distance with his back to us, hunched over a set of papers. I didn't notice him at first, my attention firmly on the marital problem at hand.

"Michael," he calls out.

The architect turns away from his sawhorses and plank slowly, reluctantly, almost. He's a tall, lean man, younger at first glance than I would have envisioned for a project of this magnitude. Unnervingly young.

Is this the first house he's ever built?

The architect smiles, making his way to us in quick, sure strides I can't help but envy considering the challenge of traipsing around the swampy ground in my impractical heels.

He exchanges a friendly greeting with Robert—his coconspirator in this audacious plan—before turning his attention to me.

"Michael Harrison at your service," he says, extending his hand to me.

"Anna Barnes," I reply, the warmth in my voice closer to New York than Miami.

You can gauge a lot about a person from their hands, and his tell the story of a man who isn't afraid to work with them, rough calluses adorning his skin. His long fingers are covered in smudged ink, and he has a bit of a zealous, dazed look in his eyes that calls to mind Frankenstein at work in his laboratory. Mr. Harrison isn't really looking at me; he's too busy surveying the landscape around him, and it's fascinating the way I can practically see his mind working on the project before him even as he's forced to engage in the social niceties at hand.

"Excuse me for a moment." Mr. Harrison releases me, reaching into the interior pocket of his suit jacket. He pulls out a tattered brown leather notebook, the edges cracked and peeling, a little pencil attached to the side, and begins scribbling something on the creamy pages, pausing every so often to gaze out at the water and back to his writing again.

It's obvious why Robert liked him for the project.

Instantly, I see our bank accounts dwindling, our days spent in this monstrosity of a home. It's clear that in this Mr. Harrison, my husband has found the partner he longs for, someone who sees his vision in a way I will never, and I have no doubt they will fuel each other until this house becomes bigger, grander, until it ruins us.

Mr. Harrison must go.

"What do you think of your new home?" Mr. Harrison asks after he has tucked away his notebook, whatever inspiration seized him swept aside.

"It's certainly large," I reply, choosing my words carefully. "A project of this scope must take a great deal of time."

And money.

I have no concept of the wealth Robert has amassed in his career—there are some things husbands do not speak of with their wives—but it certainly appears to be comfortable enough to sustain us in our days and care for us when we have no children to do so. Hopefully, it's enough to support me once Robert has left this earth and I am all alone.

That is, unless we're beggared by ambition.

Mr. Harrison's eyes widen slightly, seemingly registering the chill in my voice that doesn't match the smile on my face.

My high heels sink deeper into the muck, the wet ground darkening another inch of hemline.

It rained last night while Robert and I made love in our hotel room on Miami Beach, a violent, lashing storm that had me clutching the snowy white covers to my chin afterward while Robert lay beside me, the sound of his snores punctuated by the rolling thunder.

"Here's the gardener," Robert interjects. "Why don't you stay and talk to Mr. Harrison about the plans for the house while I speak with the gardener about some trees I'm having shipped in?"

He's already striding away before I can respond.

"How was your journey down to Miami?" Mr. Harrison asks as I stare after Robert's back. It's not the first time I've wished to strangle my husband, and it won't be the last, but the desire is there, swift and unrelenting.

Are there not enough trees surrounding us? Why on earth would he have to ship them in? And from where?

"Long, but comfortable. We came by way of Mr. Flagler's railroad, of course," I answer, my mind already untangling the massive problem of scaling down Robert's ambition. Mr. Harrison isn't the only one capable of achieving multiple aims at once.

"We owe Mr. Flagler a great debt for the effect his railroad has had," Mr. Harrison comments.

"Yes, I suppose we do."

Henry Flagler's Florida East Coast Railway has done much to boost tourism to the state, connecting the country in ways previously unimaginable. Now, passengers can travel by rail to Key West, enabling tourists to enjoy the resort towns that have cropped up along Florida's coast. Whether the railroad will convert the state into the tourist destination my husband believes it to be remains to be seen.

"What would you like for your new home to have?" Mr. Harrison asks me, turning his attention back to the house.

An address in Rhode Island.

"What did my husband suggest?"

The entire backside of the estate is almost entirely made of glass to showcase the view of the bay. The ground floor of the house opens to an enormous patio that, judging by the stones being laid out by some of the workers, is nearing completion. It's a house built for lavish parties and entertaining, an estate that is made to show off, to impress, to awe.

"He said he wanted a home fit for a king—and queen, of course." He says the last part with a smile that suggests Mr. Harrison isn't wholly unaware of my growing animosity and somehow, impossibly, now thinks to charm me. "We shared some ideas for the construction of the main residence, but he's said little about the rest of the property. I have some thoughts on that front, but I'd like to get your input as well. After all, you'll be living here, too. He mentioned that this was a surprise of sorts for you."

"It certainly was. A birthday present, if you can believe it."

He whistles low. "That's some birthday present."

"Robert has always been prone to grand gestures."

It's a trait my friends have forever envied. When their husbands were too tight to buy them that necklace they had been dreaming of, Robert invariably would present me with a grand pair of earrings that rested in a glass jewelry case next to a more modest pair I loved.

"Have you been to Florida before?" Mr. Harrison asks me.

"No. My husband has. In fact, Robert came down here on business several months ago." At the time, I didn't think much of it, but clearly, that was what set this whole thing in motion, the trips that followed his opportunity to keep up with the construction progress.

"That's how we met," Mr. Harrison replies. "At a party at Vizcaya hosted by James Deering."

"It must have made an impression on Robert to have led him to do such a thing."

"I think it did. He was quite staggered by the place. Then again, Vizcaya tends to have that effect."

"Is the home that grand?"

"It is. Vizcaya has brought the Mediterranean to Florida." A small smile touches Mr. Harrison's lips. "Now others must follow suit."

"Don't tell me my husband intends for this house to rival Vizcaya?"

"I think he does."

"And you, Mr. Harrison? What is your professional opinion?"

"Well, Vizcaya is lovely. And your estate will undoubtedly be so. But your new home should be unique. I've always thought that the projects I build should reflect the people who live in them. Up until now, I've only had a chance to get to know your husband. I'll confess I was curious about your desires for the house, to make sure that I was meeting your needs as well."

My face must show my true emotions because he asks—

"Would you prefer something smaller?"

"Maybe. Something cozy, I suppose. I always thought you should go to the beach to escape the stifling nature of society. To be alone with your thoughts and to simply enjoy the sun and the sea." I shrug. "It seems like the fashion is to make each beach home more formal than the last—after all, look at Newport."

"I wasn't aiming for something as austere as those mansions. More a house that is open, that enables you to enjoy the natural landscape around you. Gardens and the like. Glass windows so that you can admire the sea from the house's main rooms."

"A project of this scale must be challenging."

"It is."

"Robert told me that one of the men involved in the construction drowned."

Mr. Harrison frowns. "He did. It was a terrible day. Fortunately, we haven't had any other deaths. It can be a dangerous business. It isn't the first accident we've had."

"What else has happened?"

"A man fell off a scaffolding while he was working on one of the second-floor windows. Miraculously, he escaped with just a few broken bones. It's grueling, demanding work being out in the heat, going from sunrise to sunset." He gestures toward the papers on the makeshift table before him. "Would you like to see the plans?"

There's a word scrawled on the papers, the name for the house.

Marbrisa.

I trace over the letters there, recognizing the finality of them, the permanence. This house is here to stay whether I like it or not.

"Who came up with the name?" I ask him.

He flushes. "I did. I thought it was a name that suited the house. I was standing here looking at the sea and I wanted to capture the essence of the breeze on my face, the bay before me. One of the men working on the seawall helped me find the right words in Spanish. Your husband liked it, but if you wish to change it, we can."

"No, you're right. It suits."

My gaze drifts down to his renderings, trying to make sense of the proportions of the rooms, the layout that he has envisioned for how our life will be arranged. It's such an intimate thing to order someone's life like this, and Mr. Harrison has done it down to the inch.

Our home in New York is nowhere near this grand, but then again, I suppose in a tightly packed city, a sprawling manse of this size is too difficult a proposition. Those who have made their mark on New York have already done so, their legacies in brick and stone, their names forever memorialized on libraries and museums, streets and homes.

"Do you like the plans for the house?"

It feels somewhat indelicate to criticize a man's work, but I can't summon the passion for this place that he and Robert have.

"It seems silly to have a house this size for just two people. And to be honest, I've never been overly fond of elaborate parties." I know how I must sound—how boring I must seem. But the truth is, I have always been happiest when my life was simple. "Oh, I know it's what is done, and I know how badly Robert wants this, but—"

"You don't share his vision?" Mr. Harrison finishes for me.

"No. I don't. I'm not even sure this is his vision anymore. It seems like this place has taken on a life of its own."

Mr. Harrison smiles. "You've caught that, haven't you? Homes, great homes, tell their own stories. Their past, their present, and their future are written on their walls, etched in their stone pavers, dangling from the rafters in glittering chandeliers that twinkle like stars."

"I had no idea building was so poetic."

He laughs. "Maybe that's just what we tell ourselves when we spend so much of our time and labor on a project that it naturally takes on a life of its own. I like to think of the houses I build as having their own personalities. Oh, there's the people who are their custodians to consider, of course, a symbiosis in the relationship between the house and its owner, but some-times these grand estates have a way of forcing their residents to their will, of bending and shaping the trajectory of their lives. After all, when our bones turn to dust, these walls will still stand."

"My, Mr. Harrison, with imagery like that, I almost feel like I should half fear the house. You speak of it as though it is an almighty power indeed. Will it bring about my destruction or be my salvation?"

I try to inject as much humor as I can in my words, but there's also an undeniable truth in them, the feeling that we are hurtling toward some danger I wish we could avoid. This house looming behind me seems like the physical manifesta-tion of the legacy Robert was never able to create on his own—the children we were unable to have.

"The latter, if I have my way. Everyone is hoping the house will do for the area what Vizcaya did for Miami—bring jobs. A project of this size can support a great many households. Now that the Great War is over, there will be a considerable number of men in search of employment."

"Yes, but who knows what the world will look like now that the war has ended. It seems like a dangerous time to take a risk like this one."

"Is there ever truly a good time to take risks? After all, the greatest reward comes from daring in times of uncertainty."

"Has he convinced you yet?" Robert asks, striding to-ward us.

"Mr. Harrison is clearly passionate about the project." I take a deep breath. "I just hope it's not too much house for us."

"Anna's always the practical one," Robert says with a smile for his architect, more amusement than affection in his voice.

I was raised to be practical, in a household that wanted for nothing but also brooked no excess. My clothes were always well-made, but never too fine, our house comfortable but never garish.

"Is there anything you'd like me to add to the house for you?" Mr. Harrison asks me.

"I like to garden." It's not a hobby I've had much occasion to indulge in the city, but when I was a child, my mother and I loved working in her small garden.

Mr. Harrison smiles. "Then gardens you shall have."

We tour the inside of the estate, each room seemingly larger and grander than the last. Robert and Mr. Harrison speak about their plans for the house a bit longer, and I listen half-heartedly, scrambling to keep up with all the ways in which my life has changed in the span of a few hours.

On our way out, as I climb into Robert's roadster, I glance back at the house, the wind blowing my hair in my face, slashing in front of me, obscuring my vision for a moment. The house stands before me, taunting me, looming large over the men working on the grounds.

How is this to be our future home?

I keep looking back as we maneuver down the long driveway, the house growing smaller and smaller in the distance. Someone had the idea of flanking the entryway with towering palm trees, several already planted, many more to go.

The car slams to a stop.

I lurch forward, my arm jutting out to brace myself.

"What's wrong?" I ask, turning to look at Robert, my heart pounding as I think about how close I came to hitting the windshield in front of me.

"Peacock crossing," Robert announces, amusement in his voice as he watches the feathered animals prance and preen in front of our car as they cross from one side of our street to the other. "You don't see that every day in New York."

I take a deep breath, trying to still my racing heart, to catch my breath. I blink, my eyes playing tricks on me, and for a moment, I can hear the loud thud that would have sounded if my head had hit the windshield, can see the sharp crack that would have run down the glass.

How can Robert be so calm? How can he be so careless?

I open my mouth to complain about him braking too recklessly, to ask him to be more careful when he drives, to remind him that the roads are unfamiliar to us here, unused to automobile tires treading over them, all sorts of perils and twists in our path.

I'm saved the effort by more peacocks, my husband's attention firmly on their progress to the side of the road.

The male peacock passes by us, his colorful plumed feathers standing proudly as he struts in front of the car, and then we're off, my husband's folly behind us.

CHAPTER TWO

Carmen

B e careful," the boat captain shouts over the noise of the mo-
tor, the sleek little vessel cutting through the foam-capped
waves of Biscayne Bay. "We wouldn't want to lose you to the
water. It isn't that deep, but if you can't swim—"

"I can swim," I call back, but the poor man seems so unsettled by the prospect of having to tell my sister and brother-
in-law that I was injured in his care that I lean away from the
edge, the break of the waves jostling us once more.

If my plan to have my brother-in-law Asher grant me control
of my fortune is going to be successful, I need to give him the
impression that I am responsible and trustworthy, and making
a good impression on his employees seems like a prudent start.

The boat captain looks momentarily stricken by his words,
and I wonder if Asher told him what happened, prepared him
for the possibility that I would be afraid of the water.

There was a horrific accident at sea, I imagine Asher saying.
Her parents drowned.

I can understand why he might do so, considering my parents went boating and were killed in a storm. It would be natural for me to hate the thing that killed them. But if I've learned anything in the three weeks since I've become an orphan, it's that grief does not follow logic or reason. My feelings come to me in the oddest moments, my reactions wholly unpredictable. Grief is changeable, capricious, and cruel.

Off in the distance, the shoreline beckons, the estate coming into view ahead.

It's easy to see why my sister Carolina wanted to live in a place like this.

I think I'm going to like Florida.

The wind whips my hair around, blowing the gauzy scarf I hastily tied around my coiffure, momentarily obscuring the house as the boat charges toward our destination. A spray of seawater hits my face, and then another, the captain cautioning me to sit down, the ocean rough today. I've had enough of sitting lately—in church pews and funeral homes—my grief suffocating. It feels good to let go, to enjoy the feel of the air in my lungs, the wind in my face, to be away from prying eyes and whispers.

It feels good to put Cuba behind me, to set my sights on my future and the possibility of what's to come. Even before my parents passed away, I was ready to get off the island, begging them to let me attend university in the United States, to experience more of the world than what I had seen so far. I just wish it hadn't taken such a tremendous loss to set me on my way.

A gust hits the tender, lifting the scarf off my head, sending it floating through the air in front of me.

A shriek escapes my lips and I reach out, grabbing at the fabric, the house coming into view once more. I can just make out the silhouette of a figure standing somewhere on the shores of Marbrisa—a woman—my sister Carolina, perhaps. Her dress blows in the wind, the dark color a stark contrast to the palette of greens and blues of the landscape ahead.

I catch hold of the scarf, gripping it in my fist, the boat lurching once more, the house in view again.

The woman is gone, and in her place is a man, little more than a speck in the grass standing in front of the immense manse my older sister and her husband call home.

As the tender motors closer to the dock, the man grows larger, standing near the water's edge, his feet planted as though bracing himself for something singularly unpleasant, his jacket discarded somewhere along the way, his arms shoved in his pockets, his shirt rumpled.

He's slight of build and fair-haired, and I recognize him instantly from the last time we saw each other—my brother-in-law Asher Wyatt.

The small boat idles toward the dock, and the full impact of the house hits me all at once.

We have grand homes in Havana, so I can't say it's the size that makes the greatest impression or the formality of the thing, but rather it is the totality of all that Marbrisa is that stuns.

I've never seen an estate like it.

It isn't a house; it's a work of art.

The grounds are elaborate, the emphasis clearly on the gardens and the lush greenery as well as the view of the water. It looks like someone took a grand European mansion and transported it to Florida. I half expect a duke or duchess to walk out and greet me, which must suit my sister Carolina perfectly. It is an estate filled with drama and glamour, two characteristics my elder sister has in spades.

The driver turns off the boat and ties it up, helping me onto the dock before returning for my suitcases.

I take a deep breath, belatedly realizing my hair is a mess from the boat ride and the wind, the scarf I tied to keep it tidy failing to do its job. Oh well. If Asher was expecting me to be like my sister, he's bound to be disappointed.

Asher strides toward me, looking perfectly at home with the specter of the house behind him. If I were an artist, I would paint a portrait of the tableau before me. All that's missing is Carolina draped in jewels beside him.

"Carmen," he says in greeting, walking toward me. He presses a kiss to my cheek; his lips are cool against my skin, a hint of whiskey on his breath.

Despite our relation by marriage, my brother-in-law is little more than a stranger, and I can count on one hand the number of times we've met. There's one memory I have of him, the first time I ever saw him—I must have been twelve years old. He was coming to dinner, to our house in Havana, to meet our parents. Carolina had been insufferable all week in advance of his visit, so sure that the rich American she had met in Miami when she'd traveled there with family friends was going to ask our father for her hand in marriage, more temperamental than usual in case things didn't go as she planned. I had done my best to keep out of her way, the whole house had, and I pled a cold to stay in my room that evening, to escape what I assumed would be a stuffy dinner with boring adults. After all, Asher Wyatt was a full seven years older than my sister, thirteen years older than me.

But the man I caught sight of when I peered out my window at the sound of a motorcar approaching our driveway wasn't the old man my twelve-year-old self foolishly had envisioned. He looked dashing getting out of his convertible, his skin tanned, his smile wide, and I added Asher Wyatt to the list of things I envied about my exciting, glamorous sister.

I'd barely recognize him now.

Despite the strength of the Miami sun bearing down upon us, my brother-in-law looks as though he's been locked away in his office, his skin pale and papery thin. His expression is drawn, his body slighter than I remembered.

He looks terrible.

"It's good to see you again," he says, his tone devoid of any warmth or welcome, a chill in his manner that has me taking an instinctive step back.

Has something happened?

"Is Carolina alright?"

"Your sister is sorry she couldn't make it. She was unavoidably detained."

I open my mouth to ask him what has happened; surely, if Carolina couldn't be here, there must be a good reason.

Since my parents' demise three weeks ago, I've spent a lot of time considering my options, trying to comprehend how my future changed so rapidly. There were distant cousins in

Havana that I could have stayed with—our immediate family was quite small—but since my father had entrusted Asher with the administration of my inheritance, going to live with my sister and her husband seemed like the most prudent option.

Truthfully, the cousins appeared relieved.

I expected a warmer welcome, though. In my more fanciful moments, I envisioned a tender family reunion. After all, in times of loss, it seems natural that one would want to cleave to their family.

A bird caws off in the distance, somewhere on the estate, the sound cutting off my response and skating across the water until it is engulfed in the roar of the wind and the waves.

I wait for Asher to elaborate on the circumstances that kept Carolina from greeting me, but he doesn't say anything else, his lips pursed in a thin line.

I glance back at the boat captain who stands near the edge of the dock with my bags, a thread of unease filling me. Asher walks past me, heading toward the captain, his back toward me. The man's expression is hooded, and he nods at something Asher tells him, their voices too low for me to make out what they're saying.

Maybe I should have stayed at a hotel in Miami. Of course, one needs money for a hotel, and thanks to the terms of my father's will, my sister's husband is my guardian until I marry or turn twenty-one. With dim romantic prospects and three years until I reach the age my father decided would signify maturity, I'm dependent on my brother-in-law's good nature whether I like it or not. Insulting that a girl should be considered incapable of managing her own affairs despite being of legal age, but my parents were always traditional.

Asher walks back toward me, extending his arm to me.

"The staff will carry your luggage to your room. I'll show you up to the house so you can get settled in."

I hesitate for a moment before taking his arm and falling into step beside him.

"I'm sorry for your loss," Asher says, breaking the silence between us as we walk toward the main house.

I wish he hadn't said anything about the funeral; I'd nearly forgotten how upset I was when they sent word that they wouldn't be able to come, how hurt I had been that Carolina didn't see fit to let me know herself, that in a time when we should have been able to lean on each other, to share in our grief over the loss of our parents after their accident, I was left alone in Havana to deal with the aftermath of settling their affairs.

"I was surprised Carolina didn't make it."

I shouldn't have been, considering Carolina never made a return trip to Havana after her marriage. Each Christmas, I waited to see if my sister would be joining us, and each year I was left disappointed. We ferried gifts across the sea to each other and impersonal notes, so it *shouldn't* have been a surprise, and yet, when there's so much hope tied up in the promise that things could be different, it's easy to misread a situation.

Asher frowns. "Carolina—"

A scream pierces the air.

The heel of my sandal catches on the gravel path.

I lurch forward, my heart pounding madly in my breast.

Asher reaches out, his hand gripping my arm to keep me from falling to the ground. For a man who looks as though the life has been leeched from him, he moves surprisingly quickly.

I struggle to calm my racing heart, my gaze darting around the estate in the direction the noise came from.

"What was that?"

Asher releases me. "It's just the peacocks."

The paleness of his skin belies the confidence in his words. He might have concluded that there was no threat quicker than I did, but there's no doubt in my mind that for a moment he was as startled by the noise as I was.

"Peacocks?" I ask.

"They're everywhere."

"Are peacocks native to Miami?"

"No one really knows how they got here. Some people think they might have been brought by some of the early developers. They certainly add to the atmosphere of the place."

Atmosphere is something Marbrisa has in spades.

I preoccupy myself with dusting the sand off the skirt of my dress, more than a little embarrassed by my dramatic reaction to the birds' presence.

"The house is beautiful," I offer, the word floating inadequately between us.

"It is."

I wait for Asher to elaborate on the thought as one naturally would in such a conversation, but he doesn't say anything else until we reach the main staircase going up to the glass doors leading into the mansion.

"Welcome to Marbrisa."

I glance up, the enormous structure casting a long shadow the closer we get. There are stone creatures crouched atop the parapet—gargoyles, perhaps? Or other winged beasts. They're too far away for me to make out their features beyond the essentials, but they look as though they're prepared to swoop down upon me.

Whoever built this place must have had a vivid imagination.

Asher pulls open one of the glass-arched doors leading into the house.

I hesitate, the threshold yawning before me.

There's a shift in the air from the fresh scent of the ocean breeze to something I can't quite identify—the mustiness of a house that's finally being aired out after being closed for far too long. As I step into the splendor that is the main house, I cross into another world, into another time. The house's history is etched in its floors and written on its walls. There's a heaviness to Marbrisa, a weight beyond the heavy gold-framed artwork and towering chandeliers.

Growing up in a city with as rich of a history as Havana, it's hard to not be fascinated by how the past informs the present, to ignore the stories that reside in the walls of buildings and in street stones, the lingering imprint of the lives that came before us.

What stories does Marbrisa tell?

The door slams behind me, the sound booming in the cavernous space.

A chill slides down my spine.

Despite all the windows and the sunlight streaming into the house, the inside is a far cry from the exterior. Here, oppressive opulence reigns, the natural beauty and harmony of the grounds giving way to oversize furniture and grand artwork filled with haughty figures staring down at me like I am an interloper in their domain. Whether they are Asher's ancestors or simply someone else's that were available for purchase is difficult to tell, but they're an unsmiling lot adding to the macabre ambiance.

The house lacks a general lived-in appearance, the casual detritus of life that accompanies a home. Rather, it looks like a museum, a monument to another time. I see little of Carolina in the decor save for the fact that it is undeniably ostentatious. Still, there's a warmth about my sister—a charisma—that this place lacks, a sumptuousness that should be here but is not. It's like sitting down at a gleaming banquet table heaped with accoutrements and expecting to be served a feast only to discover that the plates are all bare, the food withered and decayed.

The tile floor is an intricate mosaic of colors and patterns that appear to tell a story, but I'm too close to the image to get the full picture, to understand exactly what it is that I'm looking at. It's a puzzle of sorts, and I've always been one for putting all the pieces together.

Each individual segment is a work of art, but taken together, the sheer amount of labor that must have gone into the flooring is staggering. The ceiling is equally impressive, an image that looks somewhat biblical given the clouds, rays of light, and winged creatures hovering above. The entryway is huge, the ceiling far, far above our heads; the artist must have worked on a scaffolding perched high to create such a breathtaking image.

Asher and I part ways, and the housekeeper, Mrs. Morrison, leads me up an enormous golden staircase to my bedroom.

Heavy paintings adorn the richly detailed walls, flanking the hallway, a seemingly endless row of chandeliers hanging from the ceiling.

It feels a bit like I am Alice and I have just gone through the looking glass. Because there's something about this house, something that I can't quite put my finger on, something that just feels a bit *wrong*. The house is meant to look as though it is centuries old, but the furnishings and decor don't have the same worn look as the rest of the property. In fact, the space looks as though it was redecorated much more recently.

"How long have you worked at Marbrisa?" I ask Mrs. Morrison.

"Since it was constructed. The original owners hired me to care for the house. Then Mr. Wyatt hired me back when he bought it from the state fifteen years later, in the thirties. He was determined to restore the property and the furnishings to their former glory after the house had sat vacant for so long. We had a hurricane some fifteen years back. That took its toll, too."

"It must feel a bit like working in a museum," I muse. *Or a mausoleum.* "All this marble. Not to mention the artwork. And then there's the history of the house to be preserved. I imagine that can be an overwhelming task."

"It can be. Yes."

I sneak a glance at her, trying to decode her short answers.

There's a tension emanating from her, fairly crackling around her body. She looks to be about my mother's age, perhaps a bit older, her reddish brown hair sprinkled with gray.

"You said Asher hired you. Did you begin working here when Asher and Carolina married?"

It's been six years since they wed in Havana in 1935.

She flinches nearly imperceptibly at the sound of my sister's name.

Ahh.

"No. Mr. Wyatt hired me. Before your sister came to live here."

There's a tightness to her voice when she delivers the last sentence, as though she's tasted something bitter in her mouth and is eager to spit it out.

"Well, you've done an extraordinary job. The house is lovely. It's clear you care for it a great deal."

Mrs. Morrison's eyes flicker with surprise. "Thank you."

We stop in front of one of the bedrooms. "This one is yours. Your sister picked it out for you."

Carolina's always been like that—doing a kind thing one moment, showing a different side of her personality the next. That she cared enough to pick out a room for me, and yet not enough to be here to welcome me upon my arrival, is just one of those things I've learned to take in stride no matter how much the latter stings. Part of me has always admired her fierce independence, how she has learned to hold herself accountable to no one, to live solely on her terms, but when you're the recipient of such behavior, when her interests no longer align with yours, it can hurt.

The impetus to apologize for whatever slight Carolina has caused is there on the tip of my tongue. Despite the years between us, I have always been the peacemaker in the family, striving to avoid conflict at any cost. I'm not responsible for my sister's actions, but at the same time, I've been here less than an hour and I've slipped back into the pattern of our childhood.

I take a deep breath and bite back the empty apologies that come to mind. Carolina will always be Carolina, and there's no point in me wishing she could be someone she's not or making excuses for her behavior. My parents are gone now, my sister married and in a family of her own; it's time for me to be my own person, independent of where I come from.

The housekeeper closes the door behind me, and I take in the full effect of my room. The bedding and drapes are a matching sage green silk with some floral pattern embroidered on the fabric. They look too new to be original to the house, yet they fit in perfectly with the house's grand, gilded character.

Did Carolina choose these? And was it a coincidence that she gave me this room, or did she remember that green has always been my favorite color?

It would be easy to write her off as self-absorbed if that were the whole of her personality rather than a facet. After all, that's the trouble with people—it's easy to be ensnared when you glom on to the good in them, suffering through the sharper parts.

Various paintings line the walls surrounding the guest suite, but one in particular stops me in my tracks. The artist has painted the back of Marbrisa, the view from the patio looking and leading out to the sea. There's a woman in the foreground of the painting—a pale blonde wearing a dress the color of the sea. Her hair is swept up in a loose updo, a pair of seashell combs holding it in place.

I step closer, studying the brushstrokes, the way the artist has drawn the landscape. Given the grandeur of the subject matter at hand, I would have expected the artist to focus on Marbrisa, on the stunning view of Biscayne Bay. Instead, it feels as though the house and the grounds fade into the background, pale in comparison to the brushstrokes that have seemingly, lovingly been used to capture the woman's profile.

I can't make out the artist's name amid the scrawled signature at the bottom corner of the painting, but there's a gold plate affixed just above the heavy gold frame with a name engraved there:

ANNA BARNES

Was she a guest in the house? Or one of the previous owners?

I walk over to the window, staring down at the gardens below. There's a greenhouse on the edge of the property, the stone-and-glass edifice looming large. It's in the painting, too, off on the fringes of the image.

Peacocks mill about the greenhouse—six, no, seven of them. Two of the males have all their feathers fanned out in full display as though they're posturing with each other, preening in front of the remaining females.

The greenhouse door opens, and a woman steps out. She pauses, turning back just as a man follows behind her. She calls out to him, but between the glass window and the distance, I can't hear what she says, am too far away to read the shape of her lips and the words they form.

I recognize her instantly.

Carolina.

The man walks away from the house, too much distance between us for me to make out his features, but one thing is clear by the clothing he's wearing, considering I just saw my brother-in-law not half an hour ago.

It isn't Asher.

Carolina begins walking toward the house, hips swaying.

My breath hitches as I watch her.

So much of my sister's persona is curated that it's rare to catch these glimpses of Carolina that feel like windows into who she really is rather than the version of herself that she wishes the world to see.

Carolina stops suddenly, her gaze trained toward the main house. For a moment, she stills, and then it's as though she transforms into someone else entirely. The carefree sister I knew, loved, and envied is gone, and the image staring back at me and the expression on her face are ones I no longer recognize. The easygoing woman strolling through the gardens is replaced with a woman who looks like she'd rather be anywhere but here.

How is it possible that a place that looks like paradise could bring its residents so much pain?

Carolina's head jerks up as though I've spoken the words

aloud, the question carried on the wind, through the panes of glass.

Our gazes connect.

The last thing I want is for Carolina to think I was spying on her, as I admittedly was wont to do when we were children and I followed her everywhere, hanging on her every action and word. I wish I could explain that I just happened to be looking out the window when she exited the greenhouse, wish I could assure her that no matter what, she's my sister and her secrets are safe with me.

I raise my hand to wave to her, a smile forming on my lips.

My arrival at Marbrisa is the fresh start I always hoped we could have, without the baggage of our family dynamics between us, without the foolishness of youth that followed us for so long.

Carolina holds my gaze for a heartbeat, and then she glances away, disappearing inside the house.

My hand falls to my side.

∼

I WAIT FOR Carolina to visit me in my room, but no one comes to see me save for a man who drops off my suitcases and then leaves as quickly as he came.

The urge to go in search of her is there, but I'm not a child anymore, and part of me wants Carolina to see me as an equal rather than an annoying little sister, for her to acknowledge how much I've changed and grown in the hopes that we can forge a friendship between us.

I spend the rest of the afternoon unpacking, hanging my dresses on silk-padded hangers in the enormous armoire opposite the bed. Despite the floral sachets that have been tucked in there, the furniture smells faintly of disuse—a guest room that has likely seen few guests.

When we lived in Havana, Carolina was always the life of the party. I would have thought that a house like this would have provided the perfect opportunity for her to entertain her friends, although there's a stillness about Marbrisa that suggests otherwise. It's a house that was clearly built for grand parties, for inspiring awe, but it seems to have lost its way. The estate is rather isolated, a far cry from the city environs that we were used to.

And yet, there's clearly one visitor to Marbrisa—the man Carolina met in the greenhouse.

I dress for dinner in one of my favorite gowns, the familiarity of it and the fond memories it conjures filling me with peace and much-needed confidence. I shouldn't feel this nervous to see my own sister, but Carolina's moods can run the gamut from making you feel like the most important person in the world when she bestows her attention on you to that prickling feeling that forms at your nape when a storm is about to roll in, and unfortunately, you never know what you're going to get.

Tonight, I can't help but sense clouds are on the horizon, given the lack of a warm welcome earlier.

With the age difference between us, and the fact that I gathered I was a bit of a surprise to my parents, Carolina always gave the impression that she would have been happier as an only child. Maybe it was because as the eldest, she was the one who drew the most expectation and criticism when she didn't live up to our parents' notions of what was appropriate. By the time I came around, they were too exhausted by her exploits to worry much about me and my behavior, leaving me largely unscathed. I always assumed she would have preferred to have shared none of the attention and all of the strictures.

Now that they're gone, it is surprisingly terrifying to realize the world before me is a blank canvas, my future up to me and me alone—if Asher gives me control of my inheritance, that is.

A clock chimes somewhere in the house, the long gongs like a beating heart.

I head downstairs.

～

When I enter the room, I'm surprised to find that we're not dining as a family as I imagined, but rather, there's an unfamiliar man sitting at the table in the chair opposite the one that has clearly been left empty for me.

Asher and Carolina sit across from each other at the table, like the two farthest points on a compass.

My sister rises.

The glimpse of her in the gardens earlier wasn't enough to prepare me for the shock.

She has always resembled our mother—the same dark hair, the same dark eyes, the same tall, willowy build—but now, seeing her presiding over her own table, her mannerisms so like the ones I grew up with—

A lump fills my throat, an unexpected wave of grief attacking me.

The loss of my parents has stripped me emotionally raw, and I feel more vulnerable than I ever have before, a sensation that is hardly welcome considering I have no armor to protect me from the family history I'm about to wade through. We fought when we were children—Carolina angry because I would borrow her things without asking, me desperate to get her attention and going about it in all the wrong ways. I'd hoped we'd broken out of that pattern, that in our shared grief we could be sisters once more, but seeing her again like this, all the old feelings come rushing back to me. I am once again the other Acosta sister who never quite measures up to the long shadow Carolina casts.

She's changed dresses since we saw each other through the glass panes of my bedroom window. She's wearing a gold lace gown with a tailored collar, nipped waist, and full skirt. Enormous rubies drip from her ears, her lips painted in the same crimson color.

I glance down at my dress.

There's a spot a few inches below the knee that I never noticed before, a remnant of a glass of wine I likely had the last time I wore it. The desire to run upstairs and change or at the very least take some club soda and a towel and remove the stain myself is overwhelming.

"Carmen."

She even sounds like our mother.

Tears well in my eyes.

I glance up at my sister just in time to see her eyes follow the line of the dress, to the spot in question. Her gaze lingers there a moment longer than I'd like before traveling back to my face again.

She smiles, the edges of her mouth as sharp as the stones adorning her skin, the effect no less dazzling for the brittleness in the moment.

Carolina glides toward me, Asher and the unnamed man's attention on us. I would have preferred our reunion be in private, without prying eyes, but here we are.

Carolina stops, the familiar scent of her perfume hitting me first. She embraces me, her touch featherlight against my skin, her lips hovering an inch or two away from my cheek before she pulls back to study me much as I am doing to her.

A lump forms in my throat, memories flooding me.

Carolina pulls back first.

"How are you?" she asks, her voice low, the sharp edges softened.

When I was ten and she was sixteen, I fell off my horse during a riding lesson and sprained my wrist. I was terrified of horses, but our parents insisted that we both learn to ride, and while Carolina had an excellent seat, I never took to it like she did. I remember sitting in the dirt, holding my arm, tears streaming down my cheeks at the pain. Carolina was the first to reach me, crouching down to my level, using her sleeve to wipe the tears from my cheeks. She sat with me until our mother came. It's those memories that give me hope for our relationship.

"It varies each day," I admit. "They say these sorts of things take time to get over, although I can't help but wonder if that's even possible, if distance truly does dull the pain. I miss them. So much."

I don't add the rest—the fact that I've yet to figure out what I'm supposed to do now that they're gone. While Carolina is no doubt mourning their loss, she has already made a life for herself here, a new family, thanks to her marriage to Asher.

"How are you?" I ask her.

She shrugs. "As can be expected, I suppose."

"You didn't come to the funeral."

The words escape with more accusation than I intended, the hurt I struggled to bury bubbling to the surface.

"I couldn't make it. I didn't think I would be missed. It's not like they realized I wasn't there. You were there to represent the family, which I'm sure is what they would have wanted anyway. After all, you were always the daughter they were proud of. I was the one they were eager to be rid of."

"That's not true," I sputter, surprised by the edge in her voice, the flashing anger in her eyes.

"Isn't it? I was married at your age. It seems like they weren't as eager to have you out of the house so soon."

I glance over my shoulder, praying our voices are low enough that our conversation can't be heard. What would Asher think of the implicit meaning in Carolina's words, the hint of resentment there signifying that perhaps her marriage wasn't exactly what she wanted it to be? Although, if that's truly the case, this is the first I've heard of it. While I can't say our parents were reluctant to see Carolina wed, the entire business always felt like it was driven by her desire to be Mrs. Asher Wyatt. From where I'm standing, Carolina got what she wanted and then some. There are certainly worse fates than being mistress of Marbrisa.

For his part, Asher stares down at the dinner plate, his expression hidden by the slump of his shoulders, the curve of his neck.

"You were," I murmur, turning back to face Carolina. "Missed, I mean. *I* missed you."

She shrugs again as though we're discussing a lunch date rather than our parents' funeral. "You're here now." She smiles, a slightly false note in the gesture, as though she knows I'm annoyed and she's trying to smooth the whole thing over with her charm. "Let's eat. Let me introduce you to our guest, Nathaniel Hayes."

I turn toward the stranger.

He's tall and lean, his hair an inky midnight, his skin pale. Whereas Asher looks as though the life has been slowly leeched from him, Nathaniel's face has a luminous quality to it like a pearl plucked from the sea. If I were casting a Gothic hero, Nathaniel would fit the bill nicely. It's also undeniable that if I were to place a guess as to the sort of man my sister would meet in a greenhouse, he would be at the top of my list.

He looks to be more Asher's contemporary than mine, and I can't help but wonder where he fits into this little tableau. Is he Asher's friend or Carolina's? A business associate, perhaps? I wouldn't think they would invite an acquaintance for an intimate family reunion, but maybe he's supposed to be a buffer, their way of ensuring this dinner doesn't delve into the overly personal. Maybe it'll make tonight easier.

I take a seat to Carolina's right, opposite their guest.

My gaze darts around the table, studying my fellow dining partners' faces. It feels as though I've entered at the middle of a conversation, one I was never meant to be privy to. There's a tension between them, a falseness in their mannerisms. Carolina smiles too brightly; Asher is far too occupied with the table setting before him.

And Nathaniel—

"I understand you just arrived from Havana," Nathaniel says.

Surprise fills me. I would think Asher or Carolina would be the ones to dictate the conversation, considering they're our hosts, but Nathaniel speaks with the confidence of someone who is familiar enough with the house and its inhabitants to steer the direction of the evening.

"I did. Just this morning."

"And what do you think of Marbrisa so far?"

"It's certainly grand," I say, directing my compliment and smile to my sister to draw Carolina into the conversation.

She doesn't respond, her gaze not on me, but instead on Nathaniel.

There's a hint of something in her eyes—anger, dislike, annoyance?—and then she returns her attention to the wine in front of her, sparing neither one of us another glance.

Is he the man Carolina was meeting in the greenhouse?

He's certainly handsome enough.

Up close, without the distance between us, it's hard to tell if he could be the man I saw from the window. His clothing is different, but he likely changed into more formal attire to come to dinner this evening. His clothes are elegant and fine, his manners impeccable. If I didn't know otherwise, it would be easy to mistake him as the owner of Marbrisa and Asher as his guest.

"Are you a frequent guest at Marbrisa, Mr. Hayes?" I ask, my curiosity getting the best of me.

Carolina's head snaps up as the question falls from my lips.

Mr. Hayes smiles, the effect transforming his face from Gothic hero to charmer in an instant. I swallow, more than a little unsettled. He is almost aggressively handsome, and while I can easily understand how such a quality might draw women to him, there's something disingenuous about his looks.

My mother warned me not to trust a man who was too handsome for fear he'd think too highly of himself.

"Occasionally. Asher and I did a bit of business together a few years back. We've become friends. He's kind enough to host me when I'm in Miami. I like to spend the winters here."

"It's not quite winter, Mr. Hayes."

He smiles again. "Perhaps not, but I confess, November in Boston can be markedly unpleasant. Better to be here with the bright sun and sea, and in such pleasant company."

He says the last part with a flourish I doubt he means.

I glance at Carolina, curious to see if she's moved by his patently obvious attempt at flattery, but her gaze is back on her wineglass, her lips moving ever so softly, no words audibly escaping. The mannerism tugs me back in time to when we were young girls and she used to engage in the same habit whenever she was working something out in her mind. It was almost as though she was having a silent conversation with herself, one she didn't care to share with the rest of us.

What is consuming her thoughts?

"What sort of business are you involved with?" I ask, my gaze darting back to Nathaniel Hayes. If I can't decipher Carolina's secrets, perhaps I can ascertain his.

"None I'm certain that would interest someone as lovely as you. It's all very boring. And please, call me Nathaniel."

If he thinks he can fob me off so easily and with such a poor attempt to put me in my place, he's surely mistaken.

"I wouldn't be bored at all."

"I build hotels," he drawls.

"And yet, you don't stay at them?"

Across the table, Asher's eyes widen slightly.

Nathaniel flashes me a row of perfect white teeth. "I haven't built any hotels in Miami. Yet. I'm still looking for the perfect location."

I open my mouth to reply—

A scream rips through the house.

CHAPTER THREE

Anna

The architect works like a man possessed through much of the summer—or so I'm told—Robert's excitement over Marbrisa's progress reaching a fever pitch each time he returns from a journey to Miami. We might as well have already left New York for how invested he is in our new life in Florida. Sometimes when I'm talking to him at dinner, it feels as though he is only half with me, his attention and his passion down south.

It's a strange sensation to be jealous of a house, but one that I am now uncomfortably familiar with. I may be Robert's wife, but Marbrisa is his mistress, and she holds his interest with an intense focus I cannot break. He pores over books on architecture, art, and the management of an estate into the early hours of the morning, signing off on the heaps of bills that arrive at our residence as he brings each of his dreams to fruition.

There is the copper winged horse fountain in the driveway that Robert insisted on. Why any house requires a Pegasus, I'll never understand. Ornate gates made of bronze were brought in by boat from Italy to greet visitors upon their arrival at Marbrisa, the towering structures flanked by even higher coral walls.

Now that Robert's great secret is out, he delights in updating me with each of his conquests, regaling me with tales of treasures he has collected from all over the world to send to Marbrisa. His daily business seems to have shifted from his usual affairs to his newfound avocation, and I often find myself wondering—and worrying—just who is running the investment company he worked so hard to build, the dream that was once his sole focus and that has now been cast aside in favor of the house on Biscayne Bay.

It would be easy if it were a matter of competing with a heap of stone and a magnificent view of the bay, but it's more than that. In building Marbrisa, Robert is confronting his own mortality; this is the legacy he is determined to leave behind long after we're gone, the mark he makes on the world.

Finally, it becomes clear to me that if I am to have my husband back, I must support his interests, shifting my focus to this house that has consumed him so. I do my best to share in his enthusiasm, looking over the renderings and photographs Mr. Harrison sends to update us on the progress, struggling to cover my panic and dismay with something akin to approval.

While Robert is drawn to the marble and gilt, the priceless treasures his agents source from around the world, it's the grounds that I enjoy the most. Mr. Harrison has taken to sending me pressed flowers from Marbrisa's gardens, each of his packages carrying a piece of Miami with it.

With every update, the estate transforms as Mr. Harrison

marries the natural foliage with his vision for how the exterior should complement the mansion's interior. Sometimes, he'll ask my preference, sending me two specimens to choose from, or invite me to inject my own wishes. The main house is a creature entirely of Robert's making, but the gardens are the one part of Marbrisa where my husband has been happy to abdicate responsibility.

And so, over the months, the estate wears me down, letter by letter, image by image, pressed flower by pressed flower, until finally it is done and, despite all my earlier misgivings and threads of worry, I must admit I am more than a little eager to see the finished product in the flesh.

We move in amid popping champagne bottles, our house in New York shuttered, the furniture covered in billowing white sheets, Mr. Flagler's mighty train carrying many of our remaining worldly possessions south.

It was a fight over what we should do, Robert eager to sell our New York home and make our Miami residence permanent. Finally, he relented, giving us the option of maintaining our home in New York in case his South Florida dreams soured—not that he would brook the possibility of anything other than total success.

As soon as we arrived in Miami, Robert set about planning the largest, most opulent party this town has seen, ordering champagne by the caseload, and barking orders at every member of the staff to ensure that everything goes off without a hitch. We entertained but occasionally in New York, and it's immediately evident that the sort of party Robert has in mind here is a different type of affair altogether.

He has recruited Mr. Harrison for his cause, and while I get the impression that the architect has little use for parties, it's evident that he's determined to make sure the house looks its best. They pass hours in Robert's newly completed study, putting the finishing touches on the mansion before they unveil it to the rest of the world. I've made it a point to spend as much time as I can in their company, interjecting when their plans inevitably become too grandiose.

"And what did Deering use in Vizcaya?" Robert asks, his voice bristling as he speaks of his newly found architectural nemesis, James Deering. Whether Mr. Deering is aware of it or not, Robert has made it his personal mission to best the man at all costs, and the looming specter of Vizcaya—James Deering's palatial estate north of us on Biscayne Bay—has become the target of my husband's ire. Sandwiched between James Deering's home to the north and the house his half brother Charles Deering is building to the south of us, Robert's dreams of notoriety face steep opposition.

Perhaps it was the elegant cut of Mr. James Deering's impeccable gray suit, his reputed fluency in multiple languages, and his impressive portfolio of real estate that shook Robert so. More likely, though, it was his vast wealth—inherited—that affected Robert; the reminder that even as far down as Miami, where society is being reinvented, there is still an unspoken hierarchy. That a man like Robert who came from nothing and built himself into a fearless businessman is still weighed and measured as slightly less than a man who was born into the right sort of family.

Florida is a promise to men like Robert, a place where fortunes could be made and pasts erased.

The architect replies to Robert's irate question in a routine that has become altogether too familiar since we arrived in Miami. Even though Marbrisa's construction is complete, it seems as though a house of this size and stature is never truly finished. Robert is constantly directing Mr. Harrison and his crew to make changes, his perfectionism rearing its head the more time we spend in the house. Mr. Harrison might as well be on permanent retainer for all the time he spends here. I can't help but wonder what his personal life is like, if he's married or has a family, how his wife must feel about his complete and utter devotion to Marbrisa. He doesn't wear a ring, his home temporarily in the small cottage on the border of the estate, and he and Robert have indeed proven themselves to be a match made in heaven, their enthusiasm for the house and the splash it is to make on Miami unparalleled. Each request Robert makes is more absurd than the last, but while a less devoted—or less ambitious—man would likely be exasperated by the demands, the architect never fails to rise to the occasion with equal amounts of zeal.

Tonight is as much a celebration of Mr. Harrison's efforts as it is our announcement to Miami that we have arrived.

I dress with care for our debut, as though I am a debutante to be presented to society—a slightly ridiculous event for a woman of my years—the silver spangled gown I bought in New York for the occasion one I know Robert will appreciate. The color makes my hazel eyes appear gray in the reflection staring back at me in the mirror Robert had shipped from Paris.

I fasten the diamond earbobs Robert bought me for our twentieth wedding anniversary, the bracelet he gifted to me for our tenth. I wear our marital history on my body, in the mementos that adorn it, in the lines that have developed in my face since I was a young girl when we met, in the threads of silver woven through my hair. There are memories contained in the curve of my fingers, the way they interlock with his, the wrap of my arms that fit perfectly around his shoulders. There's a familiarity, a recognition of sorts that occurs when we are together, when we are in the same room; my body has learned his, can predict his moods nearly as well as my own.

Tonight, he is nervous.

I stand on the threshold of Robert's adjoining suite, admiring how dashing he looks in his evening dress. His hair has gone from black and silver to fully silver over the years, and while I often catch his look of surprise when he studies himself in the mirror, as though he can't quite believe time had the audacity to catch up with him, my husband is a handsome man. In fact, I prefer this version of him to the one I met all those years ago. He looks better to me now that life has left its mark on him, now that I can appreciate all those changes, all the experiences he's lived, now that I know I have played a part in some of the moments that have shaped him. Despite the inevitable bumps along the road, the way life has twisted us up at times, he has given me a companionship and friendship that far exceeds any complaints I could have about our differences.

And perhaps, in the construction of this house, he was indeed correct.

Maybe Miami will turn out to be a lovely place to live.

I take a deep breath, a smile spreading on my face, enjoying the sensation that we have once again passed another hurdle in our marriage and come out together unscathed. If I've learned anything, it's that these differences between us have tested our mettle and defined the essence of who we are. It would be boring if we were too similar, if Robert played it safe as I always yearn to do. We are better for the ways in which we are different, for the inherent challenge in fitting our lives together, albeit not as neatly as one might often like.

Robert's fingers shake as he fiddles with his evening tie, a curse escaping his lips.

"Here, let me," I say, stepping out from the shadows of his room.

He turns, relief in his gaze.

"You look lovely," he murmurs, and it's silly, but even after all these years, the approval in his voice fills me with joy, my heart swelling with love and pride for the life we've built together.

I have spent over half my life being loved by this man.

His hands drop to his sides as I straighten the rumpled fabric. Tension emanates from him.

"It's just a party," I whisper, my hand sweeping down to caress his chest beneath the fine linen of his crisp white shirtfront that I selected for this evening. "We've hosted countless parties."

"Not like this."

I lean back, studying him, trying to comprehend what has him so rattled, this man who is a titan in the boardroom, who built his fortune from nothing by refusing to entertain any objection, single-handedly steamrolling over the competition.

"What's different about tonight?"

"Everything. Everyone has been talking about the house, coming by out of the pretense of being neighborly just to sneak a few peeks at the construction. You don't think I haven't heard the whispers? That I've gone mad to spend so much? They're snickering behind my back, I tell you. Waiting to see me fail. Some hoping that I do. They all want to see if the reality lives up to their imagination."

"And if it doesn't?" I thought I knew every facet of Robert's personality, but I've never seen my husband like this. How can a man who is so confident in the business arena be so shaken now? "It's just a house. A beautiful one at that, but still just a house."

He pulls away from me. "It isn't just a house. Don't you see—this is what I will be remembered for. It's not as though I have a son to—"

I take a deep breath, steadying my racing heart, suddenly feeling as though this conversation is careening into unfamiliar territory. The truth is, Robert never seemed to care much for children, accepted our inability to have them with an equanimity that matched my own. There are people who dream of being parents, of having large families, but our marriage never lacked in that regard. We were partners, and in our partnership, I found a quiet peace. So why would he bring up such a thing now?

Hurt fills me, blossoming in my chest like a wound. It's not necessarily what he said as much as it is the thought that perhaps I have been laboring under a misapprehension this entire time, that Robert has wanted things he has kept from me, that secrets have existed in our marriage that I never knew were there.

It hardly seems fair to hold something against me that I never knew he desired.

"I never knew you wanted children," I say, my voice faint, a thread of recrimination winding its way through me despite my best intentions.

Strange how the tiniest of holes can prick something that seemed so impregnable.

"What? What are you talking about?" Robert turns, facing me, and for a moment, it feels as though I am staring at a stranger for all that I can decipher the look in his eyes. He blinks, shaking himself from his stupor. "I don't. Want children, I mean. Of course I don't."

Not for the first time in our marriage, we seem to be speaking past each other, having two different conversations simultaneously, and I must take a deep breath lest my temper get the best of me.

I've found the secret to a lasting marriage lies in the breaths I take—the ones that calm me, centering me before I say something I might regret; the ones that allow me to pause the world and slow down the tempo of my marriage when it feels as though it is hurtling toward something unpleasant.

"Then what is it that you want?"

"I want to be respected," he admits, his voice nearly begrudging in the honesty contained there. "I want to be envied."

I can't claim to understand or have the same desires, but when he says it like that, I want those things for him. Still—how can you build respect on something so changeable? If we are defined by Marbrisa, what happens when someone inevitably comes along and builds a bigger, grander house? It seems like a game that's impossible to win and a sure recipe for disappointment and disaster.

I wish he could see himself as I do, understand that none of this matters, not really. The things I love about my husband aren't as flighty as the opinion or respect of others; I admire his constancy, his determination, his commitment. And at the same time, it's impossible to deny that I cannot have the good in Robert without accepting the challenges, that a man cannot work as hard as Robert has for as long without wanting to see some of the fruits of his labors come to fruition.

"You will be," I whisper, praying I am correct, the alternative momentarily unthinkable.

What will happen to Robert if he is not?

〜

THE PARTY IS already in full swing when we descend the elaborate staircase, my fingers gliding across the banister for purchase, a slight tremor in my knees, the unease that has filled me since we spoke upstairs lingering. I am at once surrounded by bright young things laughing and dancing, making me feel impossibly old. Where did Robert even meet these people? Or did they just come, dazzled by the glittering lights sparkling over the bay and the promise of free-flowing champagne and a chance to see the notorious mansion up close? This may be a dry county, but no one seems to care too much about following that particular law—or enforcing it for that matter.

Robert pauses for a moment, surveying the crowd below us like a king holding court. Curious gazes are cast our way, whispers reaching my ears.

"... *that's the wife* ..."

"... *made his money in railroads, I think* ..."

"*They say all the furniture came from Italy.*"

"*I heard it was Spain.*"

"*Have you* seen *their architect? I wouldn't mind having him design something for me.*"

This comment is followed by laughter, a group of women lingering close to where Mr. Harrison stands at the bottom of the staircase.

His cheeks are slightly pink as though he has heard their words and is more than a little embarrassed—and annoyed—to be the subject of such attention. I study him for a moment, trying to see what the women must see, to understand their admiration. He is young and pleasing enough on the eyes, I suppose, but for so long he has been a thorn in my side, the architect of all this folly, that it is impossible for me to view him as anything else even if I must begrudgingly admit that the house is indeed the feat he promised.

Robert takes a deep breath next to me, and then he releases my hand, the crowd rising to meet us, and he is immediately engulfed in congratulations and praise.

Relief floods me.

This is the response he craved, and I am grateful that people were able to see and appreciate what he and Mr. Harrison have built. Perhaps they were right and Marbrisa will succeed in bringing jobs to the area, will help in Miami's development now that the Great War is over and so many have returned home. Maybe this is the way in which we will be remembered, a place in which we can do some good despite my fears.

I descend the rest of the way down the staircase, into the mass of people.

A woman brushes past me dressed in a daring gown the color of crushed plums, an intricate necklace of bejeweled snakes wrapped around her neck. She's lovely, and so very young, this crowd in Miami different from the friends we usually socialize with, the couples we've known for ages. Our gazes connect for a moment, a hint of interest in her eyes as she takes in my dress, my necklace and earrings, before her regard lingers on my face. I get the sense that she is cataloging the cost of everything on my person, trying to see how it all stacks up against the splendor that is Marbrisa.

It's not so different from how things are done in New York, but there's an openness—a frankness—

"... *that's the wife* ..."

I shift to the side, away from the crush, happy to let Robert have his moment alone, eager to fade into the background for the remainder of the night.

Mr. Harrison stands near the balustrade sipping his glass of champagne and looking at me.

I raise my champagne glass in a silent toast. For all my

personal feelings on the matter, Mr. Harrison did all he promised and then some, and he deserves every ounce of praise for his hard work and talents.

I move toward him, exchanging an obligatory air-kiss. He's grown on me in measures, perhaps for the fact that he took such pains to ensure I was pleased with the house, listening to my thoughts and respecting my opinions. So many men are reluctant to consider a woman's perspective on so many things that his inclination to do so was enough to restore him from mortal enemy to something marginally higher in my esteem.

"It's a triumph tonight," I say in greeting. "You should be very proud of your work. I'll admit, when Robert shared this whole plan with me, I struggled to see the vision. But what you've created is extraordinary."

He flushes. "Thank you."

I've noticed that unless he's talking about building, he's often a man of few words, and while he is clearly proud of Marbrisa, he's not one to draw the spotlight on himself. It's an interesting juxtaposition between his professional ambition and personal reticence.

"Surely, you aren't nervous, too, Mr. Harrison?" I ask.

"I confess I am." He shoots me a wry smile. "Your husband has exacting standards, and I'll admit, a time or two I was afraid that I wouldn't live up to them." He tugs at his collar, casting his gaze away from the group of women who were admiring him. "I hate parties," he adds. "Socializing goes with the territory, of course, when it comes to getting new clients, to making the right connections to enable me to do projects like this one, but I can't say it makes me enjoy them any more.

Then again, maybe it's all the pressure that goes with them."
His gaze sweeps the room before returning to me. "I guess I
should consider myself in good company, then, seeing as everyone here is on the make in some way or another." He smiles.
"Present company excluded, of course."

I laugh. "You don't have to spare my feelings, Mr. Harrison."

"I wasn't trying to. Just calling it like I see it. It's clear that
you're one of the few people not trying to hustle your way
through Miami."

"I'm flattered."

He laughs. "To be honest, I wasn't trying to flatter you, either. After all, when you own all this, what's left to hustle for?"

"Touché."

"It hasn't escaped my notice that you have an aversion to my
presence," he says, his candor catching me off guard.

Embarrassment floods me. "I'd hoped you hadn't noticed."

"I did."

"It wasn't personal. It's just—this house from the start felt
like a terrible idea. And I saw all the incorrigible zeal in your
eyes and feared the influence you would have on Robert, that
if I wasn't careful, before too long, well—I'd be living like—"

"Like this?"

I flush. "It is an absurdly grand house."

"I'd say it's a work of art," he counters.

"You love it."

The pride he feels for the project is etched all over his being,
and in this moment, I realize that the house is more his than
it ever was mine and Robert's. It feels as though we are the
interlopers here.

"I do." His gaze drifts over the crowd. "In spite of whatever discomfort I might feel at affairs like this, it seems like the house was made for parties, doesn't it?"

"Indeed, it does. That's how you met Robert, isn't it? At a party?" I ask.

"Yes. He told me he was looking for a piece of property to build an estate that would change Florida. I showed up at his hotel room the next morning with the plans. I stayed up all night drafting them. Then I took him for a ride in my automobile to show him the plot of land I had in mind. I knew the previous owner—he had run into some troubles and was looking to off-load it for a song."

"Robert would have liked that."

"He did. Told me he appreciated my initiative. I didn't have much experience, but he was willing to take a chance on me."

"I'm not surprised. Robert built his fortune from scratch. He was the oldest of eight, and he started working when he was just a little boy to bring home money for his family."

Robert's history was one of the things that attracted me to him. There are those in New York society who look down on men like Robert, the clash between new money and old playing out in boardrooms and ballrooms. But I always liked that Robert knew the value of things, that no one handed his fortune to him, that he wasn't afraid to make sacrifices and work hard to get what he wanted. It gave me the hope that he would be the kind of husband who wouldn't be afraid to dig in when times in our marriage inevitably became tough, that he would understand and respect the sacrifices that came along in life.

My gaze sweeps across the ballroom as I realize just how

far we have come, my origins hardly more auspicious than my husband's.

"Where are you from?" I ask, curiosity filling me. In building our home, Mr. Harrison is privy to the intimate details of our lives, and at the same time, we know so little about him. Perhaps he and Robert have struck up a friendship of sorts and discussed more personal things, although knowing my husband and his businesslike manner, I somehow doubt it.

"Chicago."

"And how did you find yourself in Miami?"

"I fought in the war. In Europe. When I came back, I wasn't well. The doctors thought the warm climate down here would do me good. Chicago winters no longer suit me."

He offers each sentence reluctantly, biting off each piece with the bitterness of a memory he doesn't care to relive. There are things they experienced overseas that they clearly wish they had left behind, haunting moments that have inextricably followed them home. I've seen the same thing in cousins and childhood friends who returned, in those whose loved ones did not.

I reach out, gently resting my hand on the sleeve of his evening jacket, and something about the motion seems to pull him back to the here and now, a flash of gratitude in his eyes.

My hand drops to my side.

"Were you an architect in Chicago as well? Before the war?"

"I was."

"Well, if I had to make a guess, Mr. Harrison, I would say that you will have your pick of projects after tonight."

"I'm grateful," he replies, his expression earnest. "I couldn't have done it without your husband's faith in me. I owe him everything."

"I'd say you did a fair bit yourself. I don't know that many would have seen a bare plot of land and envisioned *this* in its place."

"The vision is the easy part. It's the execution that's tricky." He glances around the room. "Everyone wants to be in Miami these days. Your husband was right; construction has exploded at a pace we can barely keep up with. Money is pouring into the state. Everyone's moving south."

"Will you be leaving us, then? Heading on to other projects?"

"No," Mr. Harrison replies. "I won't be leaving you. There are still some things that your husband wants me to finish, projects he has planned now that you're in the house. Sometimes it takes settling into a place to put your true mark on it, to learn its wants and needs."

I'm struck again by the way he describes the house as though it is a living, breathing organism rather than an expensive heap of stone. What is the relationship like between creator and creation—does it border on obsession, will Marbrisa sink her teeth into Mr. Harrison and never let go, or is it possible for him to move on to the next project with little more than pride and fond memories?

"I imagine you'll receive many offers after tonight."

He smiles. "And here I thought you didn't like my architectural style. I don't think I've ever seen someone look quite so horrified when I showed them a set of plans as you did that first day."

I flush. "I have little interest in architecture, Mr. Harrison."

"Michael, please," he interjects.

I smile, feeling a bit silly clinging to such formality with the man who designed the home we live in. "Michael. You must call me Anna, then."

He takes another sip of his champagne. "Anna."

"I know what I like, I confess, but I don't have the right vocabulary to explain why I like it, to identify trends. I want my home to feel comfortable. I want to be at peace there. Beyond that I'm unsure," I say.

"And here? At Marbrisa? Do you think you could be at peace here?"

"I hope so."

It's difficult to imagine finding peace within the walls of a museum.

My life is not a peaceful one, my husband not a restful man. When you are busy building empires, you do not spend a great deal of time worrying about your own comfort because you are constantly looking to the next thing, the subsequent conquest.

"I see you walking around the gardens in the morning," Michael adds. "You look at peace there. Sometimes you even smile. You can't completely hate it."

"I *do* like the gardens," I clarify, feeling ungracious considering I know how much they have been a pet project of his. "When I'm outside, I feel like I can breathe a bit more. Inside this house—"

I wrap my arms around myself, a chill sliding through me despite the sticky humidity in the air.

"Do you have a family back in Chicago?" I ask, eager to change the subject from my silly feelings about the house.

He shakes his head, a smile playing at his lips. "No, no wife who is eagerly awaiting my return. I'm sure you've noticed that I'm dedicated to my work. I have little time—or interest—in other things. I'm certain I would make a terrible—and absent-minded—husband."

It hits me then, full force, that in all this time that I've resented the architect, I've also secretly envied him. My days are largely my own, but it feels as though I drift from activity to activity without any constant to guide me. Robert comes and goes with work, and he is the clock and calendar around which I order myself, my needs adjusting to his, my schedule conforming to his plans. There's nothing that gives me purpose, no passion that sparks the enthusiasm in my eyes I see reflected in Michael's.

I am not concerned with legacy, not in the same way that Robert is, but I can't help but think that if something happened to me, if I one day left this world, my life would have been defined by very little.

I am a wife, and it brings me peace and joy, but without Robert in my life, who am I?

I push away the maudlin thoughts, the whisper of worry, with another sip of champagne.

Robert isn't going anywhere.

A scream pierces the night.

~

CHAPTER FOUR

Carmen

For a moment, I think it's the peacocks screaming again, but then there's another loud screech, the sound of Asher pushing his chair away from the dining table.

Carolina has gone pale.

Another scream.

Definitely human. Unmistakably so.

Asher throws his napkin on the table and rises from his seat without a word for any of us, leaving me, Carolina, and Nathaniel sitting there as another bloodcurdling scream echoes throughout the house.

Good Lord—what could have happened to prompt someone making a noise such as that one?

Carolina's fork falls, the heavy silver hitting the fine china. She rises from the table, too, her skin pale. Her hands tremble.

Carolina was always prone to what our mother referred to as "nerves"—a malady that seemed to encompass all manner of ills.

I expect Carolina to follow her husband outside, but instead she heads for the staircase without a backward glance for me or Asher's friend Nathaniel, leaving us sitting awkwardly in silence before Nathaniel speaks—

"Excuse me, I'm going to see if I can be of assistance."

There's something equally strange about his motions, how smoothly he seems to be handling this bizarre situation, such that I can do little more than stare at him in shock, attempting to make sense of the tableau before me.

That scream—

When Nathaniel exits the dining room, I'm right behind him.

I follow Nathaniel to the front door, where a crowd of the staff has gathered, whispers rising to a fever pitch. It's impossible to see what they're all looking at, and by the size of the group gathered, it's clear it takes a great many people to run Marbrisa. I don't envy Asher or Carolina the task.

Mrs. Morrison stands near the front, too far away for me to hear what she's saying, but she's the closest to Asher, her position in the household clearly an important one. He says something to her, and she gives him a clipped nod.

As she turns away, our gazes connect.

Her mouth is drawn in a thin line, her cheeks flushed, her shoulders ramrod straight. I can feel the fury and tension emanating from her body all the way across the patio. For a moment, it seems like I'm glimpsing the personal side of Mrs. Morrison beneath the facade, a woman who is rattled and angry rather than the competent housekeeper who seamlessly glides down Marbrisa's corridors ensuring the house runs without a hitch.

She turns away from me.

"What happened?" I ask one of the workers standing near me.

He says nothing, making the sign of the cross over himself before walking away.

I scan the crowd—

Nathaniel has disappeared.

I slip through the throng to the front where Asher stands, his back to me, his shoulders hunched. His body blocks much of what is on the ground, but a peacock's plume peeks out, the colors instantly recognizable.

Asher whirls around.

"Don't look," he instructs, his voice grim.

"What happened?"

"One of the birds. It's dead. One of the maids found it." He pauses for a moment. Swallows. "It died badly."

I glance over his shoulder to a spot where the maid stands, her hands clutched to her chest, another woman's arm around her.

I can imagine that would be a horribly disturbing thing to find, but surely on an estate this size, animals die of natural causes. By the sound of those screams, I feared something far worse had happened.

The crowd shuffles uneasily, looking as though they've been collectively seized by something unpleasant.

"Not another one," someone mutters behind me.

I feel as though I have stepped into the middle of a play, and everyone knows the role they are supposed to adopt except for me. There's a familiarity to everyone's interactions, a re-signed weariness.

What on earth is going on?

The house's front steps seem like a strange place for a bird to be injured. Did it fall?

"What happened to it?" I ask Asher.

"I don't know, but I'm going to find out. Go back inside. Please."

"Does this often occur?" I ask, ignoring his instruction. "Do animals frequently die at Marbrisa?"

Asher takes my arm, drawing me gently away from the crowd.

"It occurs more often than it should."

There's something in his manner, in the paleness of my sister's face, in the maid's trembling body, in Mrs. Morrison's anger, in the crowd of onlookers—

"Do you think someone killed the bird?"

Asher is silent for a beat until I am sure he isn't going to answer me, and then he gives me a clipped nod. "It wouldn't be the first time."

"What do you mean?"

"Just that the animals at Marbrisa have a way of meeting nasty ends."

Suddenly, Nathaniel pops into view up ahead. I've no idea where he came from, but he's locked in conversation with the maid who first found the peacock. They're close enough to where Asher and I stand on the steps for me to make out pieces of their conversation over the din of everyone else.

"I didn't see anyone," the maid murmurs in response to whatever question Nathaniel's asked her, her shoulders shaking with a sob.

I yearn to inch closer to their conversation, to overhear

what they're saying. Once again, Nathaniel seems to have taken control of the situation, and I wonder at Asher's willingness to let him.

I study my brother-in-law more closely. "What else has happened?"

He's silent for a beat, and then he answers—

"At first it was lizards. Some snakes. Then an alligator. Now this."

"How gruesome." There's something particularly heinous about someone killing the local wildlife and displaying their trophies about the estate. What sort of person is capable of such a thing?

Is this what they've been living through? Why didn't Carolina say something? Is that why she's been acting so strangely?

"How long have these things been happening?"

"Too long. Well over a year. Maybe longer? It all sort of runs together at this point. At first, it was easy to dismiss the deaths as accidents, but then they became more frequent, harder to explain away. Almost like the culprit is thumbing their nose at us, daring us to ignore the behavior."

"You think it was intentional?"

"It's one too many coincidences for my liking."

"You should call the police."

"I have."

"And?"

"It's not like there's much they can do. We live among wildlife. These things happen."

He sounds as though he is parroting someone else's words rather than his own.

"Is that what you believe or what the police said?"

"It's what the officer who came out to investigate told us. He seemed more annoyed than anything else. This place—the locals are wary of it. It's infamous around here."

There's something almost wistful in the way he says the word "infamous," the way he scans the vast property like a man who can't quite believe his luck, that makes me reassess my earlier impression of Asher. He wears his wealth like he was born to it, but the hint of longing makes me wonder if he didn't have to work for what he has.

I know so little about the man my sister married—where he's from or how he came to own this great big house. At the time that Asher and Carolina became engaged, I was too young to be privy to much of the conversations that occurred before our parents gave their consent for the two of them to marry. Truthfully, Carolina was right—I think in a way they were eager to see her set on this new phase in her life, grateful they had so far sidestepped a major scandal given her often audacious behavior. Whatever they saw in Asher met their approval, I suppose, and it was clear that Carolina was never going to be satisfied with her life in Havana, that she was looking for something else.

They pinned their hopes on Asher making her happy, which from where I'm standing is beginning to look like a mistake.

"Who lived here before you and Carolina? There's a picture in my room of a woman at Marbrisa—Anna Barnes?"

"This has nothing to do with Anna Barnes."

"I wasn't suggesting it did. I just saw her name and thought—"

The rest of my words are cut off by the wind as Asher glances away from me, his attention on the area where the staff has gathered surrounding the poor bird's body.

He strides toward the group, and they part for him. He exchanges a few words with Nathaniel, the maid gone, and then Asher bends down, scooping the animal up. He turns, and our gazes connect for an instant. Gone is the version of Asher I saw earlier by the dock, the one who looked tired and worn down by the world. This Asher seems alight with fury; it emanates from him as though the peacock's death is a personal wrong that must be avenged.

I can't bear to lower my gaze, to see the poor animal in his arms.

Asher pivots, heading toward the gardens, and even though it is warm outside, there's a chill in the air, a sensation of rot and decay settling around Marbrisa and all her inhabitants.

∽

"I'm surprised you're not halfway to Havana by now."

I glance up from my sandwich, irritation filling me at the sight of Nathaniel strolling into the kitchen. It would figure that he would enter just as an errant piece of turkey doused in mayonnaise escapes my lips. I surreptitiously wipe at the offending poultry, hoping he didn't notice the small indignity.

No one returned to the dinner table after the peacock's discovery, and while I couldn't fathom having an appetite in the immediate aftermath, considering I haven't eaten anything since breakfast, hunger has overridden any squeamishness now that the midnight hour nears.

Thankfully, I found Marbrisa's kitchen to be well stocked and blessedly vacant when I came downstairs this evening.

Unfortunately, Nathaniel evidently had similar plans.

I swallow, carefully rising from my crouched position over the kitchen countertop, realizing how unladylike I must appear scarfing down the turkey and cheese sandwich.

He's still dressed in the same shirt and pants he was wearing hours earlier at dinner, but he's shucked his jacket and tie.

"I'm not easily scared off," I reply.

"Hmm. You'd be alone in that, then," he replies, heading for the refrigerator with the comfort and ease of someone who has clearly helped himself to a midnight snack or two in this kitchen before.

"And yet, you're not halfway to Boston."

Nathaniel smiles. "No, I'm not. I suppose you can say that I'm not easily scared off, either."

He pulls some leftover fruit salad out of the refrigerator, silently helping himself to one of the spoons from a nearby drawer.

Our house in Havana paled in size to the manse that is Marbrisa, and while my parents employed a staff—and a cook among them—our kitchen was still where we spent time as a family. My mother occasionally cooked, teaching me the basics so I would know my way around the kitchen. It was a warm, comfortable space. Marbrisa's kitchen would rival a kitchen in a hotel and then some. Whoever built this place clearly did so with a great deal of entertaining in mind. Now it looks deserted, only a fraction of the space in use. There's no warmth, none of the little details that make a house a home.

Once again, I can't help but wonder how Carolina would feel at ease here. I cast a sidelong glance at Nathaniel, hoping that the comfort he's displayed at Marbrisa thus far translates to an intimate knowledge of its secrets.

"The maid you spoke with earlier—the one who found the poor bird—she certainly seemed shaken by the entire business," I say.

Nathaniel stops eating, his spoon hovering in midair. "You're not like your sister, are you?" he asks, entirely sidestepping my comment.

I can't tell if he means it as a compliment or an insult, or understand how he could arrive at such a conclusion so quickly.

"What do you mean?"

My tone is as cold as an icebox.

"You're more direct than Carolina is," Nathaniel replies.

"I'm not sure I agree with you there. Carolina has always said exactly what came to mind with little concern for the consequences. It's one of the things I envy most about her."

And one of the things that frustrates me the most.

"The version of Carolina you're describing isn't the one I've gotten to know here."

"Do you know my sister well? I thought you were a friend of Asher's not Carolina's."

He laughs. "Like I said. You're direct."

"You didn't answer the question."

"I didn't realize I owed Carolina's little sister any explanations."

What an odious, arrogant man.

"Do you intend to stay here for the whole of the winter?" I ask, changing tack.

"Eager to be rid of me?"

"Not at all," I lie.

He smiles again, and I get the sense that he finds me amusing, as though I am a pantomime for his entertainment.

Infuriating.

"I do not intend to spend the whole of the winter here, no," Nathaniel answers after a beat. "I come and go as I please, as my affairs call me away."

"How fortunate you are to have such gracious hosts in Carolina and Asher."

"I am indeed. And you? Now that we've settled on the matter of you not leaving Marbrisa, what are your plans?"

"School. Work." None of your business.

His brow rises. "Work? No plans to follow your sister and undertake the bonds of holy matrimony?"

"You can hardly blame me, considering the example before me."

"You've picked up on the tension between them, have you?"

I hesitate, torn between my dislike for him and my desire for more information. "It's unmistakable. Things are—"

"Strained between them," he finishes.

I nod, unhappy with the prospect of Nathaniel finishing my sentences.

"Has it always been like this?" I ask him.

"I would think you would know better than anyone. After all, you're uniquely placed to be your sister's confidant."

"I'm not. And I don't know."

My words must betray some of the emotions churning inside me because he seems almost mollified by my response, as though he's remembered *why* I'm here, the tragedy lurking in my past.

"It's been like this since I've known them," Nathaniel finally replies, surprising me for the candor in his response when I had given up on him answering me at all.

He seems truly concerned, but I'm hesitant to trust him. There's something about him that gives the impression that he's trying just a smidge too hard. Whether it's merely the fact that he's potentially on the grift, enjoying the fruits of Asher's generosity, or my suspicion that he and Carolina could be having an affair, I have a feeling there's something about Nathaniel Hayes that isn't as it seems, and I've likely wrung as much of an admission of anything as I'm going to get out of him this evening.

Time for bed.

I sweep past him, taking the sandwich with me.

CHAPTER FIVE

I sleep fitfully, waking several times throughout the night. The mattress feels as unused to guests as the rest of the room, the surface hard in unusual places and soft in others. The unfamiliar noises the house makes leave me tossing and turning, the memory of that horrible scream when the peacock was found assailing me throughout the night.

After our late-night interlude, my mind wanders to the only other guest in the house—is Nathaniel's room near mine or is he in another part of the house? I've yet to glean the mansion's footprint, my strange welcome keeping me from my plans to explore Marbrisa.

Several times in the early hours of the morning, I hear footsteps down the hallway. An estate of Marbrisa's size takes a great number of people working long hours to run it, and I wonder about the poor woman who found the peacock earlier. Is the image of the bird's body haunting her dreams as much as it is haunting mine?

The sun is barely rising in the horizon when I climb out of bed and dress, determined to spend the morning exploring my new home. Despite the rocky start yesterday, I'm here for as long as it takes to convince Asher to turn my inheritance over to me.

I take the stairs quickly, eager to avoid running into anyone else. I've never been a morning person, and now, my mind muddled by a lack of sleep, it feels far too early to string coherent words together.

As soon as I step outside, I take a deep breath, the fresh air filling my lungs. It's a bright day, the sky a sparkling blue, the palm trees swaying with a light breeze. The lawn is perfectly manicured, a sea of green until the seawall hits the ocean.

There's something stale in the air inside the house, a mustiness that emanates from the walls and floors, the decay of a building that was neglected for too long before being resurrected.

Mrs. Morrison's earlier announcement that she worked for the previous owners and then returned years later when Asher hired her again comes to mind. What happened to the house in the period between the two owners? Was it vacant or did someone else live here? And why was it sold in the first place?

Mrs. Morrison might not want to talk to Carolina's sister, but it seems like she knows more about Marbrisa than most.

I glance at the water for a moment, the little boat that motored me over to Marbrisa yesterday no longer tied at the dock. I don't envy Asher and Carolina the presence of the bay at their backs. It's one thing to monitor who comes up the estate's elaborate driveway, who is lingering in the woods surrounding

Marbrisa, but the water leaves the entire shoreline exposed to whoever would want to come up to the dock. In Havana, the tightly packed city condensed us all in a manageable manner—there were only so many hiding places, so many corners for danger to lurk. But out here? The closest neighbor is miles away.

Whoever is targeting Marbrisa's animals could be someone who lives or works on the estate or someone else entirely. How do you guard against incursions when you possess so much of the land and sea that it's impossible to control who trespasses?

There's a maze off to the right of the house, beyond where the greenhouse lies, the maze's entrance just visible from my bedroom window. It's an interesting-looking structure; a lovely house is one thing, but how many people can lay claim to their own personal maze?

It seems as good of a place to start exploring as any, and I set off toward it when I spy a man crouching near one of the hedges, a set of shears in his hand.

I hesitate for a moment, watching as he hacks away at the errant branches.

He pauses and sets the garden shears down on the ground.

He rises from his crouched position. "Miss. Can I help you? I'm the gardener—George—at your service."

He looks too young to have worked here when the previous owners lived at Marbrisa, based on the timeline Mrs. Morrison gave me, but I have a feeling that if anyone is privy to the estate's secrets, it's the staff.

"It's nice to meet you. I'm Carmen," I reply. "I'm Carolina's sister."

He nods, his gaze trained to a point just above my head, his cheeks slightly pink, although whether the effect is from working in the sun all day or his discomfort in speaking with me, I can't tell.

"I know who you are. I didn't expect to see you out here, though. Your sister's not much for the outdoors."

Surprise fills me at his frank assessment. Carolina does indeed dislike the outdoors.

"I was curious about the maze. I can see the entrance from my bedroom window. I didn't realize anyone was working here, though. I'm sorry to disturb you."

"You're not disturbing me." He's silent for a moment, finally meeting my gaze. "I'll admit I've been curious about our infamous new guest."

"I'm hardly infamous," I protest.

"You'd be surprised. The house has been whispering about your visit."

"How long have you worked here?"

"A year or so, maybe? I was working at a grand estate up in Palm Beach, but my grandmother got sick, and I came home to take care of her."

"Do you like working here?"

"I've had worse jobs on estates not nearly as fine as this one." His gaze shifts from me to the house for a moment. "Marbrisa is special," he replies finally.

"Were you here yesterday? When they found the peacock?"

I don't remember seeing him in the crush, but I was so distracted by the commotion that I just as easily could have missed him.

"It was my day off. I heard about it, though. Some of the gardening crew didn't show up for work today."

"They just quit?"

How on earth is Asher going to maintain a property of this size if he can't staff it?

"Can't say I blame them given what happened to that poor animal," George replies.

"Asher mentioned this isn't the first time something like this has happened."

"That's true. Doubt it will be the last, either."

"Why do you say that?"

"It just seems like someone's intent on leaving a message of sorts. After all, why keep doing it? Takes a particular kind of sickness to mess with animals like that."

Working outside on the estate as much as he does, he must be familiar with the various animals that live here. Perhaps even cares for them as he does the greenery and flowers. There's a glint in his eyes like the one I saw in Mrs. Morrison's that suggests this isn't just a job to him, that perhaps there's something personal to it.

"Have you ever seen anything suspicious?" I ask him.

He smiles. "Are you a detective or something?"

"No, of course not. I just—something feels strange here. Like this place is—"

"Cursed?" he finishes for me.

I blink, surprised at the word he chose.

"No, I wasn't going to necessarily say that. Troubled, maybe."

He laughs, the sound low and gentle. "You've been here, what, less than twenty-four hours? Give it time."

"Is it really that bad?"

"No, I didn't say it was bad. Just complicated. Look, Marbrisa's a beautiful home. One of the finest in South Florida, if not the country."

He says it with an air of pride, and given the state of the gardens and the work he does here, I can't entirely blame him. He's young to be responsible for so much, and it's obvious he's talented at his craft. Did he get promoted by virtue of being one of the few who was willing to work under such conditions or was he hired on for the position?

"But that doesn't mean that there aren't strange things afoot, that we don't all feel it," George continues. "That there aren't rumors about the place, people who won't work here, staff who end up leaving and never look back."

I glance at the house, relieved to see that we're still in view. Farther afield, workers mill about the property. I'm grateful for the company, considering yesterday's troubles. George seems nice enough, but I'm beginning to realize that at Marbrisa, not everything is as it seems.

"You're still here," I reply.

"Like I said, Marbrisa's beautiful. There are a lot worse jobs to have than waking up to this every morning. Besides, if I don't care for her, who will?"

The reverence with which he speaks of the estate, as though it's somehow a living, breathing entity, strikes me again.

"Have you had a chance to tour the grounds yet?" he asks.

I shake my head. "I was tired when I arrived. Would you like to show me?"

"I'm not sure the lady of the house would like me escorting her sister around. Or Mr. Wyatt, for that matter."

So far, this is the most pleasant conversation I've had since I came to Marbrisa, and given Carolina's cold reception, Asher's strange manner, and Nathaniel's arrogance, I'm eager to make a friend.

"I won't tell her if you don't. And Asher won't mind. I don't get the impression that he's overly concerned with what I do."

"He's your guardian, isn't he?"

I flush. It's a little embarrassing to have a financial guardian at my age, considering I'm past my eighteenth birthday. George can't be that much older than I am, and yet, I envy him the freedom to make his own way in the world without having to ask someone else for permission.

"For the moment. My parents' affairs aren't entirely settled." I hesitate. "It seems the gossip network at Marbrisa is an active one."

He grins. "Like I said. You're the infamous sister." He's silent for a moment, considering, and then he nods. "Fine. I'll show you around."

My lips twitch slightly at the lack of enthusiasm in his voice.

"I'm sorry. I shouldn't have pushed. I understand if you have other things to do. I wouldn't want my infamy to rub off on you," I tease.

He shrugs, seemingly impervious to my half-hearted attempt at humor. "I have some time. Besides, you would do well to have someone show you the maze. It can be easy to get lost."

"How big is it?"

"Ten acres."

That does seem daunting.

He holds his hand out, indicating for me to proceed, and we walk toward the entrance of the maze.

"They used to have grand parties at the house. Rumor has it, some of the guests would go off together where no one could see them."

I blush at the implication contained there. "Do they still have parties here?"

"No. The parties stopped a long time ago, before Mr. Wyatt's time. He and your sister don't entertain much. Besides Mr. Hayes."

He says the latter's name in a hushed tone, and I get the impression that he isn't a fan of Nathaniel Hayes. If I saw Carolina sneaking off near the greenhouse, what are the odds that George might have seen something as well?

"Now the maze goes mostly unused," George adds. "Mr. Wyatt likes to come here before sunset. People say he walks the maze at all hours of the night."

"Alone?"

George nods.

"That sounds strange."

"The staff whispers about it," he admits after a pause.

I get the impression that he's hesitant to say too much about my sister and brother-in-law for fear of repercussions. Will I run into the same roadblock with Mrs. Morrison? How is it possible to get to the bottom of who is behind the strange happenings at Marbrisa if everyone is too afraid to speak about them?

"What do they say?"

He shrugs again. "Just another one of the things at Marbrisa that doesn't make a lot of sense."

What does Carolina think about her husband wandering outside at all hours of the night?

We pause at the maze's entrance. The hedges are tall, thick shrubs creating an impenetrable wall. Sharp angles and perfectly symmetrical rows show a structure that has been painstakingly manicured by someone who appears to take the job very seriously. The gravel pathways are wide enough for us to walk beside each other with some room in between.

The early-morning mist has settled around the hedges, giving the whole place a slightly ephemeral, romantic look.

George gestures for me to walk ahead once more.

"Is the maze your responsibility, too?" I ask as we step into the space.

I stop, immediately confronted with a choice—to go left or right.

I glance back at George, curious to see if he's going to give me any indication of which direction to take, but he's silent, a ghost of a smile on his lips.

I turn right, George on my heels.

George nods. "It's one of the hardest parts of the property to care for, to be honest. Mr. Wyatt doesn't care as much if the rest of the landscaping is a bit wild, says it adds to the character of this place. But the maze—well, he can be very exacting about that."

When I first saw Asher yesterday, he had the air of a man who had resigned himself to something, but I saw a flash of that determination last night when he picked up the bird's body—a sense of ownership over Marbrisa and a responsibility for all on the estate's grounds. It isn't hard to imagine that he would care a great deal about the details he can control.

Asher isn't wrong in his design; the house wouldn't be half as grand without its surroundings. Whoever built the estate must have preserved much of the natural landscaping, only razing the necessary parts to build the main house and requisite outbuildings. Some of the trees look far too old to have been recent additions, and they're lovely in their intricate trunks, their gnarled, sweeping branches. The palm trees tower high into the sky, giving the impression that they have been here for a very long time and will continue to thrive after we are gone.

George nods when I voice the thought out loud.

"Rumor has it that when this place was built, the owner oversaw every aspect of the design involved with the main house. He spared no expense shipping furnishings and decorations from all over the world to make Marbrisa the grandest home. Some say he was obsessed with his quest. While he was occupied with the main house, his wife oversaw the design of the gardens."

I stop again, another choice before me. I remember enough of my Greek history to feel as though I'm a maiden trapped in the Minotaur's labyrinth.

My heart pounds a little quicker, and this time when another choice is set before me, I don't look back at George, but instead decide to turn left on my own, curious to see which way this path will take me.

I've always liked puzzles, which I suppose is part of why history has always appealed to me so. The past feels like a tapestry that tells a story, all the events laid out just so in order to predict the future. Whoever constructed this maze must have enjoyed puzzles, too, because there's something thrilling about the experience.

"When was Marbrisa built?" I ask George.

"1918. Just as the Great War was ending."

This house has existed through two major world wars—the first shuttering at its inception and the second now as war is raging in Europe. Whether the United States will abandon its official position of neutrality and enter the conflict remains to be seen. In Cuba, there was an ongoing conversation about whether we would follow our closest ally into battle. If the United States does choose to enter the war, life will likely look far different.

"Who were they? The original owners?"

This time I take a right turn.

"Rich people who came down from up north looking to make their fortune. Lots of people like that flocked to Florida before the land boom burst in the 1920s."

"Are you from Miami?" I ask him.

"Lived here my whole life."

I stop, turning to face him. "Was one of Marbrisa's original owners Anna Barnes?"

"Who told you about Anna Barnes?"

"No one. There's a painting of a woman in my room. Her name is on it."

"I'm not surprised. Anna and her husband Robert built the house. Or rather, Robert built the house for Anna. It was his birthday gift to her, or so the rumor goes. It was before my time, obviously."

"Some birthday gift," I muse, taking in the grandeur that is Marbrisa. "He must have loved her a great deal."

"Maybe. Who knows? After all, he built Marbrisa at a time when people were only starting to develop this part of Florida. Maybe it was just a good investment."

"Still, there's something romantic about it," I reply.

The care that was taken in constructing Marbrisa is evident throughout the estate. For a husband to go to such trouble for his wife is a grand gesture, indeed. These days, it feels like a boy asking me to dance is the extent of romance I see. Anna must have been thoroughly swept off her feet.

I close my eyes for an instant, and I imagine Anna and Robert here, strolling through the maze hand in hand. Perhaps he gifted her with a flower he plucked from the gardens.

It's a shame that such a beautiful testament of their love has turned so cold.

"Some say Anna haunts Marbrisa."

It's such a ridiculous notion that I can't help but laugh.

"I'm a little too old to believe in ghosts."

George shrugs. "I doubt the ghosts care very much whether you believe in them or not. I'm just saying that there are some strange things happening in this house."

"A ghost didn't kill that peacock."

"Maybe. Maybe not."

"So that's what has the staff so scared—they really think a ghost is haunting Marbrisa?"

Is the fear what was responsible for Mrs. Morrison's strange demeanor yesterday? The housekeeper was clearly upset about something—was it history repeating itself? Were there similar occurrences during her initial time at Marbrisa? Have people always believed the house to be haunted?

"You can laugh all you want, but there's an energy here," George says, rubbing the back of his neck. "Something that just feels off. Eventually, you'll feel it, too."

I don't want to encourage this ghost nonsense by admitting that I know what he's talking about, that I *have* felt it, too.

His hand drops to the side, and George tilts his head, studying me, and suddenly, I realize since we've stopped walking we're standing uncomfortably close together.

He's even younger than I originally thought, not that much older than I am. His skin is tanned from working outside all day, brown hair peeking out from beneath his gardener's cap.

I start to ask him why people think that Anna haunts Marbrisa, the way Asher looked when I asked him about Anna coming to mind once more, but the words are stuck in my throat as I realize how close we are standing to each other.

"We should go in. It's about to rain," George murmurs, his gaze intent on mine.

His eyes are a mossy green.

I break eye contact with him, my heart pounding as I stare up at the sky. Sure enough, it's darker than it was when we first came out here, an awareness prickling in the air, a change in the wind, a hint of a warning and then—

The heavens open and the rain pours down.

I shriek, the water pelting us. The instant of notice we received before the storm rolled in was hardly enough to do us any good.

George grabs my hand, his palm slippery against mine, and pulls me through the maze, toward the house, toward shelter.

This time, he assumes charge, navigating the twists and turns with ease, taking us back to the entry point as the water assaults us. He must know the pathway by heart, given the quickness with which he decides which direction to take.

When we reach the maze's entrance, it feels as though we have left a secret world behind us, and where something seemed to have loosened within him inside the protection of the high hedges, now I can sense an impatience within George, a hesitation.

We are at once returned to our natural roles at Marbrisa— he is a member of the staff, I am a guest of the house.

He lets go of my hand.

I glance up at the house, as we run for cover, at a movement in one of the upstairs windows.

There's a reflection staring back at me through the pane, the image slightly hazy from a distance, a shape floating above us.

The closer I get, it becomes clear that the shape is a woman.

Carolina stands at the window, looking down at me, a frown on her face.

CHAPTER SIX

Anna

A crowd has gathered near the water's edge, staring down into the inky sea. We had planned for fireworks out on the back lawn as a highlight of the evening, but our guests have gathered here before the festivities were set to commence, no doubt drawn to the screams as I was.

Michael stands behind me, and I scan the crowd looking for my husband, searching for the source of all the commotion.

"Do you see Robert?" I ask Michael.

"No. Stay here, though. I'll see what's going on."

The guests have seemingly moved closer to the water, to where Marbrisa meets Biscayne Bay.

Where is Robert?

I look for a familiar face now that Michael has gone off, but I see no one I recognize, all these people strangers to me.

"What has happened?" I ask the woman standing next to me, feeling a bit like a guest at my own party.

"I'm not sure. I just followed everyone out here. Perhaps it's some planned entertainment," she adds, her voice filled with excitement.

If it is, it's something I'm certainly not privy to, but then again, it's entirely possible that my husband has a surprise or two up his sleeve. I open my mouth to tell her so, when I spy him, walking away from the water.

Robert.

I push my way to the front, heart pounding, relief filling me.

I freeze mid-step.

He looks—wrong, somehow. He's wearing an expression I've never seen on him before in all these years of marriage.

"What's happened?" I ask him.

His face is white as a sheet. "One of the guests. A woman. She fell into the bay."

I gasp.

I move forward and glance over his shoulder.

A body lies in the grass.

I take a step closer, my mind protesting the scene before me even as my feet carry me forward.

The woman rests on the ground, her dark hair wet and tangled around her. Her skin is pale in the moonlight.

It's warm out, but how cold is it in the water? And how long was she in there?

Her gown pools around her, the color nearly blending with the dark earth.

A memory comes to me, the deep purple color recognizable. It's the woman I saw earlier after I descended the staircase. The snake necklace is still wrapped around her neck.

I take a step forward to offer my assistance. Suddenly, Robert is at my elbow, pulling me back.

I whirl around to face him.

"Is she alright?" I ask. "Is there a doctor here? Should we call someone to help her?"

He swallows. "It wouldn't do any good. She's dead."

"What?" I struggle to turn around and sneak another look at the woman in question, but he holds on to me, and it isn't until I feel my legs giving way beneath me that I realize he's keeping me from falling to the ground.

I glance back at Marbrisa, the lights blazing inside, the sound of raucous laughter carrying outside.

Some of the guests have clearly come to Robert's aid, struggling to form a perimeter to hold the curious onlookers at bay.

"What happened?" I ask again.

Robert shakes his head, looking as shocked as I feel. "I don't know. I saw her earlier strolling near the water, but I didn't think anything of it. She was hardly the only guest to want to enjoy the view." He's silent for a moment. "There's been a great deal of drinking tonight. Perhaps she got too close to the edge and lost her footing."

"How awful."

Tears fill my eyes. I can't help but feel somewhat responsible. It's our house, our party. Not to mention, this is the second person now that we've lost to the bay.

"Was she alone when it happened?" I ask.

It's so crowded tonight. How did no one see her go into the water? How did no one help her?

"I have no idea," he answers, his voice grim. "I came out

when I heard the screams. One of the guests was walking by and saw her floating in the water."

"We need to go for help. Should we call the police? What can I do?"

"One of the guests is already taking care of it. I'll speak to the police," Robert replies. "You go up and rest. You needn't concern yourself with this terrible business." He glances to a spot over my shoulder. "Michael, will you take her up?"

Michael steps forward, coming to stand at my side. I didn't even realize he'd come back.

"Of course."

Robert strides away from me quickly, taking charge of the situation like he always does.

Michael offers his arm, but I shake my head. "I'm alright. Just shaken a bit, I suppose. That poor woman."

It seems too horrible to voice aloud the thoughts coursing through me—what was it like for that poor woman in the water? How long was she in there? Did she cry out for rescue, her words carried on the wind not to be heard over the sound of the band? My mind tumbles down all sorts of possibilities with macabre ease.

"Someone will have to tell her family," I say. "Was anyone with her tonight?"

We received a few visitors when we first arrived at Marbrisa, mainly the wives of friends and business associates of Robert's, but I put little effort into getting to know my neighbors, reluctant at this point in my life to start forging new friendships, making new connections. I did all that in my younger years, when I was a new bride learning how to build a marriage, and now I find the whole process of socializing rather exhausting, like a game I'd rather sit and watch from the sidelines.

"I believe she came here alone," Michael replies.

"Did you know her?" I ask him.

He's pale, just like Robert was, and given what he told me about fighting in the Great War and his manner when he said it, the tension in his body, the way he looked past me rather than at me as though he was haunted by something I couldn't see, I worry this has dredged up memories of death.

He hesitates. "I saw her around at parties and that sort of thing."

There are so many people here tonight, some with official invitations, many others likely gate-crashing, eager to catch a glimpse of Marbrisa. I'm not sure which category this woman belonged to.

"I saw her earlier. In the ballroom." I take a deep breath, surprised at how shaky my voice is.

Michael says nothing as we walk toward the main house. A couple of times, I stumble in my heels on a piece of uneven terrain, and he reaches out, steadying me.

Here I was worried about him, and he's the one taking care of me.

"Do you need a moment?" he asks me, concern in his gaze. "Before we go back in the house?"

I take a deep breath, realizing that news of the poor woman's drowning is likely to spread to the rest of the party soon, and no doubt it will become a spectacle for anyone looking to seize on the latest piece of gossip.

"Perhaps." I try to calm my racing heart. "It won't help the situation if I go in there looking a fright and rile everyone up." I glance back at where Robert stands talking to some of the guests, the woman lying on the ground beside them.

"Maybe I should go up and get a sheet or something to cover her," I murmur to Michael.

It feels wrong to leave her exposed like this for people to gawk over.

We don't even know her name.

"I can get something," he replies. "I told Robert I'd take you up to your room so you could rest."

"It's alright. I promise I'm not that fragile. You have more than discharged your duty to the Barnes family. It just caught me off guard. First that poor man drowns during the construction, and now this."

It's beginning to feel like Marbrisa is cursed.

~

HOURS LATER, THE guests long gone, Robert still hasn't come upstairs to our rooms.

I walk over to the window, pulling back the curtain, and stare below. Flashlight beams illuminate the ground, some of the officers that were called to assist with the accident still on the property.

I'm surprised they're still here, honestly, considering this is hardly a mystery to be solved. It's a tragedy that the woman fell into the water, but I'd think it was a cut-and-dried nasty business.

Finally, I can't take the suspense anymore, and I change out of the robe I slipped on earlier into a simple dress and head downstairs.

When I reach the base of the stairs, the main entryway is filled with people milling about, the woman lying on a metal stretcher, her body partially covered with a white sheet.

A man in a fedora stands near her, a small notepad and pen in hand, jotting down some notes as he leans over her.

Death has settled over her face now, her body—

I don't realize I've gasped aloud until the man jerks his head up, his gaze connecting with mine.

I reach out, gripping the banister to steady myself.

Something nags at me, a thought that comes to me quickly and is gone as soon as it arrives. Hours ago, I stood at the bottom of this same staircase and saw the woman alive. Now—

"I'm sorry." I feel as though I'm babbling, the shock of seeing her like this—hours ago, she looked peaceful, almost, but the change is noticeable, and suddenly, my head spins from the champagne I've consumed, from the horror of everything that has happened. "I didn't mean to startle you."

The man shakes his head. "It seems I'm the one who startled you. You must be Mrs. Barnes. I'm Detective Pierce. Sorry if we disturbed you. Your husband was insistent that we didn't, but police work isn't exactly a quiet business."

"It's fine."

I wrap my arms around myself, suddenly wishing I'd grabbed a shawl when I came downstairs. Despite the normally warm climate, it feels cold in this house, the woman's body lying just feet away.

"Do you know who she is?" I ask the detective.

It feels strangely intimate to see her in such a state when I have no idea what her name is.

"Her name is Lenora Watson. Some of the other guests identified her."

Lenora.

"Have you told her family?"

"We're in the process of notifying her next of kin. We're still trying to figure out what happened here."

"She fell into the water."

That's right, isn't it? That's what Robert said earlier, at least. There's something sharp about Detective Pierce, a rapid-fire impatience that has me feeling as though I am several steps behind him, my brain like the muck at the water's bank.

I blink, a memory flitting through my mind again and then escaping as quickly as it came.

"I'm sorry—I'm—I'm not myself today."

It seems unwise to admit a flaw in front of this man; he gives the impression that he is eager to seize on any such imperfection and make the most of it for his own means.

"That's understandable given all that has transpired this evening. Were you there when it happened, Mrs. Barnes?"

I shake my head, feeling a bit like a marionette, as though I am floating above my body, watching this entire precarious scene unfold. I wish that I had waited until the police were gone to come downstairs, that I could have postponed this entire business until tomorrow morning when I was more collected and poised for the inevitable questions that would come my way.

"No, I was inside the house. I had been talking to our architect, Michael Harrison. I heard the screaming and went outside to see what had happened."

"Were you with your husband as well?"

"No, Robert was with our guests."

"Do you remember who?"

"No. It was a big party. To be honest, they were all more Robert's guests than mine. As soon as we arrived, everyone wanted to speak with him about the house, to congratulate him on his triumph."

"And you didn't want to be congratulated?"

There's a touch of irony in his voice when he asks the question.

"No—I—I didn't do anything. I didn't build the house."

Detective Pierce doesn't say anything, but the expression flits across his face just the same—

Neither did your husband. He just paid the bills.

I can read the contempt in his eyes and on his face as surely as if he had just voiced the thought aloud. I wonder if he came here from elsewhere like we did, or if he grew up in Miami, if he views us as moneyed interlopers intent on transforming the hometown he knows and loves into something unrecognizable.

"It's some house," he drawls.

I open my mouth to defend Robert, all of us. I realize how this must look—this ostentatious mansion, this decadent party brimming with champagne and jewels, the dead woman—

I open my mouth to—

Her necklace is gone.

I blink, trying to remember—was she wearing it earlier? Or

was it my imagination? Did I see it because I expected it to be there?

No, it was there when they pulled her out of the water, I'm certain of it. Did the police take it?

"She was wearing a necklace. Did you remove it from her?"

Detective Pierce glances down at the body and back at me. "What do you mean she was wearing a necklace? How do you know?"

"I saw her wearing it earlier at the party."

"I thought the two of you had never met."

"We hadn't—I—"

"Your husband told me you had never met."

"We *hadn't*. I just noticed her wearing the necklace. We saw each other in passing before she drowned."

His gaze narrows. "You just said that most of the guests were your husband's, implied that you didn't know anyone very well, and yet, I'm to believe that your path just happened to cross with a woman who ended up dead less than what—an hour later?—and she left such an impression that you remembered the jewelry she was wearing?"

"I don't know what you're meant to believe, but it's the truth. I remembered the necklace because it was beautiful, distinctive."

I don't add the rest—that I remembered her in part because of how much she studied me and my own ensemble. It seems disrespectful to point out that aspect of her behavior.

"Did she say something to you?" Detective Pierce asks.

"No. It was a moment. Our gazes met and I noticed her dress and necklace. I thought she looked lovely."

"When?"

"What?"

"When did you see her?" he asks.

"I don't know. I wasn't exactly keeping track of the time. It was not long after we arrived downstairs."

He jots something down in his little notebook before turning his attention back to me.

"Was she with anyone when you saw her? Talking to someone, perhaps? Arguing with someone?"

"No. I don't know. I really didn't notice her enough to take in all that. It was a few seconds at most."

"Did she seem upset?"

"I don't think so." I wrack my brain, trying to remember that moment. I was so happy that Robert was finally relaxing, getting the credit he was due. And then I saw Michael and we began talking—

"Did she seem like she'd had too much to drink?" the detective asks me.

"Not that I could tell. But I'll be honest, I interacted with her so little, I'm not sure I'm the best person to ask. There were probably people here who spent more time with her than I did."

"What was the necklace like?"

I blink again, trying to keep up with his questions. It's late, and a slight ache is forming in my head from the champagne I drank earlier.

"It was a snake. That was why I noticed it. It was unique. Beautiful. The snakeskin was encrusted with jewels."

"Encrusted with jewels?" He arches a brow, a low whistle escaping from his lips. "Sounds expensive."

"If it was real, yes, I imagine it would have been."

"Do you think it was fake?"

I shrug helplessly. "I have no idea. I'm hardly a jeweler. She wouldn't have been the first woman to wear paste."

"Do you wear paste?"

He throws the question out there like a challenge, and I get the sense that he's trying to convict me of something, but of what, I have no idea.

I scan the room for Robert, wishing he would come sort everything out, that the officers would leave and take Lenora's body with them.

"No—I—my husband—"

"Can I help you with something, Detective?"

I turn at the sound of Michael's voice, more grateful to see him than I've ever been.

Michael walks up and stands next to me.

"Are you alright?" he asks, his voice low.

I nod. "Where is Robert?"

"He's outside dealing with some matters." Michael turns his attention toward the detective. "Are you all almost finished here?"

Surprise fills me at the hostility in his voice, the way he positions his body so he's slightly in front of me, between me and the detective. They're of a similar age, but the detective is broader of shoulder and an inch or two shorter.

I can't help but wonder if Detective Pierce served in the war as well—there's something military-like in his precise bearing.

"Not quite," Detective Pierce answers, a faint smile playing at his lips as though he's amused by the whole business, un-fazed by Michael.

There's a crashing noise somewhere behind me.

I close my eyes, taking a deep breath to steady my nerves.

The woman's bloated face and mottled skin stare back at me, the markers of death now burned in my brain.

I open my eyes.

Michael seems to be similarly affected, his gaze averted from the body as well.

"Get Robert. Please," I murmur to Michael.

Surely, there's nothing to stop the police from taking the woman's body now. I want them out of my house, want things to go back to normal, want to sleep off this nightmare.

"If you need anything from us, we're happy to help, but it's getting late," I say. "Surely, this business can wait until the morning."

"I don't think it can," Detective Pierce answers.

"I applaud your dedication, Detective, and this was a trag-edy," I reply. "But I hardly see what else there is to discuss. Accidents happen."

Detective Pierce smiles, but there's no humor in it.

"Who said this was an accident?"

CHAPTER SEVEN

Carmen

I see you got caught up in one of our thunderstorms."

As I cross the threshold into the entryway, the rain still pouring outside, I nearly collide with Nathaniel.

I can't stop a groan from escaping my lips.

I invited George to come in to escape the elements, but he shook his head no, opting instead for the comfort of the greenhouse. I can't say I entirely blame him, considering the overall lack of warmth at Marbrisa. I'd rather be among plants than be the recipient of Nathaniel's judgmental gaze.

"I was out for a stroll, exploring the property," I reply, a shiver wracking my body. "I wanted to learn a bit more about my new home."

"In this weather?"

"It's not like I predicted the rainstorm." The skirt of my dress sticks to my legs, the bodice plastered against me.

Nathaniel makes an impatient noise. He removes his jacket, draping it over my shoulders before I can protest.

It smells faintly of tobacco and spice, the fabric still warm from his body.

It's the gentlemanly thing to do, of course, and I can't fault him for it, but it irks me just the same to be in a position of taking favors from this man I dislike. Even if I am warmer now.

"Do you think that was wise?" Nathaniel asks me, his brow arched in that imperious manner of his. "I'd be worried about more than the weather, considering what happened yesterday."

"Are you saying I'm in danger at Marbrisa? I thought it was only animals who had been targeted. Am I supposed to spend all day in my room?"

"No, not necessarily. But I'd be careful just the same. Asher has had a terrible time with the staff. The turnover is high, and he takes who he can get. It's hard to know who you can trust. It's likely one of the staff members is responsible for the goings-on at Marbrisa."

"To what end? I'd think they'd want to keep their jobs above all else."

"Is that what the gardener told you?"

"Were you spying on me?" I ask incredulously, surprised at the gall he has. Just because Asher is technically the custodian of my funds doesn't give his friends the right to treat me as though I am under their care.

"Just happened to be glancing out the window when you and your friend went walking toward the maze."

Anger fills me. I shrug off the jacket, thrusting it toward Nathaniel. It hangs between us before he takes it from me, his expression inscrutable.

"Yes, George was kind enough to show me the estate. He has a great deal of pride for the work he's done in the gardens. Asher is lucky to have him."

"I think Asher counts himself lucky he has any staff left given the superstitions surrounding this place."

"Do you not believe in superstitions, Mr. Hayes?"

A ghost of a smile stretches across his face. "Why? Do you hope to scare me away?"

"Not at all. I just noticed that you seemed rather engrossed in conversation with the staff yesterday. I was surprised that a guest would have such concern over what happens at the estate."

"I care about my friends. Asher has had a rough time of it lately."

"Because of what's happening at Marbrisa?"

"Among other things."

"And my sister? Do you count her among your friends?"

"Carmen."

My name echoes throughout the grand entryway.

We both turn.

Carolina stands at the top of the staircase.

"That's my cue to leave," Nathaniel murmurs, striding off in the opposite direction.

I stare after his retreating back, studying his mannerisms, the way he moves. Could he be the man I saw leaving the greenhouse? I wish I knew for sure.

He doesn't seem like the sort of person who would be cowed by Carolina, especially considering how forward he's been with me, so why bother to go to the trouble to leave? Is it merely simple dislike between them, or is there something more at play that I'm not privy to?

"You should be careful with the company you keep," Carolina announces from her perch at the top of the staircase, a cigarette dangling from her red-lacquered fingertips.

I wince as I climb the steps to meet her, fully aware of how wet I am. The rain did its damage before we were able to make it to the house, and with each step I take, a trail of water follows me. My skirts are plastered to my legs, my hair soaked, my silk shoes no doubt ruined.

I shiver once more, regretting my impulse to return Nathaniel's jacket to him.

Carolina, of course, looks stunning—not a hair out of place. It was like that when we were kids, too—if she ever broke a sweat, I never saw it.

She takes a drag of her cigarette.

"I don't know what you're talking about," I reply, unsure if she's referring to my exploration with George, my interlude with Nathaniel, or some other sisterly slight I am unaware of. I stop when we're nearly eye level at the top of the stairs. "You've hardly been around to be my guide. I haven't seen you since that nasty business at dinner. Where did you go?"

"To my room."

"You weren't curious about what had happened?"

"No, I wasn't."

I don't believe her for a second.

The fingers resting on her cigarette tremble slightly. For all her bravado, something has her unsettled. Just what is she hiding here?

Is it an affair or something more?

"I heard it isn't the first time something like that has happened at Marbrisa."

"It isn't. I doubt it will be the last, either." She throws the second part out like a challenge. "A woman was murdered here, you know."

It's such a Carolina thing to say that for a moment, I don't react. When we were children, she was always like this—telling me stories to scare me at night. Maybe it's to be expected of older siblings—perhaps they exist to give the younger ones a hard time, to make sure we're prepared for whatever the world throws our way, or it's simply a perverse joy in having someone to push around.

"Are you going to tell me ghost stories now? I'm no longer six years old and afraid of the dark."

Carolina laughs, the sound unnaturally loud in the stillness of the house. It's like the size of the estate swallows its inhabitants, minimizing their impact, forcing its residents to confront their mortality with the inescapable fact that long after we are ash and dust, these walls will still stand.

"You never got it, did you?" Carolina takes another drag of her cigarette. "The most fun happens in the dark."

"Maybe we have different definitions of fun."

"No doubt we do. You could do with a little fun, little sister."

"Who was the woman?" I ask, ignoring the dig falsely cloaked in well-meaning advice.

"Anna Barnes. The mistress of the house. Her husband built this whole estate as a testament to their love. And then he killed her."

Anna Barnes.

Murder? How did her marriage turn bad so quickly? To go from building an estate like this out of love to murder is a horrific leap.

Carolina flings Anna's name out carelessly, as though she has no fear of ghosts or their wrath, as though there's no power in saying the woman's name, those letters strung together giving her a sort of permanence.

"How do you know?"

I'm still not ready to give up the story I've built up in my mind, the romance between Anna and Robert I imagined when I was in the maze. I don't want to believe that something so terrible could happen here, but even as I try to discount it, the truth of the matter slides into place like a puzzle piece. Everyone has told me about the superstitions that Marbrisa is haunted. I might not believe in ghosts per se, but it's easy to believe that if something as terrible as murder happened here, it would leave a mark.

Carolina shrugs. "Everyone talks about it if you go to the right places."

"And what places are those?"

Where do you go, big sister?

"The fun ones. The ones that would shock and scandalize you. Miami is more than this boring old house, you know. You should get out some time. Live a little. Before you wake up one day and realize you've missed out on everything."

"I saw you."

I didn't intend to say it, didn't intend to prove her words by acting scandalized by what I witnessed, but it's impossible for me to keep the quiet condemnation from my voice, because we're too far set in the roles we have played for so long. Carolina is the outrageous one, frequently pushing the bounds of propriety and then some, and I'm constantly torn between envy and censure.

Carolina pauses, the cigarette hovering in midair as she levels me with a stare, the amusement in her eyes replaced with steel.

"I don't know what you're talking about."

"Yes, you do. Leaving the greenhouse yesterday. With that man."

Carolina closes the distance between us, gripping my arm, shaking me, so quickly I can barely register the moment, her hold surprisingly strong for a woman who moves so languidly all the time.

"You're mistaken."

The ash from her cigarette dangles off the edge, hitting my bare arm.

I wince, struggling to free myself from her hold, but Carolina only moves closer.

"Don't follow me around. You won't like what you see, *little sister.*"

"You're playing with fire," I warn.

"You have no idea what you're inserting yourself into. You've only been here a day. You know nothing about what it's like here. You have no idea what being married is like. Especially to a man like Asher. It's so easy to judge when you've spent your life being coddled by our parents, when your every need has been taken care of. It's easy to judge when you've lived a child's life with a child's responsibilities and concerns."

"It's not like that now, is it?" I shoot back. "I was left with a funeral to arrange in Havana, affairs to settle. I'm the one who doesn't have a place to go, doesn't have a family, doesn't have anything but your husband's good graces to fall back on. You have all this. Why would you risk your future, jeopardize everything? If Asher finds out you're cheating on him—"

"Are you threatening me? What—are you going to tell Asher about what you saw?"

"No, of course not," I reply, truly appalled that she would think me capable of such a thing. "You're my sister. I won't tell Asher, but you should stop what you're doing. Do you really think it's wise carrying on with someone in the same house where you live with your husband, under his very nose? If I saw you, who else could have?"

"What are you, my conscience now?"

"No, but I am worried about you."

Now that we're closer, I can just make out the faint dark smudges under her eyes.

"Are you alright?" I ask, careful to keep my voice low lest someone overhear us. "You don't seem like yourself."

"How would you know?" she counters. "We haven't seen each other in six years."

"Why does it always have to be like this between us? You're my sister and I love you."

"Let's not pretend that we've ever been close or that we've ever seen eye to eye on things. You're here because you have nowhere else to go."

Her words sting for the truth in them because she's right— I have nowhere else to go.

"Marbrisa isn't your home. It will never be your home," Carolina continued.

"As you so accurately pointed out, I didn't exactly have anywhere else to go. So for now it must be."

"You could have stayed in Havana."

"With what money? Your husband controls my inheritance."

"You must have a plan, then, for getting the money. I've never known you to not have one."

"What is that supposed to mean?"

"Oh, come on, ever since you were a child, things have always worked out for you. You've always had a talent for getting what you want."

For a moment, I'm so surprised I can't formulate a response. The way she described me is exactly what I would have said about her.

"I do not always get what I want."

She rolls her eyes. "Please. Our parents could never say no to you."

"They never said no to you, either."

"They never said no to me because I wore them down. It's not the same thing. You were always their favorite."

"I was not."

"You were. You always did everything they said. You were the easy one."

"You could have been 'easy.' You chose not to be."

She laughs. "Is that how it is for you? Do you just tell yourself you have to behave a certain way, follow a certain set of rules, and everything just works out?"

"It's easier than the alternative—doing whatever you want, damn the consequences."

"What if I could convince Asher to turn over your inheritance? Would you go then?"

The eagerness with which she suggests me leaving Miami stings, but the freedom offered is certainly appealing.

"Could *you* convince Asher?" I retort. "Given what I saw last night, it hardly seems as though the two of you are close."

"He's my husband. And he's a man. Trust me."

There's bravado in her words, but the uncertainty in her eyes belies her confidence.

"Carolina—"

I take a step forward. The wet sole of my shoe slips on the marble staircase.

I open my mouth to scream, my arms flailing behind me to regain my balance, to brace myself from falling.

It's too late, though. I'm already leaning backward—

Carolina reaches out, her hand grabbing my shoulder, her fingers digging into my skin, her nails sharp against my flesh.

For a moment, I hover where I am, suspended between standing and falling, and then I reach out, taking hold of my sister, using her to steady myself.

My arms wrap around her, my heart pounding, and there's an instant when I think that Carolina is going to push me away, but instead she holds on tightly.

I glance back over my shoulder at the long staircase, a little dizzy at the sight of all the steps beneath me. If I'd fallen, I could have broken my neck.

A woman stands down the hall, her back to us as though she's leaving, the hem of her dark dress visible, the curve of her waist, and then she's gone, and we're alone again once more.

～～

I OPEN THE door to my room, still unsettled by the business on the staircase.

When I enter the room, my gaze immediately drifts to the painting of Anna Barnes. It's more than a little disturbing to think that I'm sleeping in the same bedroom as the image of a murdered woman.

What happened to her? Carolina said that Anna's husband killed her, but my sister has never been the most reliable source of information. Is that fact, rumor, or conjecture?

I still.

A sound emanates from the wall closest to the painting.

It's a faint thump, like muffled footsteps.

I walk over to the wall.

Silence.

The walls are papered in silk, a pattern of vines and flowers throughout. The vines are a deep mossy green like the ones growing on the stones in Marbrisa. The flowers are a crimson red. The paper is slightly faded, as though it's original to the house; the reddish color has run in some places from the elements.

I never noticed before, but up close they sort of look like bloodstains smeared against the silk panels.

I blink, staring back at the wallpaper.

They're flowers once more.

"Don't be ridiculous," I mutter to myself. It's the lack of sleep that's getting to me, the weight of all the grief that's been heaped upon me these past few weeks.

There's another thump, even fainter than before.

I place my ear to the wall.

Nothing.

I pull back.

Maybe it was the pipes. I can only imagine what the bones must be like in a house like this. By all accounts, it isn't that old, if George was right and it was built right around the end of the Great War, but there's something about the place that makes it feel older—the architecture, perhaps, that harkens back to a style centuries ago; the sensation that you are suspended in time and space, that in crossing the threshold to Marbrisa you have suddenly left 1941 for an earlier era.

I turn away, feeling more than a little silly that I was suspicious of the noise. I glance back at the painting of Anna Barnes. It's terrible what happened to her, but the tensions in this house aren't the result of a ghost, and a ghost didn't kill that peacock.

One of the maids has clearly been in my room, the tangled sheets I left on top of the bed this morning neatly made. There's something resting on my comforter.

I walk over to the bed, staring down at the object lying there.

It's a necklace made of two twisted figures encrusted in jewels.

I pick it up and run my fingers over the stones.

It's a unique piece, custom, by the look of it, and undoubtedly expensive.

Is it Carolina's? If so, I've never seen her wear it. It certainly isn't a family heirloom. Perhaps it's a gift, a peace offering of sorts, but considering our showdown on the staircase, that seems unlikely, too.

If it is a peace offering, it's a strange one.

The two figures almost look like—

Snakes.

The necklace is slightly damp to the touch, the metal cold against my skin. There's a distinctive smell coming off it, one that it takes me a moment to identify, a salty tang in the air.

It smells like the sea.

CHAPTER EIGHT

When I dream that night, I'm in the bay, underwater, falling, falling back down into the depths of the sea. I try to open my eyes, but it's blurry, and I can barely make out the surface, the hazy view of the main house staring down at me, eclipsing all else. I piston my arms, trying to pull myself up, to get my head above water, but it feels as though something keeps dragging me down, an unseen hand pulling me to the ocean floor, wrapping its fingers around my ankle and giving a good tug.

I open my mouth to scream, but the sound is stuck in my throat, and it feels like I'm choking on the sea, the salt water in my lungs—

I lurch upright in bed, struggling to catch my breath, my body heaving with the effort.

The dream felt so realistic, the sensation that I was drowning terrifying. When I was a little girl at the beach in Varadero, I once was knocked over by a wave. It carried me off for a moment before my mother scrambled over to where I was and plucked me out of the water, and I still remember the fear that I felt in that moment—I tasted it this evening in my sleep.

It's hardly the first bad dream that I've had since my parents died, but there was a sharper edge to it than the other ones. It felt altogether too real, like the darkness that seems to be settled around Marbrisa had invaded my subconscious, too.

I toss and turn on the cool linen sheets, struggling to get comfortable, but it's of no use.

I can't fall back to sleep.

The fight with Carolina turns repeatedly in my mind. She's right that I came here because I had little option, but at the same time, I had hoped that with our parents gone we would be able to bond in our shared grief, that if anyone could understand the tremendous loss I'd experienced, it would be her. I'd hoped that it would bring us closer, but now it feels as though we are perpetually meant to be apart, and if anything, my arrival is only serving to drive a wedge between us, dredging up old memories and resentments.

Carolina didn't come to dinner this evening. Neither did Asher or his friend Nathaniel.

I ate my meal in silence in Marbrisa's cavernous dining room, wishing I'd stayed in Havana. Perhaps I could have found work. Maybe the distant cousins wouldn't have been so bad after all. The excitement I experienced when the boat first motored me up to Marbrisa yesterday feels like it was ages ago.

As soon as I secure my inheritance, I can focus on the next chapter in my life—college, then a career doing something I love. The money my parents left me will support me through the next few years, but it won't last forever, and I have no desire to end up trapped in a marriage because I have no other options. I need to know that I can support myself. There's so much uncertainty in the world now with the war overseas, and it feels as though I stand on the precipice of a change I must be prepared to meet.

My stomach growls loudly.

I barely ate at dinner, the food unappealing despite the obvious talents of Marbrisa's chefs.

I turn on the lamp on the nightstand and climb out of bed, grabbing the robe I discarded earlier and slipping it on over my nightgown.

I pad over to the dresser, searching for the hair ribbon I placed there.

I still.

There's a hairbrush resting on top of the dresser, the ribbon beside it, a bottle of my perfume sitting next to them.

The necklace is gone.

I set it on my dresser after I found it in my room, intent on asking Carolina if she had left it or if she knew anything about it. But Carolina wasn't at dinner, and now the necklace isn't here, either.

Did one of the maids put it somewhere else when they came into my room? Or even more disturbing, did someone come into my room while I was sleeping and take it?

Rain begins pelting the windows, the sound filling the silence. Like earlier when I was caught outside with George, the weather changes quickly from clear skies to falling sheets of water that hit the roof with loud thuds. A crack of thunder explodes, lightning brightening the night sky.

The house is unusually quiet at this late hour. The interior is as still as a crypt, while outside the weather rages on. The wind whips against the windows, slamming the glass panes. The roar of the ocean rolls in the background.

How can anyone sleep through this racket?

I slip out of my room, heading downstairs in search of food. Hopefully, there's something to snack on in the kitchen again. I just pray Nathaniel is still abed.

Some of the lights are on in the hallway, partially illuminating the house. I assumed my room was in the guest wing, but I've yet to discover where Asher and Carolina's rooms are. As much as I wanted to explore Marbrisa's gardens, the house is still too intimidating. There are so many tensions between the people living here that I'm afraid I will inadvertently stumble onto something I shouldn't, the sheer size of the place daunting.

I miss the city.

I walk down the staircase, careful to keep hold of the railing, my earlier near-accident still fresh in my mind. The shoes were, indeed, ruined by the rain, the rest of my outfit thankfully salvageable. I have no idea how I even go about replacing my wardrobe these days; do I ask Asher for an allowance like a child? My father's will made no such provisions for how my affairs are to be handled, merely that Asher is responsible for the financial administration. Considering my parents' relatively young age when they passed away, I doubt my father spent much time contemplating the situation, believing he was preparing for a contingency that would likely never occur. But now that I'm here in this position, I can only pray that they chose wisely and that I can trust Asher. It's more than a little unsettling that his own wife doesn't seem to.

Another flash of lighting hits, followed by booming thunder, and then the house is plunged into semidarkness once more, save for a light emanating from an open doorway down the front hall.

I hesitate.

I hate to admit it, but the whole ghost business has me unsettled even though I *know* there's no such thing as ghosts. Although, I suppose in a manner of speaking, it's harder to prove that something *doesn't* exist even if I've never seen one myself.

If such things were possible, Marbrisa would certainly be a prime candidate for haunting.

It makes you wonder why someone like Nathaniel Hayes would choose to be a guest here. He may be Asher's friend, but there are plenty of hotels in Miami now, and judging by the fine cut of his clothes, he can afford to stay elsewhere. Is it merely the lure of free accommodations keeping him here or is there some other enticement?

I walk toward the light, reminding myself ghosts aren't likely to employ electricity.

The lights flicker.

I blink, wondering if my eyes are playing tricks on me when it happens again, a zap of power followed by a millisecond of darkness and illumination once more.

A creak echoes from above, the sound of weight being pressed upon the floorboards.

Is Carolina walking upstairs? Or is it something else? After this morning's encounter, I only hope it isn't Nathaniel.

The lights flicker again.

Goose bumps rise on my arms.

"It's just the storm," I whisper to myself. "Storms take out electricity all the time."

I head toward the light, stopping at the threshold.

Asher stands in the library, his back toward the open doorway, his gaze cast toward the window.

Another crack of thunder echoes throughout the house.

I jump, the noise catching me off guard, a hiss escaping my lips.

Asher whirls around at the sound.

Our gazes connect.

"Can't sleep?" he asks.

"The storm woke me. I haven't been sleeping that well anyway. Too many thoughts, I suppose. I started having bad dreams after my parents' death, and since I came to Marbrisa it's only been worse. I was on my way to the kitchen and saw the light, and well—"

"You came to investigate?"

I nod.

"I'm sorry for the troubles. For the peacock and all that. I know you've been through a lot. I certainly don't want things here to make it worse for you."

I take a few steps closer, and the full force of Marbrisa's library hits me before I can muster a response. Whoever built the room must have loved books, because the library is an homage to reading. Two out of the four walls are covered in floor-to-ceiling bookshelves. Another wall is positioned with enormous glass doors that in daylight must provide a stunning view of Biscayne Bay. The wall opposite the doors boasts a fireplace with an intricately carved mantel. It's far too warm to consider lighting it, but it looks good just the same, and there's something cozy about the sight of those logs stacked up for use even if I doubt they're employed very often.

Artwork hangs over the fireplace.

"They're the original architect's blueprints of Marbrisa," Asher says, following my gaze.

I walk toward the blueprints, studying the rendering on the wall. I know nothing about architecture, but it's fascinating to see how the house was laid out, to appreciate all the hard work and vision that must have gone into a project of this magnitude.

The estate's name is scrawled there.

MARBRISA

Beneath it is a familiar signature.

"Who drew up these plans?"

"The architect's name was Michael Harrison. Why?"

"His signature—I recognize it. It's on a painting in my bedroom."

"He dabbled in art as well, even if architecture was his first love. He was incredibly talented."

"What else did he build?"

"Some small projects here and there, but Marbrisa was his grandest design. He was my inspiration for buying the place."

"How so?"

"I was at an auction and those plans were there. I'd never seen the place, but I liked the vision in his drawings. I asked my agents to do a little research on the house, and when they did, I was fascinated by what they uncovered. The house had been dormant for well over a decade, was owned by the state after the original owner died without heirs to pass it to. I decided I needed to come down here and see Marbrisa for myself, and the rest is history."

There's something endearing in the way he tells the story, the passion that shines through his eyes. For a moment, Asher reminds me of the man who drove up to our house all those years ago to pick up my sister. I think that was what my young eyes recognized back then—Asher was a romantic. The man standing before me seems to have lost all traces of such whimsy.

"You were that taken by the plans?"

He nods, looking a bit abashed.

"I see what initially drew your interest, but what inspired you to buy it?"

"Temporary insanity?" He winces. "I don't know . . . there was just something about it. It felt like it was speaking to me, which I know sounds utterly ridiculous." He shoves his hands into his pockets, seemingly shaking himself out of his stupor. "I thought it might make a good investment, and it was a steal considering the condition it was in and its history. There, does that sound better?"

"More logical, maybe, but I know what you mean about feeling like the house is speaking to you. I felt that from the first moment I saw it. Although, the house's voice almost seems to change. Like it has different things it wants to tell me." I flush, more than a little embarrassed by how fanciful this all sounds. "I've always been interested in history," I add, hoping that explains. "I don't believe in ghosts or anything like that."

"No, I don't, either," Asher replies, and I can't tell if we're assuring each other or ourselves of that fact.

"And it doesn't feel like this place is haunted, like there's someone else here," he adds. "More like it has different lives beneath it, secret histories begging to be uncovered."

I nod. "Exactly."

"It was the scope of the project that attracted me. The house seemed like it was drawn by a dreamer, and I wanted to see what became of his vision." His cheeks flush. "It sounds silly, I know."

"Not silly. The house looks like something out of a story-book. I mean, it has actual gargoyles. I doubt you're the first person to come down here and be struck with fanciful thoughts."

He shrugs. "Well, you would have thought it was ridiculous if you'd seen the estate when I first visited. It looked like the whole place had been cursed."

"That bad?"

"It was a money pit from the start. But it was such a unique property even in a state of such sad disrepair. The years it had sat vacant had taken their toll—much of the furnishings and art had been sold off to repay the estate's debts, other pieces damaged or stolen by the teenagers who used to sneak in here on a dare. I wanted to fix it. I wanted to see what it was in its days of grandeur. I suppose I wanted a dream of my own.

Business—the kind I'm in, investments and the like—there's no beauty in them. You trade money around, but you quickly realize that there's beauty in the things you can buy with your money, in using it for the attainment of something higher. In building a dream." He gives me a conspiratorial smile. "I didn't grow up in a place like this. I worked for what I had. Every inch of this house, of the grounds. I guess it felt like a way to say I had arrived. I just needed the rest of it—the family, the wife."

Carolina certainly would have fit the bill on that account.

I can see his point to a degree, but considering the economic depression that has ravaged so many, it seems like surviving is a reward on its own. There's something likable about Asher, an earnestness I can relate to. Whereas Carolina puts up a wall between herself and the rest of the world, it feels like Asher is letting his guard down from how he behaved when I first arrived.

"Did you know about Marbrisa's history? What exactly did your agents uncover?"

He hesitates, and I realize that despite his pretense of candor, whatever he's about to tell me is not going to be the truth.

"I asked around about the house a bit. The locals were hardly forthcoming. This town has seen its share of fortunes rising and falling. Back when Marbrisa was built, everyone came to Florida looking to get rich—running to something or from something. I got the sense that people from around here were pretty fed up with rich northerners coming in, buying up land cheap, and leaving their mark on Miami, lording their good fortune over everyone else just trying to make it. So no, no one really gave me the full story. Just enough pieces for me to gather what I could already glean with my own two eyes, which is that clearly the house had fallen on hard times."

"Why did you come to Miami?" I ask him. "Were you running to something or from something?"

He smiles. "Maybe a combination of both."

He takes a long swig of his glass, swaying slightly as he sets it down on the wood with a heavy thunk.

If he isn't already drunk, it seems like he's on his way.

"Would it have made a difference?" I ask him. "If you had known what you were getting into? About how strange things would be here?"

"Would I have saved myself from my hubris and folly?" He laughs, the sound anything but funny. "Hell if I know. I'd like to think I would have. But the truth is, I wanted this place too damned bad to listen to reason. Marbrisa sank its teeth in me for one reason or another, and I wasn't going to rest until I saw the project come to fruition. I had this vision of my children playing games on the back lawn, of my wife sitting on the porch watching them, me beside her." His knuckles are white on the glass. "The house isn't the only thing that didn't turn out the way I expected."

We've officially spoken more words to each other this evening than I think we have in the entirety of being relations through marriage, and as uncomfortable as I feel seeing this vulnerable side of Asher, it's clear that the fault line that runs through Marbrisa runs through his marriage to my sister, and I can't help but be curious as to how they've gotten here in the first place. Carolina is right—I know nothing about being married, of the affairs between man and wife. I know what I've seen from the outside looking in on other people's relationships, but it's a far cry from living such experiences myself. Although, given the apparent unhappy state of my sister's marriage, I'm hardly eager to enter the bonds of matrimony myself.

"Are you alright?" I ask. It's a personal question, but he is my brother-in-law, family if only by marriage.

He shakes his head. "Sorry—I was just thinking. I fear you've caught me at a bad time. There's something about this place . . . a feeling . . ." An embarrassed laugh escapes. "You must think me mad."

"No, of course not—I'm just sorry I interrupted you. I'll leave you to it."

"Please. Stay. I didn't mean to chase you away." He takes a sip of his drink. "Here I am complaining about my problems when you've suffered a great deal. What happened—I can't imagine the shock you've been through. Some things are too horrible for words, especially when such losses happen to good people. Your parents were very kind."

"They were. Thank you."

I've received a variation of his condolences from everyone who has come to pay their respects following my parents' death, and I am still no more equipped to handle them. I wish there was a blueprint for events such as these, a map of grief to follow that would tell me how to act and what to say. Everything that comes naturally simply feels inadequate, and I constantly feel as though people expect more of me, as though they are studying me in my most intimate moments. It was like

that at my parents' funeral, the whispers and gazes nearly un-
bearable.

It's impossible to not feel like there's something wrong with
me when I see how unflappable Carolina is regarding the
whole business. However she's managing her grief, she seems
unbothered by others' opinions of her.

"I know we haven't had a chance to speak much of their
affairs, but we should discuss the terms of your father's will
and your inheritance soon," Asher says, tearing me from my
reverie. "I don't want to bother you with it while you are griev-
ing, but I want you to know, you have nothing to worry about.
It means a great deal to me that your father trusted me to help
with the administration of his estate, and I promise I'll do
right by you and by his wishes."

Relief fills me. "Thank you."

"What do you intend to do now?"

"I'd like to go to university. I've always enjoyed reading and
I've always been interested in history. I thought perhaps I could
be a teacher."

As far as plans go, it's not as fully fleshed out as I'd like, but
considering the war and the enormous question of whether the
United States will join the conflict, it's hard to know what the
world will look like in six months, much less in the autumn of
1942 when I would start university. If the men are sent off to
fight, then there will be opportunities at home and abroad for
women to join the war effort and fill the positions left behind.
It feels like the world is collectively holding its breath as more
horrific reports come out of the situation in Europe. If my
parents' death has taught me anything, it's that I can make all

the plans I'd like, but life is going to play out on its own terms regardless.

"That sounds like a fine plan," Asher replies. "You will, of course, be missed at Marbrisa."

It's clear he says the last part out of politeness and little else, no real affection in his words, but then again, we're barely more than strangers, so I can't exactly blame him. More than anything, he looks a bit relieved, as though my absence will give him one less thing to worry about here. Or perhaps I'm being unkind, and he truly is concerned about my well-being and safety. I get the sense that the mantle of duty Asher carries on his shoulders is a heavy one, and if we were closer and possessed any intimacy between us, I'd advise him to sell Marbrisa to the most willing bidder and hie off somewhere where he isn't plagued with such worries. What sort of man clings so tightly to something that causes him such trouble?

I glance back at the framed rendering over the fireplace. "The painting in my room that was done by the same man— this Michael Harrison—it's of Anna Barnes."

Asher nods. "I bought the painting at the same auction where I bought the plans for Marbrisa."

"Who had them?"

"They were sold off to settle the estate's debts and changed hands a few times over the years. There's a market for items that have, shall we say, a troubled history. It was pure chance that I was there that day; I had intended to buy a little horse statue that my art dealer said would be a good investment." He shrugs, looking somewhat abashed. "Like I said, I don't have a lot of expertise with these matters. Most of the furnishings, the artwork, were bought by agents I paid for their expertise."

I admire him for the lack of pretense, the honesty with which he admits something most people would consider to be a flaw.

"The blueprints piqued my interest, and when I saw the painting, I knew nothing about brushstrokes and the like, only that it was another part of the story, a piece of the puzzle that made me want to know more."

"People talk about Anna Barnes like she's responsible for everything that's going on here. Like she's a—"

"Ghost?" Asher finishes, his tone wry. He sighs. "I know all the rumors. That locals think Marbrisa is haunted and all that rubbish. Hell, I can't complain too much, considering I bene- fited from the stigma; the reluctance people felt about owning an estate like this certainly drove the price down. That's why it was in such a state of disrepair in the first place, why it was empty for years. People think it's cursed. After all, it's easier to chalk up whatever misfortune comes your way to the fact that there's some specter hanging over the house rather than the reality that it's a behemoth with all the costs and trials and tribulations that are associated with running such a place.

"Carolina hates it," he says almost absent-mindedly, more as an aside to himself than anything else. "She initially loved the idea of living here, of the notoriety that came with it. We own one of the grandest estates in all of Miami and everyone knows it. When I proposed, I don't think it hurt that I came with Marbrisa in tow."

No, I imagine it didn't.

"And now?" I ask, curious about my sister's innermost thoughts, the parts of herself she keeps locked away from me. It feels a bit disloyal to ask her husband if he is privy to them, but concern for my sister and for myself make me want—need—to know more.

"Hell if I know what Carolina thinks anymore. I would imagine she would confide in you more than anyone else."

"We've—we've never been close. Not really."

I would think Asher would know that, considering he's her husband. If not him, who is Carolina confiding in? I see no evidence of female friends here, no familiarity with the staff. She corresponded with our mother but rarely, me even less, and as far as I know, there were no pen pals in Havana, either. She must be incredibly lonely.

"Why aren't you close?" Asher asks.

"Do you have siblings?"

He shakes his head.

I sigh. "I don't know. The age difference, perhaps. I always felt like she was too many steps ahead and I was too many steps behind. Maybe it was in my nature, the order of things to want to catch up to her, and natural for her to want to make sure I never did. We were different. Different personalities, different interests. There was just this gulf between us that kept getting wider in every way. Our parents probably didn't help things. It's easy for siblings to be cast into certain roles, harder still to break out of them once they're set.

"Carolina wasn't happy in Havana. Found the society there and our parents' wishes for us to be too stifling."

"And you didn't?"

"I supposed it was easier to go along with things than to rock the boat."

"Carolina can be—"

"Complicated," I finish.

"Yes." He's quiet for a beat. "I met your sister in Miami. At a party at the Biltmore Hotel. It was so fast. We must have spent a total of twenty minutes together. Hardly enough to know each other, hardly enough to know my own mind."

"Then why did you—never mind, I shouldn't ask."

"She was lovely. The loveliest thing I had ever seen. And at the time, it seemed like we got along so well, that our personalities were similar, our desires the same. It was fast enough for me to be charmed. Utterly." He grimaces. "I seem to have a habit of rushing into things against reason and ending up biting off more than I can chew."

I can't help but feel a little sorry for the man and how earnest he is, how completely and miserably he misjudged my sister. Carolina is a great many things, some of which I thoroughly envy, but "lovely" is much too mild a word to describe my sister.

Sometimes I wonder if that's the trouble—everyone looks at Carolina and draws their own conclusions of who she should be rather than considering who she is.

Silence falls between us.

"I should go to sleep," Asher says. "I have an early morning meeting with the head gardener about hiring some new workers."

"I met him earlier," I say, lest Nathaniel tattle to Asher

about my stroll in the maze. "George, right? He seems dedicated to the gardens. The grounds are lovely."

Asher nods. "He's young, but he knows his business. He was already on the staff and was promoted to head gardener when his predecessor left without a word after the dead alligator."

"It must be difficult to lose staff in such a manner."

"It's certainly frustrating. I don't know how to assure the workers that they won't be next. They're convinced that this 'ghost' will eventually escalate to people."

"Admittedly, I don't know much about curses, but why do they think Anna is haunting Marbrisa?"

He's silent again, and I already know the answer by how obvious it is that he doesn't want to say it aloud.

"Because she was killed here."

So, there was some truth to what Carolina told me.

"How?"

"In the bay. She drowned. Michael Harrison found her."

"Carolina said—well, she told me Anna's husband murdered her."

"That's the rumor. That he pushed her into the bay and watched her drown."

"How horrific."

How cold. How could you do such a thing to someone you professed to love? I can't contemplate a marriage disintegrating to such a point.

"Doesn't it make you uncomfortable?" I ask. "Living in a house where someone was murdered?"

"It's another problem in a long list of them," Asher replies, his voice dry.

⸏

I RETURN TO my room, leaving Asher alone in the library. I stop in front of the painting of Anna Barnes, studying her image once more.

"What happened to you?"

What was she thinking in the moment when this was painted? There's something in her expression that looks . . . resolved? A glint of determination that suggests Anna Barnes could be a force to be reckoned with.

Tomorrow, I'll ask around and see if I can learn more about Anna and her husband. I've been so moored in my grief over the loss of my parents, my future uncertain. At least this gives me something to focus on, something to fill my days, a way to understand this strange place a little better. Mrs. Morrison wasn't in the house this evening, but tomorrow I'll talk to her as well. If she worked for the Barnes family, then she must know more about what happened to Anna.

I walk over to the window. It's a full moon tonight. The weather has finally calmed down; the rain stopped as quickly as it started.

I pull the curtain back in place, turning away from the window when I spy movement out of the corner of my eye.

A woman in a dark blue dress heads in the direction of the gardens, walking toward the hedge maze, her strides quick.

Carolina.

She lifts her skirts, running now, her dark hair trailing behind her.

Is she meeting her lover? At this hour? Was she waiting for the storm to lift all evening, waiting for her opportunity to sneak out of the house?

I just left Asher; he's likely still awake. What if he looks out the window at this precise moment and sees the same thing?

I can't blame Carolina for chasing happiness; if losing our parents the way we did a few weeks ago taught me anything, it's that life is short, and it can all be taken away from you in the blink of an eye. But I'm worried about her all the same.

I move away from the window, sweeping the curtain closed.

I climb back into bed, leaning over and turning off the lamp on my nightstand. I lie down on my side, pulling the covers over my body.

A peacock shrieks off in the distance, the loud noise piercing the night.

I groan.

The peacocks seemingly have little concern for normal waking hours, and I've already learned that they have no problem squawking whenever they please, even if the rest of the house is sleeping. It's the most disconcerting thing to be lying in bed and to hear the unusual noises they make.

I pray they will quiet down soon so I can finally sleep. It feels like it's been weeks since I got a proper night's rest, and while tonight is going to be another night in a string of them when I'm awake more than I'm asleep, I hope I can at least get a few hours before the sun breaks through the curtains.

Another scream, this one different in tone and immediately recognizable.

I bolt upright.

Carolina.

I lurch out of bed and head toward the window, yanking back the curtain. I can no longer see Carolina outside the maze, only the entrance visible to me now. There are a few gas lanterns lit around the entrance, giving off a warm glow, but it's impossible to see the twists and turns I walked just this morning.

I run down the hallway, to the staircase, my bare feet slipping against the marble, my nightgown swirling around me. I race through the house, my heart pounding, legs pumping as fast as they can carry me.

When I reach a set of back doors leading out to the patio, one of them is already yawning open. I push my way outside, the stone terrace scratching at my bare feet until I hit the soft grass.

The scream came from the direction of the maze, where I last saw Carolina near the entrance, and I head there now, belatedly realizing that not only did I fail to put on shoes, it's also possible that I'm running into a situation I might not be prepared for if Carolina is indeed in danger. As soon as I heard her cry, all I could think was that my sister needed me.

Did she find another dead animal? Or did she see something else?

The maze's entrance comes into view.

I hesitate for a moment. In the morning light, the maze looked enchanted. Now, cloaked in darkness, only a hint of illumination to guide the way, it looks menacing.

I wish I'd grabbed a flashlight.

I wish I'd brought a weapon.

"Carolina!" I call out, desperate to see my sister emerge from the maze.

I take a step forward, my heart pounding, the entrance before me. I'm out of breath from the mad dash from the house, the eeriness of the maze in darkness making the hairs on the back of my neck stand on end.

The sound of footsteps crunching on gravel fills the air.

Relief fills me.

Thank God.

"You scared me," I call out to Carolina. "I heard you scream."

The sound of crunching footsteps gets closer, and a figure emerges from the maze.

It takes a moment for my brain to catch up with what my eyes see. I expected Carolina to round the corner of the maze.

Asher walks toward me.

He looks—stricken, shell-shocked—as though he's seen a ghost.

His snowy white shirtfront is covered in red.

He carries a bundle in his arms.

It's so reminiscent of how he looked on the patio with the peacock, that for a split second I convince myself that he's found another bird somewhere in the bowels of the maze.

He staggers, his knees giving out beneath him, and he falls to the ground, just as he looks up, as our eyes meet, and a heaviness floods my veins.

I glance down at what he's carrying.

"Carmen," he croaks.

"No." I barely recognize my voice or the sound I make as I stumble toward him, my limbs moving as of their own volition, my mind struggling to keep up.

Carolina lies in Asher's arms, her dress marred with blood.

"Carmen," he says again, but his voice sounds so small, far away, as though I am being pulled underwater like in my nightmares and I'm struggling to come up for air.

My hands tremble as I reach out, sliding them up to her neck, searching for a pulse, desperate to feel her life beating beneath my fingers.

She's gone.

CHAPTER NINE

Anna

"There's a detective here to see you," the housekeeper, Mrs. Morrison, announces, wringing her hands together.

The whole house has been unsettled since the night of the party, the poor woman's death rattling even the steadiest of nerves. The frequent coming and going of the police certainly hasn't helped matters.

"Which one?" I ask.

"The lead one. Detective Pierce."

I grimace.

"Is he waiting for me now?"

"He is. I asked him if he'd like to wait for you in the green salon, but he said he'd rather walk the property. I take it he meant for you to find him." She says this last part with a sniff, and if it wasn't for the dread filling me at the mere mention of Detective Pierce's name, I'd almost be amused by her horror over his lack of good manners, although I'm not sure Mrs. Morrison holds us in much higher esteem.

Our money is new, and the staff knows it.

I have no idea where Robert found Mrs. Morrison when he hired her. He intimated that he stole her away from another large household with the promise of a hefty salary and the honor of presiding over Marbrisa. Given how skilled she is at running things, I can't imagine what we would do without her. While she seemingly barely tolerates us, her devotion to Marbrisa is absolute. I asked her once about Mr. Morrison, and she told me her husband died fighting in France.

We never spoke of it again.

"Well, I suppose I'll go find him, then," I reply. "Did he say which direction he planned on taking?"

"He was headed toward the greenhouse when I last saw him."

"And Robert?" I ask.

"He's still out of the house."

I'd much rather have my husband beside me when I face the detective once again, but if I'm to be on my own, at least it's here, in my own home, rather than stuck in a cramped police station.

I take off in search of Detective Pierce, using the back entrance off the entry hall to make my way toward the greenhouse, the path reminding me of that awful night when I took the same steps out of the party. The stunning view of Biscayne Bay is entirely lost on me now. Ever since Lenora Watson drowned in the water, I haven't been able to go near the edge, my gaze trained off in the distance, focusing on anything other than the place where she lost her life.

I find Detective Pierce near the greenhouse, watching the peacocks mill about.

"I almost hit one of these damned things driving in," he says by way of greeting before turning to face me. "They act like they own everything around here, don't they?"

"Are we talking about the peacocks now, Detective Pierce?"

I haven't the energy for pretense today, to ignore the obvious fact that he doesn't like us, and we all know it.

"I suppose we aren't." He smiles, little joy or humor in the gesture. "Who handled the invitations for the party?"

I blink, trying to keep up with his sudden change in topic. "My husband's secretary. He sent her a list and she invited those people."

"Did you put any names on the list?"

"No, I didn't really know anyone down here. We invited Robert's friends, business associates, that sort of thing."

"Was it normal for you and Robert to socialize independently of each other? You say you invited your husband's friends; did you not know them yourself?"

"Did you really come here to interrogate my social habits, Detective Pierce? I had no idea police work was so dull. Now really, this is becoming ridiculous. We've been more than happy to help, and we're all very sorry for what happened to that poor woman, but you're grasping at straws here. What does my social life have to do with Lenora Watson drowning in the bay?"

"No one invited her to the party. She wasn't on the official list of invites that your husband's secretary sent out."

"I'm hardly surprised. It was one of the biggest events of the Miami social season. Many people were curious about the house. It sounds like Ms. Watson was one of them. That's not particularly suspicious."

"You know what I find strange?"

I take a deep breath, struggling to keep my temper at bay. For once, I'm glad Robert isn't here; he'd be frustrated with this line of questioning, his patience over the police's scrutiny growing with each day.

He resents us. The fact that we're here, the house, the money, all of it. Mark my words, he'll make a stink about this just because he can and because he wants to cause trouble, Robert warned me.

I'm beginning to think he was right.

I don't respond to Detective Pierce's question.

"I find it strange that Lenora argued with your husband before her death," he continues. "After all, you just said that she wasn't an invited guest. You didn't know her. So, what business did she have with your husband?"

"What are you talking about? She didn't have any business with Robert. He didn't know her."

The look Detective Pierce gives me is almost pitying.

"They fought. The night of the party."

It takes everything in me to keep my expression neutral, my heart beating wildly in my chest.

"According to whom?"

"A guest who saw them. He said it looked quite heated."

"He must be mistaken. Robert didn't know Lenora Watson."

"Funny, your husband told us the same thing when we interviewed him."

"Just what are you suggesting?" I snap.

"I'm not suggesting anything, merely attempting to answer a few questions that have been nagging me since that night."

"Well, I don't see why you keep coming back here looking for answers. I've told you everything I know. I don't have any answers left to give you."

"Actually, you were more helpful than you might think. That necklace you mentioned—could you draw it for me?"

"Why?"

"The way you described it—" He flips through his notebook. "'Encrusted with jewels,' you said. That sounds expensive. Lenora Watson was a waitress at a hotel on Miami Beach. She wasn't buying herself jewel-encrusted necklaces. But maybe someone gave it to her. Someone she was involved with."

He doesn't say anything else, but then again, he doesn't have to. His words hang ominously between us, the implication blatant.

You don't make it through more than two decades in a society marriage without learning that people like to gossip, that because some couples have their own affairs, people will accuse you of doing the same. But I know my husband. I know him with a certainty that resides in my bones. Robert might not be a perfect man, but he is a good one—a faithful and honorable husband. I won't let Detective Pierce besmirch that, won't let him try to tear down what we've worked so hard to build.

"Robert wasn't having an affair with Lenora Watson." My voice shakes, anger filling me. "I know my husband. I've been married to him over half my life. You can make whatever accusations you'd like, but my husband is a good man. Maybe some men have women on the side, but Robert isn't like that. My marriage isn't like that."

How dare he threaten the foundation I've built my life upon.

"Mrs. Barnes—"

"No. You've said enough. You came here looking to stir things up, and it isn't going to work. You have no proof that Lenora Watson wasn't the victim of a tragic accident. She drowned. She wasn't the first person to drown in that bay, as I'm sure you've learned by now. So you can keep fishing for answers all you want, but you're never going to convince me that Robert was involved with her. And even if he was—which he *wasn't*—then I can promise you that Robert would never have hurt her. My husband isn't capable of that."

"Everyone is capable of murder under the right circumstances."

"How sad it is if you really believe that. I can't pretend to imagine the kinds of things you see in your work each day, but I can promise you that you're barking up the wrong tree here. When will you leave us in peace?"

The question comes out angrier than I intended for it to, the tight rein I had told myself that I would keep on my emotions disappearing with each word that falls from his lips. For the first time since the night of the party, worry fills me—not that my husband is guilty, but that we might have attracted the wrong kind of attention, that in building such an ostentatious house, in being so overt in our presence here, we might have just painted a target on our backs for anyone who takes issue with Marbrisa and with us.

"I need a sketch of the necklace, Mrs. Barnes, and then I'll be going. You seem to remember it better than anyone else. We'd like to know who gave it to her. We're hoping that the image can help jog a jeweler's memory."

"And if you think that Robert was involved with her, you're essentially asking me to help you vilify my husband."

"And if you think he's innocent, then your recollection could help exonerate him. After all, if he didn't give her the necklace, we can rule him out and find the person who did."

I don't for a second believe that's his intent, but I also can't envision Robert being capable of the things Detective Pierce suggests. You get to know someone when you spend over half your life with them. You see them at their best and worst moments, and even at his worst, Robert is still a good man.

"Fine. I'll draw it."

He hands me the notebook wordlessly along with a pen.

I hesitate for a moment, trying to remember that night, what the necklace looked like.

"I'm not much of an artist," I warn.

"I'm not looking for a masterpiece. Just something that can help us identify the necklace."

I take a deep breath, setting pen to paper, trying my best to re-create the piece of jewelry that I saw. When I'm finished, I hand him the notebook.

"I hope it helps."

He merely quirks a brow at me.

"I do. We're not monsters, you know. Regardless of what you might think. I feel sorry for her. And I do feel some responsibility to her. After all, she died at my party, in my home. But that's where it ends. It was an accident."

"You keep saying it was an accident. But you weren't there. You don't know. Tell me this—is there a chance that the whole reason you're pushing this accident narrative is because you don't want to look too close to home and realize that something terrible could have happened here?"

"A woman drowning is terrible enough."

"It is. But it isn't murder. I bet that'll interfere with the parties you throw in the future." He grimaces. "Or maybe it won't. There are folks drawn to all manner of strange things."

"Why are you so intent to make this into something nefarious? Why are you pushing so hard and looking for skeletons where there might not be any?"

He's silent for a moment, looking over my shoulder and staring at the house behind me. "Because this is hardly the first time people like you and your husband have moved down here. You might have the biggest mansion, but we've been seeing the likes of you for a while now. You treat Miami and the locals like they're disposable, like they simply exist to fulfill your needs. They're my people. My neighbors, my friends. This is my home. I'm responsible for them. Lenora is one of mine. I owe it to her to find out what happened to her."

"And if Lenora Watson was nothing more than an accidental drowning?"

"Then at least I will sleep at night knowing that I have discharged my duty to her family, that I didn't sweep all of this under the rug merely because it happened at Marbrisa."

CHAPTER TEN

Robert still isn't home.

I glance at the clock in my bedroom, watching the seconds tick by. It's nearly midnight now, the staff long abed.

Detective Pierce left hours ago, but his visit has haunted me. I keep hearing his voice in my head, keep seeing the suspicion in his gaze. I'm ashamed to admit that it's lingered longer than I'd like.

What if I'm wrong?

I would swear on my life that my husband is a good man. After all, what is the institution of marriage if not that very thing—pledging before God to live out the rest of your days with one person, putting your future hopes, dreams in their hands?

But what if I'm wrong?

I walk over to the window, staring at the grounds below. When Robert and Michael designed the house, they situated our bedrooms on the backside of the house so that the view from our windows looks out over the coral patio and the lawn and sea beyond. The moon is full tonight, the light reflecting off the water.

I hate these nights when I'm by myself, Robert traveling for business or off making deals. It feels so empty out here, our closest neighbor miles away. It's easy for the darkness and silence to creep in, to feel like no one would notice if I disappeared. It's easy to wonder if we made the right choice coming here, if we would have been happier tucked away in our life in New York. Should I have voiced my concerns to Robert more insistently? And would he have listened?

Why didn't Robert tell me that he fought with Lenora Watson? And what would they have to fight over?

It's possible the witness was confused. There were so many men in evening dress at the party. Perhaps they simply mistook Robert for someone else.

The wind begins to kick up outside, a whooshing sound rattling the windows. The peacocks protest, their screeching something I've yet to grow used to.

I glance out the window. Some of the lamps on the back patio are illuminated, casting long shadows down on the ground. The palm trees sway back and forth, the wind knocking the enormous fronds about, the play of light and movement making it appear as though dark shadow monsters walk the grounds of Marbrisa.

I shake the fanciful thought away, stepping back from the glass pane, turning toward the clock again.

Next, I'll see ghosts walking the halls.

Silly.

But if Detective Pierce is correct, and Lenora Watson's

death wasn't an accident, then a killer was here at Marbrisa. Did someone push her into the water? Or did they simply see her fall and fail to help? Did they walk up behind her and put their hands around her neck or grab her waist and shove? If Detective Pierce is right and someone murdered her, then what will they do to get away with it?

And if the police do find a lead from the necklace I sketched for them, will I be in a killer's crosshairs?

I switch on the lamp on my nightstand, bathing the room in light.

The house feels slightly less ominous now without shadows in the room.

The clock chimes midnight.

What's keeping Robert?

My mind races with all the things that could be going wrong—a car accident on his way home, some other malady befalling him without me knowing it.

A creak sounds in the house.

Then a thud.

The sound of footsteps up the stairs.

I walk to my bedroom door, heart pounding.

I tug on the knob, opening it.

Robert stands in the hallway outside our bedrooms.

"Where were you?"

There's more accusation in my voice than I'd like, but it's built up with each accumulated minute, each hour that has ticked by.

"You're still up?" he asks, his eyes widening in surprise.

"I couldn't sleep. I was waiting for you."

I never wanted to be a jealous wife, to make Robert feel as though I was a jailer of sorts, but Detective Pierce's recriminations run through my mind on a loop I can't escape, and suddenly, this evening's late arrival strikes me a bit differently.

Where has he been and who has he been with?

"If I'd known you were waiting, I would have come home earlier."

Robert walks toward me and puts his arms around me, and for a moment, I allow myself to relax into the familiar curve of his embrace.

He smells of gin and cigar smoke.

I wait for the scent of a woman's perfume to hit me, search his collar for the telltale cliché of lipstick on his shirt, but when I pull back and study him, he's still just my Robert.

"Where were you?" I whisper, burrowing my head into the curve of his shoulder, threading my fingers through the thick head of hair at the base of his neck.

"I had lunch with some developers. They wanted to show me some properties, and after that we grabbed some dinner up by Miami Beach." He sighs, releasing me. "I didn't mean for it to go so late, but it's a good opportunity, and some of those guys are talkers. I left as soon as I could without being rude. They were still going strong when I departed."

It's a plausible story, certainly, and still, I can't shake the questions Detective Pierce asked me.

"Where did you go for dinner?"

"A cute little restaurant with the best stone crabs you've ever eaten. I'll take you there this weekend. You can wear that new red dress you bought. We'll put the top down on the car. I think you'd like the restaurant—and the stone crabs. Good pie, too.

"I'm sorry it's so late. I know things have been difficult since the party, and I didn't mean to worry you. Next time, I'll make it back at a reasonable hour. Promise." He smiles. "It wasn't nearly as much fun as it would have been if you were with me. You should have come."

You didn't invite me.

"Detective Pierce stopped by again," I announce.

"Why?"

"He wanted to ask me about the necklace Lenora Watson was wearing the night she drowned."

"Damn it. This is what I was afraid of when he started poking around. I don't want him bothering you with this. You've been through enough. Tomorrow, I'm going to go down to the station and have a talk with them."

"No, don't. Please."

"Why not? He's becoming a nuisance. The poor woman drowned. Why does he insist on dragging this out?"

"He seems to think you were involved."

"Excuse me?"

"He thinks you were having an affair with Lenora Watson."

"How dare he. Now he's gone too far. With what proof?"

"As far as I can tell, he doesn't seem to have much."

"Of course not. Because it never happened. He's digging, then. Fine. If he wants to waste his time on a fool's errand, that's his business, but I won't have him upsetting you in the process. There's enough speculation about us down here without him adding fuel to the fire."

"I'm scared," I admit. "He seemed insistent. I don't think he's going to let this go."

"I'll handle it. Don't worry. None of this is going to touch you."

Robert leans forward, taking me into his arms once more. His lips find mine, and all the doubts leave my mind.

～

MY HANDS TREMBLE as I drive down Cutler Road, unfamiliar behind the wheel of Robert's roadster.

I've never been one for automobiles, my husband teasing me that I was born for another time, that if I had my way I'd be driven in a horse-drawn carriage everywhere I went. He isn't wrong.

I know how to drive; Robert himself taught me over several lazy afternoons in Newport, his patience abundant even if I never took to it with the same enthusiasm he did. I'd rather not fold my body into a tiny machine, hurtling at ungodly speeds on roads filled with alligators and potholes. Life is risky enough without engaging in such folly.

Cars are few and far between on this stretch of road, and I pray the roadster doesn't give me any trouble, that I'm able to make it back to Marbrisa before it's dark.

Ever since Detective Pierce's visit two days ago, I haven't been able to stop thinking about Lenora Watson. I'd always intended to pay my respects to her family, but it was all too easy for me to put it off until now. I'm embarrassed by how long it's been. As far as I know, Robert hasn't made this drive north, and our silence feels particularly egregious considering the woman died at our home.

And if I'm being completely honest with myself—there's a possibility that I'm here for less than charitable reasons. Surely, if Lenora was involved with someone like Detective Pierce suspected, then her family would know about it.

I went through our guest list for the party until I found someone who knew of Lenora's family and was able to give me directions to where Lenora's next of kin live. It's miles away from Marbrisa, but it isn't the geography as much as the stark contrast in the grandeur of the estate compared to my surroundings now that makes the distance seem so vast.

I can't help but feel that I'm validating Detective Pierce's position by going to see the family, and I wonder if this is what he wanted all along, further entangling me in this situation.

It's not that I doubt Robert; it's just that there's something about this entire business that's gnawing at me, and I can't shake it loose.

I head north, outside the environs I've come to know, following the turns described to me.

I slam on the brakes.

An enormous alligator lies in the middle of the road, the sun beating down on its back.

I hesitate for a moment, peering over the windshield to get a better look at the animal. From this vantage point, it's hard to tell if the beast is asleep or dead, its body unmoving.

I've heard about the alligators ever since we moved here, their ability to consume small animals and then some; horror-inducing, but I've never seen one this close.

Its body is all hard ridges and angles, and I suppose there are some who might find something beautiful in its appearance, but I certainly wouldn't share their enthusiasm. It quite frankly terrifies me.

The beast twitches, its tail undulating in the dirt.

Not dead.

His head swivels, and he stares balefully at me, as though reproaching me for invading his natural habitat.

He can have it.

Please don't come any closer.

For a moment, I think he's going to do just that—charge the car. He certainly looks as though he's considering it, and while the roadster may have the size advantage, the magnitude of damage an animal that massive can do to Robert's prized car isn't to be taken lightly.

The last thing I want is to be stranded out here.

I offer another prayer to the heavens.

His tail swishes again.

I wait patiently as the alligator decides that he wishes to continue his forward progress, shuddering as his body slithers by.

Once he's blessedly gone, I follow a dirt road east, the path cut out by grooves set forth by others that have trodden this path before me. The foliage is thick with mangroves on either side, the roadway narrow and winding in some places. The roadster is heavy beneath my hands, awkwardly navigating the twists and turns. I wince as the tire hits a hole in the road, the car jerking about. Driving was difficult enough on Cutler Road, but here I'm beginning to wish I had just parked and walked.

The space is barely wide enough for one vehicle, and I pray no one else is coming in the opposite direction.

An oath escapes my lips as I swerve to avoid a chicken scurrying across the road.

There's a break in the landscape, a house coming into view ahead.

I can smell the salt air, the faint scent of fish not altogether unpleasant.

Lenora Watson's mother lives in a little A-frame near the water. Despite the small size, the outside is painted in a bright white that looks fresh, the grass patchy, but clearly someone has spent some time pulling weeds, working with the natural landscape—the enormous tree roots bisecting the lawn—to make the property look as neat as possible.

There's a mango tree in the front yard, ripe-looking fruit hanging down from the branches.

I park the roadster and turn off the engine.

For a moment, I sit in the car, studying the house, wondering why on earth I thought it was a good idea to come. There were quite a few moments along the drive when I considered turning around and heading back to Marbrisa, and faced with the prospect of seeing Lenora Watson's family, I can't help but regret that I didn't. It's entirely possible that my arrival here will be far from welcome, that they'll blame me since she died at my home.

The front door opens, and a woman in a white housedress steps out from the screened-in porch.

It's too late to turn back now.

"Can I help you?" she calls out.

I exit the roadster on slightly shaky legs, my nerves getting the best of me now that I am here. I close the car door behind me, smoothing my skirt down with damp palms.

Loud barking fills the air, and before I can ascertain the direction that it's coming from, an enormous black dog the size of a small pony bounds toward me.

I grab the car handle, ready to leap back inside, when the dog suddenly stops in front of me, its tail wagging, looking up expectantly toward me.

"He's friendly," the woman says. "Just excited for company."

She calls the dog to her, and he turns immediately, my presence forgotten.

The woman climbs down the steps, the dog at her side.

I take a deep breath, recognition dawning.

Her hair is the same beautiful dark auburn color as Lenora's, but hers has gone silver in strands. Her face is her daughter's, echoing the glimpses I had at the party. She looks to be about my age.

It's a shock for a moment to see her and realize that we've likely lived the same number of years on this earth, and if life had turned out differently, I might have had a child Lenora's age.

"I came to pay my respects. I'm so very sorry for your loss. My name is Anna. Anna Barnes."

Her shoulders seem to sag as I say the words, as though she

is constantly being forced to relive one of the most horrible moments of her life. If she recognizes my name, she doesn't give any indication.

"Were you friends with my Lenora?" she asks, her voice breaking slightly over her daughter's name.

I swallow, more than a little uncomfortable with the quiet grief on display before me. It feels intensely personal to see Lenora's mother like this. I wanted her to know that her daughter's death was being marked, to honor her loss, but now I worry that all I'm doing is stirring up emotions I can't fathom.

"No, I never had the pleasure of meeting her. Not officially, at least. I saw her at a party."

"And you came all the way out here to pay your condolences?"

I hesitate. "She was at my home when the accident happened. I felt—responsible, somewhat."

Her eyes widen. "You live at that big house on Biscayne Bay?"

"Yes. I wanted—I wanted to tell you how sorry I am for what happened to her."

"I told her. Not to go messing with rich folk like that."

"I—"

"No offense," she adds, "but her place wasn't there. She always had big dreams, but she never understood that some things weren't possible. That there aren't happy endings for people like us."

"I'm sorry," I say, realizing how hollow the words sound, that for all the good intentions I had, I never should have come here. Truth be told, I came here to assuage my own guilt and get answers to questions I shouldn't even have. But seeing Lenora's family's grief up close, I feel like a vulture of sorts, preying on the carrion of their loss.

"When the police came and told me what had happened to her—" Her voice breaks off, her gaze carrying to some unseen point in the horizon. "I worried about her. Constantly. I didn't like that job she had. I worried that working in that hotel, being around all those flashy things, she'd lose sight of what was important, what mattered. That she'd be reaching for things she'd never have.

"Do you have children?" she asks me.

I shake my head.

"Lenora was my last child," she says. "I lost a son in the war, and now, well . . . You worry about your kids. Constantly. From the first moment when they come into this world, you listen to their cries, trying to read their moods, attempting to understand what they need. And then they're walking, running all around the place, and you worry about them falling and hurting themselves, and then they grow older and it's like there's a whole other kind of worry, a whole other kind of hurt you must be afraid of."

Being a mother sounds quite terrifying.

"Did she seem happy?" she asks me. "The night she died?"

I try to remember that moment as best I can, wanting to honor this woman's loss with as much truth and kindness as I can muster.

"She did. She seemed—" I search for the right word, trying to understand what it was about Lenora Watson that captured my attention in a sea of people, even for a moment. "She was vibrant. So full of life. I could tell that even from a distance."

She smiles sadly. "Yes. She was like that. She had a knack for people. They wanted to talk to her. She had a way of making them laugh. She was funny, Lord, she was funny. Not in a mean way, not like she was making fun of you, but like she thought life was a big adventure, and she was out to make the most of it. She was too big for this place."

She glances around, shaking her head, slightly dazed like whatever she's seeing isn't the property around us, but something else, some secret, private memory I'll never be privy to, a history that haunts her now.

Shame fills me.

"The police think it might not have been an accident," she says, as though she's testing the theory out and hasn't quite decided how she feels about it.

To lose your child in an accident must be heartbreaking, but to lose them in a violent, intentional manner seems unfathomably cruel.

"They told me the same," I admit, waiting to see if she says anything about Robert, if Detective Pierce went so far as to suggest to her family that he was involved with Lenora.

"I can't imagine why anyone would want to hurt her. I worried about her, yes, but murder? I can't see something like that happening to Lenora. If you had known her—she was a lovely girl."

Tears fill her eyes.

"It's a terrible thing," I reply, because what else is there to say? I yearn to give her some form of reassurance; I came here searching for answers that I'm never going to find.

"If you need anything, anything at all, you can always visit me at Marbrisa."

"Thank you."

I can tell she says it more out of politeness than anything else, no intention of taking me up on my offer.

I walk back to the car, turning in time to see the screen door slap closed.

A lump forms in my throat as I drive away from Lenora's home. There's a pressure building in my chest, a tightness in my lungs. I take a deep breath, then another, trying to steady myself, my fingers trembling on the steering wheel.

"Damn it," I whisper.

I pull the roadster over onto the shoulder of the road.

Tears well in my eyes, spilling down my cheeks.

I don't know exactly what I'm crying for—for Lenora Watson, the tragedy of a life cut short, a mother's grief, or another emotion I can't quite put a finger on, a sense of melancholy and dread that settles over my shoulders like a mantle I can't shake.

CHAPTER ELEVEN

Carmen

What do you know about your sister's marriage?"

I stare down at the floor, nausea filling me. I can't get the image of Carolina out of my mind.

Did she suffer? Was she alone and scared? Was she waiting for me to come to her aid?

My sister is dead.

It feels like a nightmare I can't wake from.

I wrap my arms around myself, my body shaking.

"Miss Acosta?"

The detective's voice, more insistent now, pulls me out of my reverie, and I glance up, meeting his gaze.

"I'm sorry—what was the question?"

"What can you tell me about your sister's marriage?"

The image of Asher carrying Carolina is burned in my mind.

"Not much. I haven't been here very long. I was in Havana and Carolina was here."

The detective scribbles something in his notepad, and then he pauses, his pen hovering in midair.

"Were you and your sister close?"

The truth is on my lips, the urge to confess that I've always wished I was closer to my sister, that despite being raised in the same household, I've often felt as though we are strangers, that there were things about Carolina I struggled to understand, but there's a sharpness in the detective's eyes that makes me nervous.

I'm a stranger here in Miami, no friends or family to speak of save for Asher. In Havana, the police could be friend or foe depending on their agenda, and my father was always careful in his dealings with them, lest he end up on the wrong side of someone who had taken a bribe or couldn't be trusted. I can't tell if the detective is crooked or not, but in the absence of certainty, it seems best to proceed with caution.

"She was my sister. The last family I have left. What do you think, Detective?"

"Were your sister and Mr. Wyatt close?"

"I—I don't know." Considering I've only been at Marbrisa for a couple days, pleading ignorance seems to be the best policy. I don't want to be caught in a lie by this man. "They were married," I offer, feeling a bit helpless, Carolina's earlier words coming back to me. What do I know about relations between husbands and wives?

"That doesn't mean they were happily married," the detective counters.

"Just what are you implying? Do you think Asher killed Carolina?"

It's the question that's been running through my mind since I found Asher carrying her body.

"Do *you* think he killed your sister?"

"I—I don't know. He told me he heard a scream and went to investigate."

It's certainly plausible considering the same thing happened to me, and yet, I can't accept it as the truth, either.

"Do you believe that?"

"I don't know. He was carrying her when I found them."

There was so much blood.

Do I believe Asher is capable of murder? I'd like to think he isn't, but I don't really *know* him, and I'm not sure how well Carolina did, either.

You have no idea what being married is like. Especially to a man like Asher.

My conversation with Carolina on the stairs—my last conversation with her—runs through my mind like a warning.

If I had known that I would never see her again, never speak to her again, I would have handled things differently. Now it seems like such a waste that we spent so much time fighting over imagined slights, holding on to resentments that developed when we were children and bubbled up years later.

Regret fills me, piercing through the haze of shock and grief that has settled over me like a miasma.

Emotion clogs my throat as I ask the question that has been plaguing me since I first saw her. "What happened to Carolina?"

How long has it been since I found Asher carrying Carolina's body? Hours? Time exists in a suspended state.

He hesitates. "She was stabbed."

Tears fill my eyes.

It makes sense considering all the blood, but there's a gruesome finality to it, hearing the words fall from the detective's lips, that I wasn't quite prepared for.

"We're searching for the weapon now. We'll find it." He glances down at his notebook once more before looking back at me.

Some of the sharpness in his gaze has softened, sympathy lingering there.

How many times has he had to deliver news like this to victims' families? It can't get any easier. There's a distance in his manner as though he's afraid I'm going to fall apart at any moment and is ill-equipped to deal with the aftermath.

"The staff thinks your sister and Asher had problems in their marriage."

How many people have they questioned?

"I don't know. I don't think anyone can really know what goes on in a marriage besides the people who are in it. Carolina didn't confide in me about her relationship with Asher."

You have no idea what being married is like. Especially to a man like Asher.

"Did they seem happy?" he asks.

"Carolina seemed off. We hadn't seen each other in years, so I can't claim to be an expert on my sister's moods, but she was upset about something. There's a tension in the house, among the staff and everyone. A couple of days ago, one of the maids found a dead peacock on the front steps of the house.

From what I understand, it wasn't the first time something like that has happened here."

He makes a noise, but whether of acknowledgment or dismissal, I can't tell.

"Asher said that he told the police about it."

The detective is silent, his gaze inscrutable.

Fine, let him keep his secrets. Or try, at least. But if he's going to investigate this case, he's going to need people to talk to him, and they're not going to do it unless he offers something in return.

"Do you think Asher is responsible? That he killed Carolina? Has he been arrested?" I ask.

"We're still investigating."

There's some hesitancy in the detective's manner, a caution that makes me wonder if he's afraid to accuse someone as wealthy as Asher appears to be. Because this happened at Marbrisa, it will no doubt be a source of speculation and gossip in the area. If it had happened elsewhere, at a home less fine, would he have been quicker to consider this matter resolved and Asher guilty of murder?

Do I believe Asher to be capable of murder? Maybe? I don't know how to judge such a thing.

"Wait—you said you haven't found the weapon yet?"

"It's a big estate. And then there's the bay. Plenty of places for her killer to have dumped it. Like I said, we're searching."

"Asher wouldn't have had much time to hide the weapon. Hardly any at all. As soon as I heard my sister scream, I ran to find her. The back of the house looks over the bay. If he had dumped the weapon there, I would have seen him. Did you search him?"

The detective hesitates for a moment and then he nods.

At least he's sharing something.

"But he didn't have the weapon on him?"

"No."

"Did you search around where the body was found? Did you search the maze?"

"Miss Acosta, I've been a detective for longer than you've been alive. This isn't my first murder investigation. Of course I searched near the body. And we're searching the maze. We are continuing to look for it. We will find it."

"How could Asher have disposed of it so quickly—in what, less than a minute?—and so well that hours later you haven't been able to find it?"

Maddeningly, he doesn't answer me this time.

He crosses his arms in front of his chest, staring down at me on the sofa.

"The staff mentioned that you spent an hour alone with your brother-in-law tonight. What were you discussing?"

"Excuse me?"

"You were in the library with your sister's husband for quite some time."

Anger fills me, piercing through the haze of sadness.

"He is my brother-in-law," I snap. "Also, the custodian of my inheritance thanks to my parents' wishes. It's not unusual for us to have things to discuss."

The detective writes something in his notebook before turning his attention back to me.

"In the middle of the night?"

"I couldn't sleep. The storm woke me."

The house had seemed so quiet, and like the detective pointed out, it *was* the middle of the night. Who saw me and Asher in the library? And why would they think it was suspicious enough to merit telling the police about it?

I try to remember if the door was open when we were in the library or if we had closed it. Did someone see me walking around earlier tonight and follow me downstairs? The notion that someone was watching me move through the house is more than a little unsettling.

"Have you considered that the person who was skulking around Marbrisa, the person who told you this, might have been the person who Carolina was meeting?"

"We're considering all angles." He pauses. "What makes you think Carolina was meeting someone?"

I think back to what I saw earlier tonight, trying to recall my sister's behavior. "Her mannerisms. She was in a hurry, like she was late for something. And she was dressed nicely."

"Like she was coming from a party?"

"Maybe? I don't know. She wasn't at dinner this evening."

"Did she often miss dinner?"

"I have no idea. I only just arrived. We've only dined together once since I've been here."

His brow arches. "Why was that?"

"I don't know. Look, things with Carolina could be"—I search for the word Asher and I settled on earlier—"complicated," I finish. "Do you have siblings, Detective?"

"I do."

I sit quietly, expectantly.

He sighs, the sound so low that I nearly miss it.

"A brother."

"Younger or older?"

"Younger."

"And do the two of you get along?"

"When he's not being a pain in the ass."

I don't say anything, but then again I don't have to. There's a crack in the facade, a softening, and for a moment I almost see the man behind the badge.

"Does that happen often?" the detective asks.

"What?"

"You not being able to sleep."

"Since I lost my parents?"

He looks momentarily abashed.

"Yes," I reply. "Not to mention, things here were a bit unsettling what with the dead animal and all the rumors flying around. My dreams weren't exactly pleasant."

"Rumors?"

I hesitate, feeling more than a little silly telling him about the ghosts and the rest of it. Although surely, if he's from around here, he's heard it all before, and if it's helpful at all in terms of finding my sister's killer, then I want him to understand.

"About the house—being haunted."

He casts his gaze toward heaven as though asking for patience or divine intervention, before leveling his stare at me.

I study him for a moment, trying to make sense of the man standing before me. Maybe it's just his manner or his line of questioning, but he doesn't feel like an ally or a friend, and he certainly doesn't seem like someone I can trust. Rather, I get the sense that he's suspicious of everyone and everything, likely good qualities to be had in a detective, but it gives me pause because I can't help but wonder if he considers me to be a suspect as well.

Just what are people telling him?

"This house isn't haunted. Cursed, perhaps, but not haunted," he replies. "There's a very real person who is responsible for your sister's death, and I promise you I won't rest until I see the perpetrator behind bars."

There's a hint of both a threat and a promise in his words that makes the hair on the back of my neck stand up.

"Was Carolina afraid?" he asks me.

"I don't know. If she was, she didn't tell me about it." My voice cracks and I take a deep breath, trying to steady myself. "My sister died today, Detective. I've lost the only family member I have left. I haven't slept. Is it possible for us to continue this conversation another time? If you don't have any more questions for me, I'd really like to rest."

"I would think you would be eager to see your sister's death avenged."

"I am. But I thought finding her killer was your job. After all, you're the professional."

"Often it's the people who know a victim best who can help steer us in the right direction."

I do want to know who killed Carolina, but this is all happening so quickly, and it's hard to know who to trust. I'm afraid that in my tiredness I might say something I will later regret, might give him some ammunition to use against me. And the more time that passes, the more the reality of Carolina's death settles in.

It wasn't so long ago that I was sitting on another sofa, in another living room, listening to a police officer tell me that I'd lost my parents.

If I don't get out of here soon, I fear I'll break.

"Fine, then. I'll come back later today in the afternoon." The detective rises from his chair, slipping his notepad into the pocket of his jacket.

Relief fills me. He makes me nervous, and right now, more than anything, I need to keep my bearings about me.

"Be careful."

I still. "Pardon me?"

"Your sister was killed at Marbrisa. Chances are whoever did it knows the house intimately well. I'd lock your door tonight, Miss Acosta."

My heart pounds.

"I've always hated this house," he mutters under his breath. His voice is so low that I get the impression he says it more to himself than for me, but still, I'm surprised by his candor—and his vehemence.

"Good night, Detective—" I flush. "I'm sorry. I didn't catch your name."

He glances around the room for a moment, taking one last look, and then the strangest thing happens. Even in my sleep-deprived state, I swear he shudders.

"It's Pierce. Detective Pierce."

CHAPTER TWELVE

My fingers tremble as I turn the lock on my bedroom door. Carolina is dead.

I can't wrap my mind around it.

Just hours ago, she was standing at the top of the stairs looking so *alive*. How can she be dead?

I always knew that one day my parents would no longer be on this earth, that it was the natural order of things, but I thought that I would have Carolina. And then their accident happened, and the event that had seemed decades away caught me completely unawares.

How many tragedies can happen in such a short span?

Now that Carolina is gone, I have no one.

My legs give way beneath me, and I sink down to the floor.

Carolina is dead.

Stabbed.

Murdered.

A sob escapes my lips.

I always hoped the rift between us would heal, that eventually all the little disagreements would disappear, and we would find a way to embrace each other as sisters. I kept telling myself that we just needed more time. Now there's no time left, and the way we ended things—

The last time I spoke to my sister, we fought on the staircase. Tears roll down my cheeks as I remember the things we said to each other.

It's raining outside again, the water hitting Marbrisa's tile roof with loud thuds. The weather isn't discouraging the police; the sound of their dogs braying outside fills the night. Have they found the weapon that killed Carolina or are they still out there searching for it?

A knocking sound comes from the wall, followed by muffled noises—

I blink, convinced that my eyes are deceiving me because it almost looks like—it almost looks like the wall is moving.

I open my mouth to scream—

The wall opens, revealing a dark passageway.

Asher stands near the entrance.

He's changed from the clothes he was wearing earlier—perhaps the police took them away. His hair is wet.

"I'm sorry to startle you. I didn't mean to scare you. I tried knocking."

"From the wall?"

My mind races as I remember the necklace I found on my bed earlier and then how it disappeared. Has someone been coming into my room? Has Asher?

"The police are still in the house, and I thought it best under

the circumstances for them to not realize we're in here talking."
He hesitates. "There's a police officer standing guard at the top
of the stairway."

I walk toward the bedroom door and open it slightly, peeking through the crack. Sure enough, a uniformed officer is
standing exactly where Asher said he would be, the officer's back
to me. Whether he's there for my protection or to monitor my
movements, though, I can't tell. I can only pray it's the former and
not the latter.

I shut the door behind me quietly and quickly.

At least if Asher tries anything, the officer is close enough
to come to my aid. As long as I can scream in time.

Asher gestures to the opening in the wall behind him. "I'm
sorry, I should have warned you. There are passageways throughout the house."

My heart pounds as I think back to the weird noises I've
heard. It never occurred to me that there would be secret pas-
sages in the house, but now that he says it, I'm not entirely
surprised that a Gothic mansion such as this one would have
something as arcane as secret passageways. They match the
gargoyles perfectly. Still—

"They aren't on the blueprints framed in your office."

"No, they aren't. I'm not sure why Michael Harrison kept
them a secret. I don't even know if they were a secret when the
house was originally built. I asked Mrs. Morrison, but she said
she didn't know anything about them. I discovered them by
accident when we were doing some renovations in the master
suite. There was a wall that had some water damage from a
leak that had formed over the years when the house was aban-

doned, and when the workers repaired it, they found a passageway."

How thoroughly creepy.

"Where does it go?"

"It runs behind many of the main rooms, connecting them in various ways. My builder who handled some of the restoration thought they could have been used so servants could travel throughout the mansion without being seen, although if that was the case, I'm not sure why the architect wouldn't have included them on the renderings or why Mrs. Morrison didn't know about them, considering she was the housekeeper back then. Perhaps they were a whimsy of the owners, or the architect's own desire. I don't know. I thought about closing them up; there was something unsettling about the ability to move throughout the house so stealthily, but at the same time, the passageways feel like a piece of Marbrisa's history that I didn't want to ignore. I tried as best I could when I bought the house to preserve as much of its integrity and past as possible."

I know what he told me when we spoke earlier in the library, but why is Asher so devoted to Marbrisa?

"It was the thick of the Depression, and it felt like a good thing to bring some jobs here," he adds.

We saw the effects of America's economic depression in Cuba as well, but it was undeniable that while it ravaged the lives of so many, there were others like Asher who apparently remained largely unscathed.

"Who knows about the passageways?"

"I'm not sure. I didn't advertise the fact that there was work being done in my rooms, but it was hardly a secret, either. The workers knew, certainly."

"How many men worked on the passageways?"

"A dozen, maybe?"

"Did Carolina know about the passageways?"

Was that how she would slip out to meet her mystery man undetected?

"I don't know. We never discussed them."

There are too many secrets here, too much happening behind the scenes, and it feels as though I'm a few steps behind where I should be.

I'd lock your door tonight, Miss Acosta.

Detective Pierce's words return to me, but his advice is only marginally helpful now that I know how easy it is for someone to get into my room. Asher has never been anything other than friendly toward me, but what if I've read him wrong all along? He could easily have snuck into my room those other times, and if anyone has a motive to kill Carolina—

"I'm sorry for scaring you earlier," Asher adds. "That wasn't my intention. I wanted to talk to you, to see how you're doing. I wanted to warn you, too."

"Warn me about what?" It's a struggle to keep the tremor of fear from my voice.

"Detective Pierce told me that some of the staff had been talking about us spending time together in the library earlier. The way he made it sound—it was like he twisted it into something nefarious, like we had done something wrong."

My heart pounds. "He told me the same thing. He asked a

lot of questions about you. About my relationship with you. And your relationship with Carolina."

"He asked me the same questions about *you*," Asher replies.

Am I seriously a suspect? What are people saying to give the detective the impression that I could murder my own sister?

"Do you know which staff members talked to him?" I ask Asher.

"No. He wouldn't tell me."

"What did you tell the detectives?"

"Nothing." He rubs his face. "I'm going to speak to my attorney later today about the best way to proceed. I don't like the way the detective looked at me or the way he spoke about you. I'm worried he's searching in the wrong places, and if he focuses on us, he's never going to find the person responsible for Carolina's death."

Is Asher really concerned about me? Or is he more concerned about protecting himself? It's reassuring that he doesn't think I'm responsible for my sister's death, but at the same time, I can't help but worry that the only way he can know for certain that I didn't kill Carolina is if he knows who did.

"How are you?" Asher asks, his tone softening. "We haven't had a chance to talk since . . ."

Tears fill my eyes.

"It doesn't feel real," I say.

"No, it doesn't."

"How are you doing?" I ask, feeling a little guilty for being so focused on my grief when he is likely grappling with some of his own. I lost a sister, but he lost a wife.

"I don't know. I'm in shock, I think. I never—I can't believe she's gone."

He looks stricken, but it's hard to tell what's real and pretend here.

"How did you find her?" I ask.

He takes a deep breath as though he's steeling himself for an unpleasant memory. "I went outside to clear my head. Sometimes I walk the maze."

I remember what George told me about Asher walking the maze at night.

"I was headed to the maze when I heard a scream, like someone was in trouble," Asher continues. "She was already gone by the time I found her inside the maze."

"She must have just entered. I saw her outside only minutes before from my bedroom window."

He nods. "She'd only made it past the first turn."

Her killer was likely already lying in wait.

Carolina must have been terrified. Did she see her attacker coming or did they take her by surprise? Was it someone she knew or a stranger? She was by herself in those final moments. To call for help and not have anyone come to her aid, to die so violently . . .

Given the size of the estate and its remoteness, it seems unlikely that it was a random crime. What are the odds that Carolina was outside in the middle of the night and a killer just happened upon her?

Infinitesimal.

"Your friend Nathaniel. I saw him at Marbrisa yesterday morning, but he wasn't at dinner. Was he here tonight?"

I try to keep my tone light, torn between an obligation to not accuse an innocent man and my desire to see my sister's death avenged.

"He was out. He said he had a party to attend up in Palm Beach." Asher flushes slightly as though he's embarrassed to say more. "Sometimes, he stays the night elsewhere after such events. Why?"

How do you tell a widower that you think their wife was having an affair?

I feel terrible prying into my sister's secrets, but if it helps the police find who killed her . . .

"The day I arrived at Marbrisa, I saw Carolina leaving the greenhouse. There was a man with her."

If Asher is shocked by my announcement, he doesn't let it show.

"I'm so sorry," I continue, "but I think she might have been—"

"Having an affair?" he finishes for me.

I nod miserably.

"I know."

"You knew?"

What will Detective Pierce think when he realizes Asher knew Carolina had a lover? Jealousy is certainly a powerful motive for murder.

"I did. We didn't—we didn't have a traditional sort of marriage. We tried when we first married." He flushes, looking away from me, his gaze settling on the picture of Anna. "It became clear quite early on that we weren't well suited. I often wished that we'd had more time to get to know each other. Maybe we would have realized we weren't a good fit. But your sister returned to Cuba, and I was here, so the opportunities were few and far between. I was of an age when it seemed time to get married, and I think Carolina felt the same way. We should have been a good match, but we just weren't."

It feels intensely personal to get these details of my sister's marriage, but at the same time, I'm beginning to understand a little better what it was like for her here and why she seemed so unhappy.

"In the beginning, that first year, we fought, but even that disappeared quickly. There wasn't anything to fight about. I couldn't blame Carolina for not being who I wanted her to be, and she couldn't make me into the person she needed. The romance we had embarked upon fizzled so quickly that there wasn't even a shared connection to fight over. If Carolina was involved with someone else, I'm not surprised. It wasn't the first time on either of our parts." He looks uncomfortable again and then he pauses. "Wait—are you suggesting that Nathaniel and Carolina might have been involved?"

"There was tension between them that night at dinner. I don't know. He's handsome and charming, and he seemed like the sort of man Carolina might have been attracted to."

"Whoever she was involved with, I promise you it wasn't Nathaniel. They weren't having an affair. Nathaniel certainly has had his share of women, but Carolina was not within their number." Asher rubs his face. He looks as tired as I feel. "I don't mean to speak ill of the dead, but Nathaniel wasn't particularly fond of your sister. He isn't a friend. Not exactly, at least."

"What do you mean?"

He hesitates again. "When the accidents started happening at Marbrisa—the animals dying and the like—the police didn't take it as seriously as I wanted them to. But I felt a responsibility to the estate and to the people who live and work here. So, I asked around among some business associates and they recommended Nathaniel. He's a private detective. I hoped that if I was paying him, he would take this business more seriously than the police did."

Now that I can put the pieces together, it makes perfect sense. There was always something officious about Nathaniel's manner, an arrogance I wrote off as being a result of his supposed wealth and apparent handsomeness. But it was none of that. He was likely investigating me along with everyone else at Marbrisa. No wonder he watched things and asked so many questions.

Asher must see the question in my eyes because he adds—

"When we learned that you were coming here, I asked Nathaniel to stay as my guest for a few days. I was worried something would happen while you were here, and I wanted him to keep an eye on things."

Asher looks like he's going to be sick.

"If it wasn't Nathaniel, then who?" I ask.

"I don't know."

Did I get it all wrong? That day I saw Carolina leaving the greenhouse, I was so convinced the man she was meeting was her lover. What if it was tied to something else entirely?

"What if she didn't even have a lover?"

He stares at me wordlessly, as though I'm asking for answers he can't give.

"You were never curious?" I ask, pressing on. There's too much happening right now, too many unknowns, too many things occurring behind the scenes, and suddenly, I'm terrified that my sister's death is going to go unavenged, that Carolina's life is going to be lost in the mix.

Asher might be her husband, but he doesn't seem motivated enough to fight for justice for her.

Am I the only person left who loved Carolina?

Guilt fills me. She could have had better, considering the tensions between us.

"No. I told you. We've been living separate lives for some time. It hardly mattered to me. It was Carolina's business."

"Do you know who she was involved with in the past?"

He shakes his head. "There were rumors, but nothing I ever saw with my own eyes."

"It matters now. It matters if her lover killed her. You had to have had some suspicions."

"I didn't spend a great deal of time thinking about it, to be honest."

My emotions must show across my face because he winces.

"I know how that sounds. And I know it seems hard to believe, but it's the truth."

"Why did she stay?"

It's the question I never got to ask my sister, and now, politeness be damned, I want to take Asher's measure.

I want to avenge my sister's death.

It's an undeniably personal conversation, but I can't help but be curious about this side of my sister, to try to understand why Carolina did the things she did.

"I don't know," he replies.

"What did Carolina want?" I ask him.

"I don't know. Honestly. I wanted to start a family, but she had no interest in having children. Not yet, at least. We fought about it. She said that I was trying to control her, that I didn't understand. She was right; I didn't. I wanted a peaceful life, and Carolina was anything but peaceful. Maybe if I had understood her better, maybe if I had known what she needed from me, we could have been happy."

Everything he says makes sense, every explanation certainly seems plausible. But the incontrovertible truth is that my sister is gone, and someone killed her. And right now, no one has a stronger motive than Asher. I didn't mention the affair to Detective Pierce because I was too shocked by Carolina's death to think of it, but eventually he's going to learn about it if he doesn't have his suspicions already, and then he's really going to set his sights on Asher.

"When this gets out—"

"The police are going to think I had a motive to kill Carolina," he finishes for me.

I nod.

Asher's expression is grim. "I know."

"What are you going to do?"

"Hope Detective Pierce finds the real killer first."

He seems genuinely upset, and I want to believe him, but I can't discard Detective Pierce's suspicions so easily.

"With all the strange things that have been going on here—the dead animals and the like—did Carolina ever mention anyone threatening her?"

"No, nothing."

"Did you tell her you hired Nathaniel?"

"He thought it best I didn't."

"She seemed rattled by the peacock. On edge about something."

"I don't think she felt safe here. Toward the end. As a husband, I felt like I'd failed her. Our marriage was already so fractured, and then on top of it, for her to hate it here so much . . . I suggested she go away for a while, tried to get her to travel to Havana for the funeral, but she wouldn't leave. As much as she seemed to loathe Marbrisa, something tied her here, something I never understood. When you asked about Anna Barnes—"

"Surely, you don't think a ghost killed Carolina."

"No, but Carolina was . . ." He seems to be searching for the right words. "Obsessed with Anna Barnes."

Surprise fills me at his choice of words.

"She was the one who told me about Anna's husband killing her. She mentioned it to me just hours before she died."

"I'm not surprised," Asher replies. "I don't know what sparked her interest in the subject, to be honest. But she wanted to know everything about that period in Marbrisa's history. It was a strange topic for Carolina, but at first, I thought it was because she wanted to learn more about our home. Then I realized it was much darker than that. It consumed her."

I wish I'd paid more attention to it when she brought up Anna Barnes, wished I'd asked her more questions.

"She always believed in spirits," I add, remembering moments in our childhood. "Believed that they were around us.

But this—I don't know—I just don't understand why Anna would grip her so."

Did Carolina see herself in Anna's story? Did she relate to her because Carolina was locked in an unhappy marriage, too? And if so, does that mean Asher is capable of the same horrific crime as Anna's husband? Is this a case of history repeating itself?

"Do you think what happened to Anna Barnes could have something to do with all of this?" I ask.

"I don't know. It seems unlikely. After all, they never knew each other. They have little in common. They lived decades apart. Anna died in 1919. Carolina was a little girl in Havana then."

"But they both lived at Marbrisa."

"They did."

"And there have been strange things happening here."

I tell him about the necklace I found in my room and how it disappeared later.

"Are you sure? Maybe it was just misplaced."

"Perhaps. I forgot to tell Detective Pierce about it. I should let him know. The police believe whoever killed her was probably someone familiar with Marbrisa. The secret passageways would give them an advantage when it comes to navigating the estate."

"I know." He meets my gaze. "What do you think?"

I can tell what he's really asking, the question lurking beneath the surface.

Do I think he's capable of killing my sister?

The truth is—I don't know. I want to believe that he isn't,

but if I've learned anything at Marbrisa, it's that nothing is exactly as it seems.

Perhaps that extends to Asher, too.

What do I really know about my sister's husband besides the seemingly salient fact that neither one of them was happy in their marriage?

"I don't know."

Hurt flashes in his eyes for an instant, so quickly I nearly miss it, and then they're back to being the same pale liquid gray as before. He takes a step back as though I've physically shoved him.

"I should let you get some rest." He's silent for a beat. "I'm so sorry."

I nod, unable to speak past the lump forming in my throat and all the emotions tightly wound inside me.

"Block the passageway entrance after I leave," he instructs. "It's the only one that leads into your room. With the police out in the hallway, you should be safe tonight. And Carmen, when Detective Pierce questions you later today—"

Disappointment fills me. I had hoped that Asher would be as eager as me to see Carolina's killer brought to justice, but he's just eager to have me cover for him.

"Be careful what you tell him. They're looking at people who are close to Carolina, and I'm worried Detective Pierce considers you to be a prime suspect."

CHAPTER THIRTEEN

I manage a few hours of sleep, the armoire I pushed in front of the wall panel doing a little to assuage my nerves, the heavy police presence playing a role, too.

I wake, the morning sun shining through the curtains. My head pounds, my eyesight bleary. I glance over at the clock, surprised to see that it's nearly eleven in the morning. I've slept through breakfast. Carolina and Asher will likely already—

It crashes into me like a wave.

Carolina's body lying on the ground.

The detective questioning me.

My sister is gone forever.

I scramble out of bed, heading to the window to see if the police are still searching the grounds. I can't see them or hear the dogs.

It feels like I'm walking through a nightmare.

I dress quickly and head downstairs to see if there are any updates.

The house is preternaturally quiet.

If a dead peacock caused a mass exodus of staff, how many have fled after a murder?

"Miss Acosta."

I whirl around at the sound of my name.

Mrs. Morrison stands outside the library. Her hands are clutched against her chest. She normally favors simple gray dresses, but today she has opted for an austere black, and the sight of the mourning color threatens tears once more.

I glance down at my own skirt, belatedly realizing that the green skirt and white shirtfront are livelier than I should have chosen for myself. My grief is hardly rational or expedient.

Mrs. Morrison's gaze runs over my skirt, but she doesn't say anything about my inappropriate choice of outfit.

"I'm sorry for your loss," she murmurs, not quite meeting my gaze.

"Thank you."

It's staggering to think of how many times people have said that phrase to me in the last few weeks.

"I'm surprised you're still here. I imagine a great deal of the staff have left. Understandably so."

She stiffens. "Mr. Wyatt hired me to care for the house. I would never abandon my post."

Is she loyal to Asher or to Marbrisa? And why did she seemingly dislike Carolina so?

"Can we speak, Mrs. Morrison? Privately? I understand that you worked at Marbrisa right after it was built by the previous owners. I heard a bit about the unpleasantness that happened back then. Do you think there could be a connection between the two events?"

"Of course not," she sputters.

"I want to talk about Anna Barnes."

"I don't gossip about my employers."

"Anna Barnes is no longer with us. And if she was, and there was some connection between her death and what is happening now, don't you think she would want you to do something about it?"

"You're just like your sister, aren't you?"

She doesn't necessarily say it like an insult, but it's clear it isn't a compliment, either.

"Did Carolina ask you about Anna?"

"She did. And I told her the same thing that I'm telling you. What happened to Anna Barnes was fodder for gossip for long enough. Let the woman rest in peace."

"And Carolina? How can my sister rest in peace if her killer is on the loose? Help me. Please. There might be something in the past, something that you know that could be helpful."

She sighs. "Fine. I have an interview with Detective Pierce right now. I'll come see you after."

I pray she doesn't tell Detective Pierce that I was asking about Anna Barnes. He already seems suspicious enough as it is.

I walk outside, belatedly realizing that I'm retracing my steps from last night, traversing the same path. I veer off to the front of the mansion, not yet ready to be reminded of what happened, unable to look at the spot where my sister was killed.

George is pruning the hedges near the front door, the police nowhere to be found.

He sets the shears down when he catches sight of me.

"I heard about your sister. I'm so sorry."

"Thank you."

"Is there anything you need?"

I shake my head.

"Did the police question you?" I ask him.

"This morning. I was supposed to have a meeting with Mr. Wyatt about the gardens. When I arrived, the police were here."

"Did you see Asher?"

"No. They questioned all the staff. The ones who were around, at least. Word of the murder got out quickly, and more people decided they didn't want to risk working here anymore. Some were afraid, some didn't take kindly to being questioned about a murder."

"What did you tell the police?" I ask, struggling to keep my voice steady. "What did they ask you?"

"I didn't tell them much. I work in the gardens—it's not like I'm aware of what's going on inside the house."

"But you heard gossip, surely."

"I did. I'm not going to repeat it to the police, though. I don't want to accuse someone who is innocent."

"Did you ever see Carolina in the gardens?"

"Not really. Your sister didn't seem like the type to get her hands dirty."

"How about the greenhouse? Maybe she wasn't alone," I press. "Perhaps she was meeting someone there. A man?"

He's silent for a beat. "I saw her coming out of the greenhouse once. The day you arrived at Marbrisa. She was with a man. It wasn't Asher. I didn't think much of it—I figured it was a friend of theirs."

My heart pounds. "Are you sure you didn't recognize him?"

"I don't know. I'm sorry. Like I said, I work in the gardens. They've never introduced me to their friends and the like. I just remember thinking it was strange that your sister would go to the greenhouse, considering she'd never shown an interest in it before."

"Did you tell the police any of this?"

"No."

"You need to. It can help with the investigation."

"What is there to say? I saw your sister talking to someone. That's hardly a crime. If I accuse the wrong person . . ." He shifts uncomfortably. "Despite all the strange happenings, this is a good job, and I can use the work . . ."

His voice trails off, but I can hear the unspoken fear there, can see how nervous my question has made him. In my efforts to try so hard to treat him as though we are equals, eradicating the social barrier between us, I failed to realize and acknowledge that we are not the same. He has so much more to lose than I do.

Is that how the rest of the staff feels?

The Depression has ended, yes, and many have left the job of their own volition, but I wonder if there are some like George and Mrs. Morrison who are now placed in the awkward position of having to risk their futures by testifying against people who are wealthy and powerful, the fear of retaliation breathing down their necks.

"Do you think she was killed by someone she knew?" George asks me.

"That makes the most sense, doesn't it? What are the odds that someone just happened to stumble upon her in the gardens and decided to kill her?"

"She could have interrupted something she wasn't meant to see. A robbery, perhaps? After all, Marbrisa has a reputation. Everyone has heard about the house's legendary art. Not to mention your sister's extensive jewelry collection."

That's true. I hadn't even considered the robbery angle, but given the house's notoriety and Asher's wealth, it makes sense. But if it was a robbery, why didn't they take anything? Did Asher's appearance interrupt them in the act?

"Maybe it was a robbery. But why the maze, then? Why not just break into the house and be done with it?"

"She could have interrupted them before they could reach the house."

I suppose he's right, but there's something about it that just feels *off*, wrong. This seems personal in a way I can't quite put my finger on. It's like the mosaic in the house's entryway—I can see the individual pieces, but I can't figure out how they connect.

"Are you sure you never saw anything else? I understand your reluctance to incriminate someone with the police, but you can tell me. Even something small could be helpful."

"Are you investigating her murder now?" he asks incredulously.

"She was my sister. How can I not see this through to the end? There were so many times in life that I failed her by not being the sister I wanted to be. Our last conversation was a fight. We said terrible things to each other. I owe her this."

"I mostly tried to steer clear of your sister. I'm sorry, but she wasn't the easiest person to work for. She and Mr. Wyatt would fight and the whole house would feel the tension. The staff would walk around on eggshells, trying not to upset either one of them, trying not to get in the way. He threatened to fire me once over a hedge that he said wasn't symmetrical in the maze. I need this job. I need the money. But I can't say I blame everyone who has quit."

My stomach sinks at the mention of Asher's name. I remember how strange it felt when I first arrived here. How uneasy the staff was, the sensation that they were all tiptoeing around a bomb that was ready to explode. The man George describes—the sort of man who would lose his temper over something so trivial as an uneven hedge—isn't the man I've come to know over the past couple of days. Was I wrong to trust Asher?

"Asher told me they didn't fight."

"And you believed him?"

"I don't know. He seemed credible. I thought he was telling the truth."

"Well, he was lying. They did fight. Enough that everyone knew that they were unhappy in their marriage. Even someone like me who stayed confined to the gardens." He hesitates. "You should be careful in that house."

"What's that supposed to mean?"

"The police are here," he murmurs, my question left unanswered between us.

I whirl around. Detective Pierce walks toward us from the main house, flanked by two other officers in uniform.

I turn back toward George.

"I'll come find you later. Be careful, Carmen."

~~~

"You fought with your sister before she died, didn't you?"

I glance up at Detective Pierce from my vantage point on the blue silk couch in the drawing room. Initially, when we came in the room, I was eager for the chance to sit, my body exhausted by the weight of the events of the last few days. Now, it feels as though he has the advantage over me once more.

I have a feeling that it's an investigative trick he learned along the way. Now that I've had the benefit of a few hours of sleep, my mind slightly less muddled, it's clear that he's a man who takes his job very seriously, and each of his movements is methodically planned.

Surprise fills me. "Who told you that?"

"That doesn't matter. Someone heard you fighting. What were you fighting about?"

Was it Mrs. Morrison? When I saw her earlier, she said she had to talk to Detective Pierce. And yesterday while Carolina and I were arguing, I saw a woman wearing a dark dress in the hallway. It could have been Mrs. Morrison. What else did she tell him?

"We were sisters. We argued. We loved each other, but that didn't mean we always agreed on things."

It's so hard to know what's the right thing to do; should I be honest with the detective and just admit that Carolina and I were arguing? Or should I hold back and see if he is bluffing? More than anything, I want my sister's killer to be brought to justice, and if telling the truth helps—

"I was worried about Carolina," I admit.

"You accused her of having an affair. Our witness says you threatened your sister."

"What? No. Of course I didn't threaten Carolina. Whoever told you that is mistaken."

"But you did accuse her of having an affair."

"No—I just—I saw her with someone the day that I got here. In the greenhouse. She knew I saw her."

"Who was she with?"

"A man. Beyond that, I don't know. It was too far away to get a good look at him. I saw them from my bedroom window. The greenhouse is just on the edges of the view from my room. He moved quickly."

"Like he didn't want to be seen?"

"Yes. Or like he was in a hurry. I don't know. It was quick, and at the time, I didn't realize the significance of what I'd seen. I wish I could go back and take a more careful mental image of the situation, but unfortunately I can't."

It's on the tip of my tongue to tell him that George saw the man, too, but I remember how worried he was about losing his position. It's not my story to tell.

"And Carolina?" Detective Pierce asks. "Did it look like she was hiding something too?"

"No. I didn't get the impression she was in a hurry at all.

But Carolina was like that. She did as she pleased. She always did."

"Did that make you jealous?"

"Of course not. I loved my sister. We were very different people, but I never would have harmed her."

"My witness said that Carolina didn't necessarily feel the same way about you. We received a report that she tried to push you down the stairs."

What did Mrs. Morrison tell the police? And why would she make them think Carolina tried to push me?

"No—it wasn't like that. At all. We were standing on the stairs talking and I slipped on one of the steps. My shoes were wet. I had been outside, and I was caught in the rain. If anything, Carolina saved me. She kept me from falling backward."

"Yet, you don't have any proof of this. It was just you and Carolina. Who's to say that's what happened?"

"I'm saying it. I'm telling the truth."

He doesn't respond.

"Did you find the weapon?" I ask him.

"We didn't. It's a big property. We'll keep looking."

"And what if you never find it?"

"I imagine that's what the killer wants. But it's no matter; good detective work involves many different avenues."

If he's pursuing all avenues, then I hope he's considering the possibility that Carolina's murder could be tied to what happened here before.

"Do you know about the house's history? About Anna Barnes's murder? Were you on the force then?"

His eyes widen slightly. "Who told you Anna Barnes was murdered?"

"Carolina. Right before she died."

"Robert Barnes was never found guilty of his wife's murder. He died before it could go to trial. I told your sister the same thing when she came to see me."

"Carolina asked you about Anna Barnes?"

"She did."

"You never mentioned that you knew Carolina."

He doesn't reply.

"Why did she go to see you?"

"Because I was the lead detective on Anna's case. And on Lenora Watson's."

"Wait. Who was Lenora Watson?"

For a moment, I think he isn't going to answer me.

"The first woman to drown at Marbrisa," he finally replies.

My heart pounds. Three women have died under suspicious circumstances at Marbrisa.

"Not the first person, mind you," he continues. "That poor soul was one of the laborers who built the house. But Lenora Watson died here at the party the Barneses held to celebrate the completion of their new home. It was supposed to be their introduction into Miami society, a chance for the neighbors to come from far and wide and gawk at the wealth Robert Barnes had accumulated throughout the course of his career."

It's easy to read between the lines. "You didn't like them."

"No, I didn't. They were rich people who were more concerned with appearances and status than anything else. Robert Barnes, especially."

"How did Lenora Watson drown in the bay?"

"That's the question, isn't it? Robert and Anna claimed that she'd had too much to drink—it was a very wild party—and she must have fallen into the bay. After all, it was dark, she was wearing heels, and it wasn't the first time something like that had happened."

"You didn't believe them."

"I did not." His gaze turns speculative. "Why all the questions about Anna and Lenora?"

"You said that my sister took an interest in Anna, that she came to see you to ask about her. Doesn't that seem strange to you?"

"No stranger than all the other things you people do. With all due respect, Miss Acosta, your sister seemed bored and like she was looking for a little scandal she could use to titillate her guests at dinner parties, maybe hire a medium to try to commune with the dead."

By the way he says the last words with a snort, I'm certain Detective Pierce does not believe in ghosts.

"She asked me a few questions, I gave her the answers I could considering they're both still active investigations, but that was it."

"Maybe you should investigate a connection between Carolina, Anna, and Lenora? It just seems unlikely that *three* women would meet a similar fate at Marbrisa."

"Are you telling me how to do my job, Miss Acosta? I assure you we're exhausting all possible leads, but I will tell you this, we don't have to go digging up ghosts to figure out what happened to your sister."

"What's that supposed to mean?"

"Your sister was a very wealthy woman."

"Of course she was." I glance around the room at all the finery on display. The gold and crystal chandelier alone must have cost a fortune, not to mention the artwork on display. I'm no expert, but they all look like museum-quality pieces. "A home like this doesn't come cheaply."

He shakes his head. "I wasn't talking about Marbrisa. The estate is only in Asher's name. Carolina has no claim to the property. I'm talking about the money she inherited from your parents. It's her husband's now."

Surprise fills me. It makes sense given the terms of our father's will that Carolina would have received the money outright since she was married, but I didn't consider the fact that it would have passed to Asher. Truthfully, with the shock of Carolina's murder, I completely forgot about our inheritance.

"It's a nice sum that will pass to your brother-in-law," Detective Pierce adds.

"I suppose it is. Not in comparison to all of this, though. My parents did well enough, and we grew up comfortably, but nothing like this. We're hardly heiresses, and I doubt Asher needs the money. Carolina's inheritance would be a small thing in comparison."

The detective smiles, but it's a joyless gesture.

I don't like him.

More accurately, I don't trust him.

He seems like he has an agenda, and until I figure out what it is, I'm going to follow Asher's advice and be very careful in how much I disclose to him.

"You would think, wouldn't you?" Detective Pierce says. "That's the funny thing about old houses, though. They're very expensive to maintain. Especially one that was in the condition Marbrisa was when Asher bought it. Like her previous owners, Marbrisa had run into a string of bad luck. It was no longer the grand house that was once the envy of Miami."

"Yes—I know that. Asher admitted the same thing to me himself."

"Turns out your brother-in-law blew through nearly his entire fortune buying this place. He was lucky—very few people wanted it, considering its history. But still, it was hardly a cheap investment, particularly given the cost it requires to keep the place running and how much he sank into it in the first place to get it up to snuff."

"What are you saying?"

"That perhaps your brother-in-law isn't as wealthy as you think he is, as he wants everyone to believe he is. Maybe Carolina discovered that for herself. I saw your sister; she was very beautiful, very glamorous. Not the kind of woman I can imagine being happy in reduced circumstances. Maybe that's what drove your sister to look for another man. That's not easy on a man's ego—losing his fortune and his wife at the same time."

"I don't know about the money, but I never saw anything that gave me the impression that Asher was a jealous man. To the contrary."

"So, you did discuss your sister's marriage with her husband. Last night you gave me the impression that you knew nothing about it."

"Last night I suffered a great shock," I protest.

"Maybe you only saw what Asher wanted you to see. After all, no one knows what goes on behind closed doors. They were in an unhappy marriage. She was having an affair. Maybe he was, too. Your sister had the funds to keep this place running a bit longer. Where I come from that's called motive. In fact, some people think Mr. Wyatt had turned his sights to *you*."

Anger fills me. "That's absurd. Asher did no such thing."

"You were seen having private conversations with him on several occasions that witnesses described as 'intense' in nature."

This must be coming from Mrs. Morrison . . . or Nathaniel.

"Not to mention the time you spent together in the library on the night your sister was murdered," he adds.

"How dare you. I've lost my sister, the only family member I had left, and you have the audacity to stand here and sling mud at me, for what?" Now I do rise from my seated position, my legs no longer as shaky as they once were, indignation fueling my body. "You can see yourself out, Detective."

"Fine. I'll go. But I'll be back. I'll be honest with you, Miss Acosta, I still don't know quite how this thing played out. If Asher did the deed himself or if you both conspired together. It's mighty convenient how you're each other's alibis, what with you arguing that there wouldn't have been enough time for Asher to hide the weapon and him insisting that you arrived on the scene after your sister was dead. Don't think it hasn't occurred to us that it would have been possible to hide the weapon if you had an accomplice."

"I didn't kill my sister."

"Then I'd think long and hard about whether you want to protect that brother-in-law of yours. Because the evidence is what it is, and the odds are weighing heavily in favor of the fact that it was one or both of you. If it were me, and I was innocent, then I'd sure as hell be concerned for my own safety."

There's a speculative gleam in his eyes that I can't quite decipher—does he think I'm a victim or an accomplice? And no matter how many times he suggests it, there's something about that whole thing that makes it a bit difficult for me to imagine Asher—mild-mannered Asher—as a murderer. But then again, maybe that's the whole point. Is it all just an act, a mask he wears? If nothing at Marbrisa is as it seems, then is Asher really the killer Detective Pierce suggests he is?

"After all, Miss Acosta, there's still your inheritance left, and as I recall, Mr. Wyatt has control over your fortune. I wonder what would happen to that money if you died, too?"

CHAPTER FOURTEEN

Anna

Tonight is to be another party—it seems as though ever since we arrived in Miami, all we do is attend parties. Ever since that tragic night at Marbrisa when Lenora Watson died, I've yet to host another one, objecting over Robert's protestations that we must move past the accident. I can't imagine enjoying fireworks and champagne on the back lawn; the image of her dead body and the memory of her mother's grief are still too fresh in my mind.

We've heard little from Detective Pierce and his fellow officers. Whatever Robert's lawyers did to threaten them seems to have worked, because there have been no more impromptu visits, and while I've not heard that Lenora's death was officially ruled an accident, it seems as though they're finally chasing down other leads. I've thought about stopping by the station myself once or twice to see if they made any progress with the sketch of the necklace that I provided to them, but the truth is that even as I've insisted to Robert that I'm not ready to move on, for things to go back to normal, I want to put the past behind us and look to a future together that once seemed so bright.

And so, I don another gown—blue, this time, to match the sapphires Robert bought me for our anniversary this year to commemorate our marriage turning another year older.

Tonight's event is a raucous affair, the party already in full swing by the time we arrive, the drinks flowing fully, make-shift gambling tables set up in the adjoining ballroom. We certainly never drank this much champagne in New York. There's a whiff of danger in the air, rumored gangsters in attendance tonight, everyone looking to capitalize on all Miami has to offer. It's a constant hustle here, people trying to pull one over on someone else, to ensure that the attention is on them when they walk into a room.

It's utterly exhausting.

Robert seems to feed off the energy in the city, this new society giving him a newfound zest for life. For me, it has the opposite effect. I feel older now than I ever have, uncomfortably aware that I could be a mother to many of the guests who attend these parties, the late hours leaving me beyond tired the following day. The more Robert throws himself into our new social circle with gusto, the more I yearn to retreat to a place where I can find peace, away from the loud noise and posturing.

Robert's different down here—younger somehow. He laughs a bit louder, drinks a bit more. There's something about this place that lowers one's inhibitions if you let it, and my husband seems to have embraced this city and all that it has to offer with the hopes that it will remake him into a new man.

Miami is a giant party, filled with people daring enough to come down here and try to make their mark on the world. On the surface, it's an intriguing proposition, a place far apart from the old guard. But the problem with Miami is that when everyone has come down here bold as brass, ready to take risks, to claw their way to the top, it only becomes more difficult to do so. The competition is steep, the lengths one needs to go to great indeed until I'm not sure it is easier than it is back in New York, that the society is all that different, the hallmarks of success ubiquitous.

It feels like it's all a giant roulette wheel, fate waiting to intervene at any moment and knock everyone off their pedestal.

What will happen to the glittering crowd, the bright young things, then?

What will happen to us?

As soon as we arrive, we drift apart, Robert throwing himself into the thick of things whereas I like to stand near a wall, sipping on my drink in hand, watching the crowd and all their eccentricities. You learn things at a party like this, watching the guests. You realize who is having an affair, which businessman is nearly bankrupt, which one has sold the same swampy, bug-infested plot of land to five unsuspecting buyers who will eventually leave Florida with their tails tucked between their legs and a story of how they tried to make it in Miami and were swindled instead. It's like watching a play—a Greek tragedy of sorts—seeing the human condition at its worst. And in these moments, I think of Lenora Watson, who put on her best dress and a dazzling necklace and came all the way to Marbrisa looking for—what?

I wish I could tell her that I saw more honesty in her mother's grief than I ever have at any one of these parties. I wish she had never come to Marbrisa that night, that our paths had never crossed, that instead of lying in a grave, she was home with her mother who so clearly loved her.

That's what's missing here—everyone is chasing something, but I've come to realize that if you're always looking for something better, always waiting for the next thing to happen, for the die to roll, then you don't appreciate the things you have.

There's little true happiness here among all these jewels and all this pretense.

I glance around the room. I spy a few acquaintances, people who we've seen at parties and the like, a few who were at Marbrisa that infamous night. We have become notorious whether we wished it or not, and now when my gaze connects with someone across the way there is a pause, and then a turn, a bevy of whispers between them and the people surrounding them. Sometimes, I just want to shout, *Yes, it was a terrible thing that happened. No, we still don't know if it was an accident.*

Given the right amount of liquid courage, they'll occasionally approach me themselves with questions that I know will eventually be used as fodder at the next party.

We own one of the most enviable houses in the entire state of Florida.

Most people now believe it to be either haunted or cursed. Staff has fled in droves, leaving Robert perpetually concerned about the estate's management. The loyal ones who have stayed like Michael Harrison and Mrs. Morrison have become firmly entrenched in my husband's inner circle because of their fidelity.

My gaze sweeps from the group of people now whispering among themselves, across the room, to—

Michael Harrison stands there, a glass of scotch in hand, staring at me. As our gazes connect, he raises his drink in a toast, a ghost of a smile playing at his lips.

We've seen little of him since the night of the party; even though he's maintained his residence in the guest cottage, our paths rarely cross, his business with my husband. Robert mentioned that the architect was traveling for a spell, but he never told me where he went or that he'd returned.

For a moment, we both look at each other, too far away for words, and it feels as though an understanding passes between us, that we have both been through something difficult that few would comprehend unless they'd been in that position themselves.

I step forward to cross the distance of the ballroom and greet Michael, when out of the corner of my eye I spy Robert.

My husband stands off to the side of the room wearing the new tuxedo I had his tailor send over, a glass of champagne in hand. His hair is a bit overlong, the sides grazing his ears more than he likes, and I make a mental note to let his barber know, otherwise it'll be weeks before Robert remembers himself to tell the man to cut it.

Love swells inside me like a crescendo.

He is, unquestionably, a handsome man. Perhaps not the stuff of fairy tales, but there is something solid and distinguished about him. I can't say that marriage has always been easy, but we have been happy more often than not, and for that I am eternally grateful.

I smile, Michael momentarily forgotten, and wait for Robert's gaze to drift over to me, for us to exchange one of our private smiles as we have done so often throughout the years, capable of conducting an entire conversation without one word spoken between us. I wait for his gaze to meet mine so that I can feel like myself again when I see twenty-three years of marriage reflected in his eyes, his own amusement and discomfort over the fact that we are decades older than most of the crowd here and it is far too late in the evening. I wait for the company of the man who has been my home for twenty-three years.

He turns, and I step forward, only to stop in my tracks.

A woman walks up beside him. Her hand settles on his arm, five perfectly manicured fingers resting on the sleeve of his tuxedo jacket that I ordered for him.

The air leaves my lungs.

I've never been a jealous wife, never worried overmuch about Robert straying.

I've been a fool.

Her red-lacquered fingernails only graze my husband's arm for a moment, but there's something about the gesture that's so familiar to me. There's no artifice to it; she does it almost absent-mindedly, as though she's done it dozens of times, hundreds of times. It's a gesture a wife would make getting her husband's attention, one that is innocent in how naturally it comes. I know—I've rested my hand in that position myself.

The woman takes a step back, her hand dropping to her side, and Robert smiles at her, the stance of his body mirroring hers.

She's stunningly beautiful.

She's young.

Very, very young.

If I had to guess, she's about the age I was when Robert and I married. She can't be twenty.

One of the bright young things.

Just like I once was.

He takes her hand—quickly, surreptitiously—and then the crowd shifts, and they're gone.

It nearly brings me to my knees.

I stagger forward, desiring to call after them, to walk up to her and tell her that whatever she thinks she sees in Robert's eyes, she can't trust it. That one day she will be where I am, standing at the edge of the party, wondering how many of the guests know, how long it has been going on, whether he has told the other woman that he loves her, her heart in her throat as she realizes she was played for a fool, traded in for someone younger, twenty-three years of marriage discarded without a care.

Rage fills me nearly as swiftly as the hurt.

That he had the temerity to carry on with a woman at the same party where I am in attendance adds insult to injury. Was Detective Pierce right all along? Was Robert having an affair with Lenora Watson? I wrack my brain, trying to find clues, to pick apart moments in our marriage as if they could shed light on how we've gotten to this place. Were there nights when he stayed out late, business trips? Of course. But those things were always present in our marriage. The subtle changes I've seen in him since he built Marbrisa I always attributed to our new life in Miami, but now I can't help but wonder if I was unbearably naïve all along to not realize that he might have been enamored by more than just the raucous parties.

I turn, tears pricking my eyes, and head outside, eager for the night to cloak me in its darkness and to provide some anonymity. Guests mill about outside, but it's far less crowded than it was inside. Our hosts have left a few lanterns lit, but like me, most people seem to have come outside searching for privacy, couples holding hands and sneaking off together to darkened alcoves.

This whole time, I was convinced that people watched us and whispered because of Lenora's accident, because Marbrisa is ours, but now I realize the horrible possibility that they watch us and whisper because everyone knows of Robert's infidelity and my ignorance of it.

"Are you alright?"

I whirl around at the sound of Michael's voice.

It takes but a glance for me to confirm my suspicions that I just might be the last person in Miami to know my husband is cheating on me.

It's the compassion in Michael's expression that does it for me.

"Does everyone know?" I ask, careful to keep my voice low. There's no one nearby, but I figure the Barnes family has provided Miami with more than enough scandal. There's no need to add to it.

"I'm so sorry." He winces. "Would you prefer the truth or a lie?"

"I suppose that answers it, then. How did you find out? Gossip?"

He nods. "I wasn't sure if it was true or not. You know how people are—they'll say anything. But I heard it from enough sources that it seemed credible. I didn't know if it was better to stay silent or to say something to you. I didn't want to cause you unnecessary pain or create problems between you and Robert if the rumors were merely born of malice. I'm sorry to see that they're not. I'm sorry that I didn't say something to you sooner. Houses are easy. People not so much."

Well.

I'm surprised by how conflicted he sounds, by how much this has clearly been weighing on his mind.

"Do you know how long it has been going on? How long have there been rumors?"

Belatedly, I realize my voice is cracking. Horror fills me as a tear trickles down my cheek, and then another.

Wordlessly, Michael hands a crisp white handkerchief to me, the fabric folded in neat lines and angles like the plans he drafts.

"Awhile, I think."

Truthfully, it's hardly as though the timing really matters. Whether it's been weeks or months or years, the effect is the same.

"When did you start hearing the rumors?"

He hesitates. "When I was working on Marbrisa."

That long?

"Did you hear rumors about Lenora Watson?"

He doesn't look as surprised as I would think he would be when I toss out the name, which answers my unspoken question of if he ever considered the possibility that Robert and Lenora were involved.

"No. Not about her specifically. I never heard a name. Just that he had a mistress."

A *mistress*.

Somehow the word makes it more real. It's a role in his life, a tangible connection to him. I am his wife, which makes me responsible for making sure that his clothes are laundered to his satisfaction, for seeing to his needs, and she is his mistress— the inspiration for his passions, the sharer of intimacies, and what—love?

A sob sneaks from my lips, catching me wholly unawares.

"Did you wonder, though, when she drowned if they had been involved?"

He hesitates. "For a moment, maybe. I'm sure the police had the same suspicions."

"Yes, Detective Pierce certainly intimated as much to me."

"What do you think?" Michael asks.

"To be honest, I don't trust my own thinking on much of anything right now."

"What will you do?" he asks me.

"I don't know. I need to talk to Robert."

Part of me wants to leave this place and never look back. Simply pack up and disappear. And at the same time, how do you throw away twenty-three years of marriage in a blink of an eye? I wish I knew.

"I'm sorry. I'm sorry you're hurting. I'm sorry I don't know what to say in a situation like this one other than that he's a fool, although I doubt that's much consolation considering he's still your husband whether he's a fool or not."

He sounds angry, and I welcome it, this indignation on my behalf. I welcome the intensity of the emotion while I just feel numb with grief and shock.

"It's such a cliché, isn't it?" I ask. "Wealthy married older man has an affair with a woman young enough to be his daughter—or granddaughter in this case."

Poor Michael Harrison looks like he wishes the ground would open and swallow him whole. If the situation wasn't so dire, it would almost be funny how uncomfortable he seems to be. After all, these aren't the sorts of conversations that people typically subscribe to in polite society, but at the moment, I don't give a damn.

I'm angry and feeling more than a little bit reckless. And while it may be unfair to paint all men with the same brush as Robert, I don't really care about that, either, right now, given what has just happened.

"I suppose clichés exist because there's some truth to them," Michael replies.

"Touché." I take a deep breath, feeling as though I'll either fall apart or scream if I stay at this party another moment. "I'd like to go home. Do you have a car here? Would you mind terribly driving me back to Marbrisa?"

"Of course not. I would be happy to drive you."

"Thank you."

He hesitates. "And Robert—"

I might have come here with my husband, but I have no intention of leaving with him. Not after tonight.

"At the moment, he can hang for all I care."

∼

THIS TIME, WHEN I wait for my husband to come home, I welcome the delay, running through all the things I want to say to him in my mind. I have a dozen fictional conversations with Robert in the time it takes him to return to Marbrisa, some rational, others not. In some of them, I tell him that I am leaving him, that I will not suffer this indignity a moment longer. In others, I am prepared to fight for our marriage, to ask him to give this other woman up. It's a sobering thought to realize that she has aided in tearing my life apart and I don't even know her name.

I can't help but wonder about her, too, trying to guess what she thinks about this whole business, if she even thinks of me at all. Is it love? Or merely a physical connection between them? I'm not sure it matters, really, but I still feel as though I must know all the details—sordid or not. Maybe then I can understand and decide what I'm going to do next.

I sit on the settee in Robert's room, watching the hours tick by, wondering when he realized that I'd left the party, whether he'd worried, or if he even cared. Maybe I should have told him I was leaving with Michael, but considering the circumstances, I was hardly feeling charitable.

My heart pounds as I hear footsteps coming up the front staircase, getting louder and louder, until finally the doorknob turns, the door swinging open.

Robert strides through looking no worse for wear.

His gaze settles on me, and he exhales. "I was worried when I couldn't find you at the Sheffields'. I spent nearly an hour looking for you before someone told me that they saw you leaving the party with Michael. What happened? Are you feeling alright?"

"I saw you with that woman tonight."

An emotion flashes in his eyes, too quickly for me to catch it—surprise, panic—and then it's gone.

"What are you talking about?" he replies smoothly.

"Don't. Don't lie to me. Don't make more of a fool of me than you already have. I know what I saw, and I know what's being said. I need to hear it from you now."

He's silent, not meeting my gaze.

"Please."

It's humiliating to have to beg him for the truth like this, insulting to our marriage and the trust I thought we had built between us to be reduced to this. How did we get here? How is it possible that in the span of an evening, my life and everything I thought I knew about it with certainty has been so upended? This morning I was a happily married woman with a husband I respected and trusted.

Now I'm living a lie.

For a moment, I think Robert is going to tell me that I'm mistaken, that I'm worrying over nothing. For a moment, I think he's going to deny it.

Instead, he sinks down on the enormous bed we've made love on countless times since we came to Marbrisa, holding his head between his hands.

"I'm sorry. So sorry. I never meant for you to find out like this. I never meant to hurt you. I kept telling myself that I was going to end things, that I was going to stop."

"Why didn't you?"

He glances up at me, and it feels as though I'm looking at a stranger. "I don't know. I don't have a good explanation for why I did what I did. It was easy with her. With you—"

It feels like a knife thrust into my heart to hear him string our two relationships together in the same breath, as if he can equate this dalliance with twenty-three years of marriage. Did he compare us in other ways, too? When he kissed me, did he think about what it was like kissing her, and vice versa? When we made love did he think about her?

"I worried all the time about disappointing you," Robert adds. "I knew how much you hated the house. When I bought it, I wanted to surprise you. I thought you would love it as much as I did. And when it became clear that you didn't, it felt like I had ruined everything between us. And then that woman drowning." He grimaces. "It was horrible. I saw how upset you were that night. It felt like I had built this house for us, it was supposed to be our dream, and then there was this dark cloud hanging over it with the police sniffing around and the memory of that woman's death."

"Did you have an affair with Lenora Watson?"

Shock flashes across his face. "No—God, no. Of course not. I told you—I'd never met that woman until that night. This thing with Julie—"

Her name is Julie.

"It started recently. A few weeks ago. I've been so stressed. I just wanted an escape, to forget about everything. And still, I knew I needed to end it as soon as it started. I wanted to end it."

"Were there others? Have there been other women throughout our marriage? Have I been a fool this whole time? There have been rumors."

"No, of course not. I swear it. You know me, Anna. Better

than anyone. Do you really think I would lie to you for so long? That I could be successful in such a deception?"

I don't know what I believe anymore, and maybe that's the worst part of this. Robert's infidelity doesn't just make me question him; it makes me question myself. I don't feel like I can trust any of my memories now, can trust my own opinion on things. I always considered myself to be sensible, to be a good judge of character, but to have missed something so glaring that was going on under my own roof—

What else was I wrong about?

Robert takes a deep breath. "I need to tell you something. Something I've been keeping from you for a while now."

What else am I to learn tonight? How many lies exist in our marriage? I'm not sure I can bear any more revelations like the one he just shared with me.

Robert rises from the bed, walking over to the bar cart in the corner of the room. He uncorks a decanter of scotch and pours himself two fingers. He downs it quickly before pouring himself another.

"We're ruined."

The syllables in the word crack like gunshots echoing through the cavernous space.

Robert drains the glass in another fell swoop, his face shockingly pale. There's a tremor in his fingers.

For a moment, I can't comprehend his words.

"The money—it's gone. All of it."

"What money? Surely not—"

He's silent.

"How is that possible?"

Robert has never presented me with a full accounting of the status of our bank accounts, and I never had the temerity—or inclination—to ask, but this—

How is it possible that we've gone from building a house such as this one to nothing in just over a year?

"Where did it go?"

He opens his mouth as though he is going to answer me, crystal glass in hand, and then he turns and chucks it at the wood-paneled wall, liquid exploding and dripping down on the marble floors Michael chose for the master bedroom.

I freeze, my gaze trained to the broken glass, the dark liquid running down the wall like rivulets of blood.

"Where do you think it went?" he spits out, misery etched all over his face, and of course, there's no need to voice the answer aloud, to rub his nose in his mistakes. It's visible in the antique desk, in the gold that covers every inch of this palatial estate. Perhaps Marbrisa didn't ruin us on its own, but it's impossible not to see it as the beginning of our downfall.

"The house must be worth something," I add. "Why, look at all this art, the antiques."

I'm so tired. My body feels as though it will collapse under the weight of this devolving lifestyle, this decaying marriage. I am tired of pretending that everything will be okay, that I am able to play this role in which I have been cast. I am tired of this town that makes you fight for every inch.

I'm tired. I'm tired of trying so hard, tired of trying to be this version of myself that Robert seems to want here.

"I can't sell the house. Marbrisa is all I have."

You used to have me.

"I stretched us building the house," he continues. "When we first came up with the plan, it seemed affordable. Manageable. Everything was cheaper down here, or so everyone told me. I got the land for a song. But then problems started creeping up. And fixing them cost money. So much money. And the bigger this house became, the grander it became as well. I thought that if we had the grandest house in Miami, it would open opportunities for us, that if we could leverage the expense of the house to bigger and better things, then our fortune would be made."

I remember how nervous he was on the night of our party; I remember how desperate he was to receive praise. I had no idea these were the stakes he was betting on.

"But the house was a success. Everyone raved about it. It was all anyone talked about."

At least, until Lenora Watson drowned.

"I know. Some men came to me with a proposition. I met with them months ago in Miami Beach."

I remember the night he came back home late, the night I told him about Detective Pierce's theories about Lenora Watson. Perhaps Robert had been telling the truth when he said it was a business meeting.

"They wanted to build a hotel along the bay. Asked me to invest some money. It seemed like a good investment; after all, look how Marbrisa turned out."

Dread fills me. I've heard the same rumors he has about unscrupulous people who have come to Miami to steal their fortunes. Everyone knows someone who has been defrauded here.

He must read my expression because he nods. "An acquaintance vouched for them, but it turns out he was fooled, too. They ran off with everything."

"Robert."

He looks as though he has aged a decade, and as angry as I am with him for his infidelity, a part of me can't help but feel sorry for him.

"It hasn't gotten out yet, but when it does—I used credit for much of the construction of the house. The money I lost was going to pay those debts off. The lenders are going to start calling in my loans."

I close my eyes.

"I thought my investment would make up for how much I'd sunk into Marbrisa. I didn't see how we could lose."

He sounds like a gambler, betting everything on a town that can be cutthroat and unforgiving.

"I haven't known how to tell you. I wanted to. I started to, hundreds of times, but each time, I was just afraid that you would leave me. With Julie, I didn't have to worry about any of that, didn't have to fear that I'd ruined her future. I could forget about everything with her. I was so ashamed, Anna. I'm so ashamed. I know that I've let you down."

I can't speak. I don't even know what to say.

He rises from his position on the bed and comes to kneel before me, his legs brushing against the hem of my robe.

"Forgive me. Please. I understand if you don't want to stay married. If you want to leave me and go back to New York. I wouldn't want to be married to a man like me, either. Especially now that our financial straits are dire.

"The thing with Julie—"

An affair. It was an affair.

"It's nothing. It's over. I'll never see her again. I promise. I'll do anything to earn back your trust, Anna. Please. Please don't leave me. I love you. I've only ever loved you. I can't make it through this life without you."

I've never seen Robert like this, never witnessed such vulnerability in him. When he asked me to marry him, he did it as equals without getting down on bended knee. Now it's like he's lowering himself before me, and as angry as I am, I have never been cruel.

It would be easier if I had fallen out of love with him the moment I learned about his affair, but I've spent twenty-three years loving him. It's hard to unlearn something like that, for one mistake to erase the life we've built together.

I want to believe him when he says he will end things with her, that it didn't mean anything. I want to understand, but right now I'm too numb for anything.

"How have we gotten here?" I ask him.

"I don't know."

"I thought we were happy. I thought we loved each other."

"I did—I do love you. Always, Anna."

I don't know what I want anymore. I want to be left alone. I want to weep. I want to rage. I want to travel back in time and pretend none of this ever happened, that I am the same person I was before we came to Miami, that somehow our marriage can be salvaged.

"Even if I could forgive you, how could I forget? Everyone knows. I saw you with her with my own two eyes. I can't just move past all of that, pretend it never happened no matter how much I wish I could."

"I'm not asking you to forget. Just to stay. If you can't, what are you saying, then? That our marriage is over? That you're going to throw away everything we had together, the decades together because I had a fling?"

"What choice have you left me? You've broken us."

"I broke us? What about you? You don't think I knew how much you hated it here? How much you despised this house?"

"You never asked me. This house was your dream, not mine. You never even gave me a choice. We were happy in New York."

"You were happy in New York. I was stuck."

"You never told me."

"You never asked."

I stare at him wordlessly, unsure of how we've gotten to this place, how two people who professed to love each other so much and should have known each other so well got so lost along the way. Before I saw Robert go off with that girl, I would have said that we had a good marriage, that we were happy.

Now look at us.

CHAPTER FIFTEEN

Carmen

Detective Pierce's gaze bores into my retreating back as I leave the room. It takes every ounce of self-preservation to keep me from running, the desire to be as far away as possible from Detective Pierce and his suspicions and accusations great indeed.

I allow my steps to quicken as I reach the staircase that leads up to my room.

As I climb to the top, the memory hits me—of that fight with Carolina. Of our last moments together. I would have done everything differently if I had known what was going to happen. I wish she had come to dinner that night. I wish I had made amends.

Something was clearly bothering her. I wish I had tried harder to know what it was. I turn down my hallway and freeze.

Nathaniel stands outside my door, the police detective who was posted in the hallway last night nowhere to be found.

"I'm sorry," he says.

I nod, too emotionally wrung out from my conversation with Detective Pierce for much else.

"Can we talk?" Nathaniel asks.

I nod again, walking past him so that he trails behind me as I open my bedroom door. He follows me inside, and I close the door behind me.

It's more intimate than I'd like, but the police are all over the house, and now that I know Nathaniel was working for Asher to investigate all the strange occurrences at Marbrisa, I want to know just what he's uncovered.

Nathaniel glances at the painting of Anna on my wall for a moment, his gaze resting there as though he, too, understands the significance of who she is to this place.

"I saw Asher this morning," he says. "Right before I spoke to the police. He told me what happened. He also told me that you now know what I'm really doing here."

"I do. Where is Asher now?"

"With his lawyers at their offices on Coral Way. The police questioned him again this morning. It's beginning to look like they'll arrest him. He's worried that they're developing a theory that you were somehow his accomplice. He asked me to look after you if something happened to him."

"Will they arrest him?"

"I don't know. Probably. The evidence is relatively thin, but arrests have been made on less."

"Do you think Carolina's death is tied to the animals that have been killed at Marbrisa?"

"I'm not sure. It's a jump to go from killing a peacock to

killing a woman, and at the same time, if you throw out all that rot about this place being cursed, what you're left with is a string of murders and gruesome happenings. It's hard not to think that they would be connected."

"Did you have any suspects in your prior investigation for Asher?"

"Everyone? That was the problem. I never could figure out a motive. It seemed so random. The only clear pattern that began to emerge was that each time something like that happened, the stories about this place grew worse, scaring people away." He shrugs. "My best guess was that it was always a business rival of Asher's. It didn't feel personal to me. Carolina feels personal."

"You didn't like Carolina."

"Their relationship was strained. I had to look at all potential suspects."

"You thought my sister was killing alligators?" If the situation wasn't so horrible, I'd almost laugh at the absurdity of it.

"You'd be surprised. I learned a long time ago not to assume anything in my investigations. People can always prove you wrong. You were about the only person I ruled out as a suspect, and that was because you were in Havana when all this was happening."

"And if I hadn't been in Havana?"

"Then, yes, I would have considered you a suspect."

"And now? Do you share in Detective Pierce's suspicions— do you think Asher and I colluded to . . ."

I can't even finish the sentence.

I sink down on the edge of the bed.

"I told Asher I would watch over you. And I will." His mouth tightens. "I know Detective Pierce by reputation. He's tenacious. That doesn't always mean he comes to the right conclusion. I want to find out who killed your sister."

"Why do you care so much?"

"Because Asher hired me to do a job. It feels like I failed. I don't like to fail."

"And Asher?" I ask. "Do you think he's innocent?"

If Detective Pierce was right, and Asher's finances are as bad as he said they were—

If George was right, and Asher and Carolina did fight—

"I hope he is," Nathaniel says, moving toward the door to leave.

"And if he isn't?"

"Then I'll I turn him over to the police."

There's more I want to ask him, so much of my conversation with Detective Pierce nagging me, but investigator or not, I still can't trust him. He could just as easily be working with Asher, protecting Asher's interests. After all, he is receiving a paycheck for all of this.

It's time to take matters into my own hands.

〜

Mrs. Morrison sighs. "As I said earlier, I don't like to talk about my employers."

We sit beside each other in the gazebo, our hands folded in our laps, facing the house. The conversations with Detective

Pierce and Nathaniel have filled me with a sense of urgency. If they're to be believed, I'm somewhere between suspect and potential future victim, and either way, I need to get up to speed on the history of Marbrisa sooner rather than later, and at the moment, Mrs. Morrison is the only person besides Detective Pierce—who is clearly not inclined to share—who can possibly connect the events of the past with what is happening in the present. It's a risk confiding in her, considering she likely told Detective Pierce about my fight with Carolina, but I'm not sure what other option I have.

For her part, she looks equally unsettled sitting outside with me, and I can't help but wonder based on the statement she gave the police if she's filled with worry that she might be visiting with a potential murderer.

"Of course," I reply. "I can understand that. But in this case, perhaps you'd be willing to make an exception."

"I really don't know what help I could give. Or how it would affect what happened to your sister."

"Please. Anything could be helpful."

She sighs. "There's a great deal of sadness in this house."

"What happened back then?"

There are so many questions that I want to ask her, but it seems wiser to let her memories unfold as she sees fit. Now that she's begun talking, it looks like she's loosening up, the tight hold she has kept on her emotions gone, the past bubbling over into the present.

"They seemed nice enough when I first met them—the Barneses. She wasn't friendly, but she was kind, if you know what I mean. The sort of woman who mostly kept to herself and seemed to have little interest in making friends, but was always polite and gracious when she interacted with others. She was never rude or dismissive to the staff as so many can be. He was fine as well. Busy and important was the impression I got. But no one had a bad word to say about them in the house. No screaming matches between them."

"What changed?"

"I'd say Miami changed them. It attracted a wild crowd back then. There were parties the likes of which you've never seen. Extravagant, wild parties."

"At Marbrisa?"

"Just the one, the night that Lenora Watson drowned. They attended plenty, though. I always got the impression Mr. Barnes enjoyed them more than his wife did. Then again, she never made her feelings on the matter known much. She was a quiet one. You got the sense she was holding a great deal in." Mrs. Morrison looks down at her hands, twisting them together. "I worried eventually she would explode."

"Who came to that party—the night Lenora Watson drowned?"

"Oh, everybody did. It was a mark of pride to be seen at Marbrisa. After all, it was one of the grandest homes in all of Miami. The official guest list numbered over five hundred, and that didn't include the many who gate-crashed like Lenora. If you don't think I'm forward for saying so, it was clear that Robert Barnes enjoyed the attention, the respect he received, the deference. And of course, there were women."

"He had a mistress?"

Growing up, I wasn't supposed to know about such things,

the concept too scandalous for my young, delicate ears. But my mother and her cousins talked, and I was a little in awe of them, how glamorous and worldly they seemed, and I couldn't resist the urge to eavesdrop on their conversations as they shared the latest gossip circulating in Havana, often lamenting the plight of one of their friends or an acquaintance.

"He did. Her name was Julie, if I'm remembering correctly. I don't recall her last name. But the staff had their own circles where we shared information, and it was common knowledge at the time in Miami. Of course, a lot of this became public after Anna's death."

"Did Anna know? About his mistress?"

"I don't know. Like I said, she wasn't the sort to be overly familiar with anyone, and she was inscrutable. If I've ever met a more self-contained person, I don't remember it. She spent many of her days in that house, in the gardens."

"Alone?"

She sighs, sidestepping my question. "I felt bad for her, you know. Whether or not she was aware of her husband's affair, eventually the whole town was. It was a humiliating situation. Not to mention, I always got the feeling that she loved her husband. That she was dedicated to the marriage."

My parents' marriage appeared tranquil on the surface. I never got the impression that there was any infidelity between them, never overheard any loud arguments. If there were tense moments, they shielded me and Carolina from them. They were never overly affectionate, either, but considering they had been married nearly thirty years when they died, my impression was always that they had a happy union. What Mrs. Morrison describes between Robert and Anna sounds incredibly tragic.

"I thought he loved her," I say, feeling naïve. "After all, he built this house for her."

She snorts. "I always thought he built the house for himself, not for her. She certainly never seemed to take much pleasure in it. He might have loved her in his own way, but he made some foolish mistakes. They both paid for them." She hesitates. "I shouldn't say anything, although I suppose it doesn't matter as much now that they're all gone. There was one visitor Anna entertained a great deal. Just before she died. In the beginning, the staff didn't think much of it because it seemed natural that he would be at Marbrisa. But then, as time went on, well, people suspected they were more than just friends."

"Who was it?"

"The architect—Michael Harrison."

"She had an affair with the architect?"

It must have been a well-kept secret, considering this is the first I've heard of it. I think back to the painting of Anna hanging in my bedroom, to Michael Harrison's name scrawled there. I want to run back upstairs to my room, wish to study the image and Anna's expression with fresh eyes now that I have this new piece of information.

"I think so. I saw them together in the greenhouse once. He was clasping her hand. It could have been a perfectly innocent gesture, but there was something about it that made me think otherwise."

"What happened between them?"

Did history repeat itself? Is that why Carolina was so drawn to Anna's story? Because she was also involved in an affair? Did she fear Asher would hurt her the way Robert hurt Anna?

"I don't know. I'm sorry. Like I said, I only saw them together the one time."

"Do you think Robert killed Anna because she had an affair with his architect?"

"That was the police's theory, certainly. Robert Barnes died before the murder trial for Anna's death. A heart attack. I always wondered if a jury would have found him guilty."

"Do you think Lenora Watson's death was an accident?"

She hesitates for a long time. "I just don't know," she finally replies.

CHAPTER SIXTEEN

There's a rhythm that develops to my days at Marbrisa after Carolina's death. I wake early in the mornings, never able to sleep more than a few hours at night.

The house seems to come alive when everyone goes to sleep. There are creaks and thuds at all hours, the wind banging against the windows, the roar of the ocean waking me. I dream that I am running through the maze, chasing after Carolina, but no matter how hard or fast I run, my legs pumping madly beneath me, it's never enough for me to catch her as she disappears into the mist.

When I wake each morning, there's always a moment, a heartbeat or two, when I forget that she's gone, when all that has happened simply fades away. And then, almost instantly, it comes crashing back to me, pulling me under.

If Marbrisa seemed haunted before, now it is a ghost town. I have no idea what Nathaniel is up to, but the one time I sought him out to discuss my meeting with Mrs. Morrison, he was nowhere to be found.

Only a handful of staff remain, Mrs. Morrison among them. No one will work here now, and given Detective Pierce's pronouncement regarding Asher's finances, I gather he's not able to raise their wages to a level that would entice them to return despite the circumstances surrounding the estate—if such a thing were even possible.

I've been unable to forget Detective Pierce's other warnings about my safety and the possibility that Asher might be a threat. At night, I make sure to keep the secret passageway entrance blocked by furniture, my bedroom door locked. I see little of Asher regardless, his days spent in strategy sessions with his attorneys. He's agreed to turn my inheritance over to me, although I've yet to see any official paperwork providing me access to my funds, and I exist in a state of limbo in this house—waiting to bury my sister, waiting to receive my inheritance, trying to decide where I'll go next and what my future will look like now that my life has irrevocably changed.

When I head into the dining room for breakfast, I'm surprised to see Asher sitting there, a bowl of oatmeal in front of him. My gaze naturally goes to the spot across from him, to the place where Carolina sat, the empty chair a stark reminder that my sister isn't coming back. It's been four days since she was killed, and as far as we know, the police still don't have a strong lead.

Asher follows my gaze to the empty seat. "I've been avoiding this room," he confesses. "Most of them, really. She had a way of leaving a mark on places."

"She did."

In a way, it's easier for me being here because I don't have the same ties to this house that he does, my life with Carolina the one we lived in Havana when we were children. My memories of Carolina here are more fleeting, although haunting just the same.

I slide into the seat I occupied the first—and last—time we dined here together.

This morning, Nathaniel is absent again. Is he following leads or was it all talk, and has he disappeared as well?

"My attorneys have some paperwork that they need me to fill out to transfer your inheritance," Asher says. "We'll also need to go to the bank later and I'll help you open an account in your name."

"Thank you."

"Of course. It's the least I can do considering everything you've been through." He takes a deep breath. "I feel responsible somewhat for adding to your troubles. I should have protected your sister. I was her husband. What happened here, happened under my watch. We might not have had the kind of marriage either of us wanted, but she was still my wife."

His jaw is clenched, the same anger I saw in him the day the dead peacock was found at Marbrisa etched all over his face.

It's hard to know how much of his grief is real or if it's an act he's putting on.

"I feel like what happened to her is my fault," he adds, his voice low.

I still, my fork hovering in midair.

"When these accidents started—the animals and the like—I worried. It seemed like someone was targeting us, this house, and the incidents kept escalating." He rubs his hands over his face, his skin incredibly pale. "I worried it would eventually come to this. That someone would get hurt. That's why I hired Nathaniel. I wish he'd been able to uncover the perpetrator."

"Where is Nathaniel? I haven't seen him around in a few days."

"I let him go. There didn't seem to be a point to keeping him on considering what's happened. Besides, Detective Pierce is handling the case now. He gave me the impression that he considered civilian interference to be inappropriate." He flushes. "They've focused on me now. My attorneys didn't think it wise to provoke them by continuing to employ Nathaniel. Besides—his fees weren't exactly cheap."

"Why didn't the police investigate more back then? You went to a great deal of trouble to hire an investigator of your own."

"I don't know. Most of the incidents were the sorts of things that could be chalked up to natural causes. They never seemed particularly concerned. A lizard whose body has been shredded to bits isn't particularly surprising on an estate this size with all manner of wildlife prowling around. Detective Pierce even suggested that I was worried because I was from Chicago—a city boy. That I needed to understand what Florida was like.

"There was just something about it that felt like a threat to me. Like we were being stalked. And the more things happened, the more staff began to quit, the more pressure I began to feel."

"Do you have any enemies?"

This whole time I've been focused on Carolina's life. Maybe I should have been looking at Asher's.

"Nothing like this. At least, not that I know of. If I wronged anyone to the degree that they would strike at me in such a manner, I'm unaware of it."

"I spoke with Detective Pierce," I say. "He told me that Anna Barnes wasn't the first woman to drown here. There was another woman before her. By the name of Lenora Watson. She was a guest at a party here. Detective Pierce investigated her death. I confirmed it with Mrs. Morrison. She was the housekeeper at the time. Did you know anything about this?"

"No. But that would have been, what, twenty years ago? I'm not entirely surprised I've never heard of her. Miami changed a lot in the 1920s when the land boom went bust. Who knows how many people who moved down here looking to make their fortune left and never returned, not to mention the impact the Depression had on the area."

"Detective Pierce thinks you're in some kind of financial trouble."

He flushes again. "How kind of Detective Pierce to worry about my finances."

"Is it true?"

I try my hardest to keep from injecting any judgment into my voice.

"It is, actually. This house is proving to be the biggest mistake of my life. I've poured money into it and gotten nothing in return. Part of why I've been meeting with my attorneys these past few days is that I realized that I must sell it. There's no other hope. If I don't, I will be ruined financially. It just remains to be seen if anyone will want to buy a house with such a storied history. After all, two—no wait, three, apparently— women have died here." He hesitates. "I think you should stay at a hotel."

"Pardon me?"

Is he throwing me out because I've angered him?

"I don't think it's wise for you to stay here any longer. It isn't safe. I'd like to say that I will protect you, but I think there's enough evidence to the contrary that you should do the prudent thing and get the hell out of here. I have a meeting at the house this afternoon, but after that, I'll drive you into town. You can stay at the Biltmore. It's a lovely hotel, and I have enough funds to afford a room there until you can figure out where you want to go next."

I'm torn between relief and refusal. Lord knows I haven't been able to sleep here, but there's something that feels off about leaving this place with so much uncertainty hanging in the balance. It feels like I'm leaving a part of my sister behind here, too.

"What else did Detective Pierce say about me?" Asher asks the question quietly, but it's clear that he can read the indecision in my expression, saw the dart of relief that flashed in my eyes when he suggested me leaving Marbrisa.

"He has his suspicions. You know that."

"Let me guess, he told you that I killed your sister because she was cheating on me, and that because I was suffering financial difficulties, I, what, killed her for her inheritance?"

I nod.

"I don't give a damn what Detective Pierce thinks. What do you think?"

"I don't know."

"So that's it, then. You believe I'm capable of murder."

There's a thread of hurt and disappointment in his voice, something fairly accusing in his eyes.

"There are things that don't add up," I reply.

"Such as?"

"You made it sound like your marriage to Carolina was amicable enough. That you had both accepted the way things were between you. But that's not what I've heard from people who saw the two of you together," I say, careful to keep George's name out of it. "They say that the two of you fought. That there was tension between you. Anger."

"Oh, so now you're going off rumor."

"It's not like I'm getting any different information than the police will."

"Do you know what we fought about most recently? You."

"Me?"

"Yes. Initially, it was because of the funeral. Carolina didn't want to go to Havana for the funeral, told me she couldn't bear the thought of seeing her parents like that. I sympathized with her, understood where she was coming from, but I knew that meant that you would be alone dealing with your parents' affairs. I didn't think that was right. I volunteered to go and lend my assistance, but Carolina didn't want that." He hesitates. "The truth is going to come out anyway, so here it is. Carolina didn't want you coming to stay with us after your parents died."

"What do you mean?"

"We fought about that, too. I don't know why. She didn't tell me. I always got the impression that she loved you; you were her sister. But it always seemed like there was a rivalry between you, like she forever saw herself as being in competition with you and she didn't like it."

His words find their mark because I know exactly what he means; I've experienced it myself. There *was* a rivalry between us no matter how many times I cared to pretend otherwise. I always felt like I was in her shadow, and I suppose she always felt like I was nipping at her heels.

"Is that what you told Detective Pierce?"

"No, I didn't tell him anything. He was suspicious enough without adding family drama to the mix. He seems like the type who will seize on all the wrong answers before he finds the right one, and I don't want you to end up as collateral damage."

～

I USUALLY TAKE a morning walk around the estate, often seeking out George when he's doing his morning gardening work.

This morning, George is nowhere to be seen.

Disappointment fills me. After breakfast with Asher, I could use some company, would love a distraction from the talk we just had. I want to believe that he's sincere and protecting me; I hate knowing that in my last few days with her, Carolina didn't want me here, even though I already suspected it based on the fight we had on the stairs, the disagreements between us.

I wish I could go back in time and tell her that I wasn't coming here to upend the life she had created for herself, wish I understood what she was fighting so hard to protect.

I search for George a little longer before giving up entirely and setting off on my own.

In ordinary circumstances, our friendship would likely draw some raised eyebrows, considering his position at the house, but given the horrible things that have happened here recently, no one seems to care much what I do. With Carolina gone, I have no family left to shame, and it's a strange sensation to know that I have finally achieved the freedom I craved at an unspeakably horrible cost.

Avoiding the maze like I usually do, I walk toward the front of the house, making my way to the immense driveway that leads up to Marbrisa. There are two ways to arrive at the estate—by land or water—and each way highlights the grandeur of Michael Harrison's architectural vision. The driveway is lined with towering palm trees that terminate right before an enormous circular driveway, the fountain dominating the view, and yet still, it looks positively miniature compared to the three stories of the main house piled on top of one another, the parapet above the house.

Peacocks mill about the entrance, the males posturing and fanning their feathers out in a colorful arc.

By day, the house nearly looks like paradise.

At night, it's the stuff of my nightmares.

At least tonight, I'll be safely ensconced at the Biltmore, away from all the memories this place conjures.

"Carmen."

A shriek escapes my lips as I whirl around in the direction of the voice.

"You startled me."

I've been on edge since Carolina was killed, the warnings Detective Pierce gave me fresh in my mind.

George stands behind me. He's not dressed for work, the wide-brimmed hat he usually wears to protect himself from the sun absent. Instead, he's wearing a worn pair of biscuit-colored linen trousers and a lighter-colored linen shirt.

"Would you like to go for a walk?" he asks me.

I nod.

I can't bear the thought of being cooped up inside the house and having to face Asher again. There's tension simmering beneath the surface of all our interactions now, any hope of the casual friendship I thought we might be building before Carolina was murdered forever tarnished.

It's a lovely day, Miami's weather showing off with a light November breeze, the sun shining, the air crystal clear. It's easy to see how the climate would draw people here, how the promise of such gorgeous weather would lure even the most skeptical northerner to Florida.

"Is it your day off?" I ask George as we head off to the western side of the estate.

"No, but I have an hour before I need to oversee a flower delivery." He shrugs. "To be honest, I don't think anyone is really paying attention. Asher certainly doesn't seem to be concerned overmuch with the grounds, considering the circumstances. When I woke up this morning and saw what a beautiful day it was, I thought I'd see if you wanted to go for a walk. That seemed like a far better use of my time than trimming shrubs."

He takes my hand, tugging me forward, and I'm grateful for the distraction.

"Have the police been by to question you again?" he asks me.

"No. I haven't seen Detective Pierce again. It worries me," I admit. "The silence is almost worse than his questions."

"They can't possibly think you had something to do with what happened to your sister."

"I don't know anymore. Some of the questions he asked me and Asher—he seemed suspicious. But now, considering we haven't heard anything from him, maybe he's moved on to other suspects. I keep thinking that I should stop by the station and see if he has any new leads, but I'll admit, he isn't exactly the sort of man you feel inspired to seek out."

"And they haven't found the weapon that killed her yet?" George asks.

"No."

I don't tell him the rest, that I dream about finding the knife that killed my sister. That in my dreams, it's lying on my bed covered in Carolina's blood when I return to my room in the evening, that in my nightmares when I sit at Marbrisa's immense dining table and pick up my silverware, it isn't a steak knife in my hands but the blade that killed my sister. I don't tell him that sometimes when I am awake, I almost think I'm hallucinating, that I often think I see it when I go about my day only to blink and realize that I was mistaken.

The less I sleep, the more it feels like I'm going mad.

"And the funeral?"

"It's on Saturday."

Just three days away.

"And after the funeral?" He casts a sidelong glance my way. "What will you do?"

"I haven't decided."

What will happen to George if Asher does succeed in selling Marbrisa like he plans? Will the new owners keep him on, or will George be forced to secure employment elsewhere? I consider warning him, but despite everything, I still feel a loyalty to Asher, to keep some of his business private until he has sorted out his own affairs.

"Do you think Asher killed Carolina?" I ask.

"I'm not sure, but there was always something about him that I didn't trust."

"What do you mean?"

I'm curious to hear George's take on the situation, considering he's known my brother-in-law better than I have. Maybe I've misjudged Asher.

"I just wonder what the likelihood is of amassing a fortune grand enough to buy a place like this, particularly considering the rest of the country was starving and desperate during the Depression, and not leaving a few bodies along the way?"

"You're probably right, of course. I don't know. There's something about Asher that I trust. But maybe I'm wrong."

"I don't like the idea of you in the house with him."

"Actually, I'm to be leaving tonight. Asher suggested it. He's rented me a room at the Biltmore."

George whistles. "Some digs. I'm glad you'll be out of the house, though. With all the things going on there, it's best for you to stay away."

We walk on, the foliage growing more dense, enormous trees creating a forest on the outskirts of Marbrisa.

"Did they clear the existing trees when they built the main house and the gardens?" I ask. "It feels like this part of the grounds is a departure from the rest of it."

He nods. "The architect who built Marbrisa was instructed to create a grand European estate in the middle of Miami. But he loved the natural landscape and tried to preserve as much of it as possible."

"The trees are certainly beautiful."

They look old and grand in their own way, their trunks spindly, roots bisecting the ground.

I trip, and George is instantly there, holding me, his body inches away, his breath on my neck.

"Be careful. I wouldn't want you to turn an ankle."

I can smell his soap on his skin, a hint of the scent of the flowers he spends his days tending to on his clothes. There's something charming about a man who is devoted to caring for things.

We break apart, and I glance over his shoulder. There's a cottage off in the distance, partially hidden by the trees, just out of view from the main house.

"Whose house is that?"

He turns toward the direction of my gaze.

"It's mine. Traditionally, it was meant to be the caretaker's. It was here before the main house. When Marbrisa was being built, Michael Harrison lived there so he could oversee the construction. When Asher hired me, he offered me the cottage."

I had no idea George lived on the estate; I'm embarrassed to admit that in all our acquaintance, I never asked him where he lived or much about his life outside of Marbrisa. It feels comforting to know that he is nearby.

"I'm here if you need anything," he vows. "If you ever feel unsafe in the house, come find me."

"Thank you."

We walk back toward the main house together.

I glance up at the roar of an engine, a bottle green convertible speeding down Marbrisa's driveway, a man behind the wheel.

Nathaniel.

When Asher mentioned a meeting, he never told me it was with Nathaniel. I got the impression that he had let him go a couple days ago. What business could they still have between them? Perhaps final payment for services rendered?

Nathaniel pulls into the circular driveway in front of the house.

Nathaniel cuts a handsome figure, even from a distance, his clothing impeccable, nary a hair out of place. Even though I can't say I personally find him to be particularly attractive, I can easily understand the appeal he might have.

Despite what Asher said, I'm still not completely convinced

he and Carolina didn't have an affair. Just because he was hired here as an investigator doesn't rule out the possibility that there was something going on between him and my sister. He's exactly Carolina's type.

Nathaniel gets out of the car, slamming the door shut without a backward glance, and as he walks up the front steps to the house, there's something in his mannerisms, in the hurried grace he exudes—

My heart pounds. "Is that the man you saw Carolina meeting that day in the greenhouse?" I ask George.

Nathaniel disappears inside the house, the door slamming shut behind him.

I'd stake my life that it was him.

George is silent for a moment, staring after his retreating back. "Maybe. Yes. It could have been. He's certainly the right height and build. I can't say for sure, though. It was so fast. And besides, even if it was him, how do you know that's the person she was having an affair with? Maybe they both just happened to be walking the grounds and came across each other."

"It's enough for the police to investigate, at least."

"I don't want to condemn an innocent man."

"And if he isn't innocent? My sister was murdered. Likely by someone she trusted. She would have trusted their friend and houseguest. And Nathaniel is exactly the sort of man I could see Carolina being interested in."

"Fine. I'll say something to Detective Pierce. I'm not going to tell him that I saw Nathaniel Hayes, because I can't say so with certainty, but I'll let him know it could have been him."

"Thank you."

We say our goodbyes, and I climb the house's front steps alone, belatedly realizing that the hem of my skirt is filthy from the morning spent hiking the grounds. A hot bath and a change of clothes sounds perfect right about now. I still need to pack up my belongings for my hotel stay.

When I cross the threshold, Mrs. Morrison is standing in the hallway. Nathaniel is nowhere to be seen.

"Miss Acosta."

She seems surprised to see me, her body fairly vibrating with tension, a note of panic in her voice.

"Is everything alright?"

She wrings her hands. "No. No, it isn't. I'd hoped you were the lawyer."

"The lawyer?"

Mrs. Morrison grimaces. "The police have arrested Mr. Wyatt for your sister's murder."

CHAPTER SEVENTEEN

Anna

Robert is gone now more than ever. Away on business. He seemingly works harder than he ever has before, as though he can regain his fortune through sheer force of will. News of the swindle has gotten out, creditors nipping at our heels, forcing Robert to slowly sell off some of the magnificent pieces that adorn Marbrisa's rooms.

The walls are now marked by blank spaces where masterpieces used to hang.

At the same time, Robert is more solicitous than ever, quick to tell me where he is headed and when he will return. When he is home, he is tolerant and affectionate, going out of his way to woo me.

Each day, I feel like I lose a bit more of myself in the process.

It's just me and the staff alone in this house, the rooms threatening to swallow me whole. I'm not sure I've ever been lonelier in my life. I wanted a quiet home, something cozy where we could retreat from the pressures and frenetic pace of society. I should have been careful in what I wished for. I have gotten solitude in spades, and now I long for company.

I no longer avoid the bay; instead, I walk the seawall, talking to the air, to Lenora, as though we are old friends. It is silly, for we never knew each other in life, but in a strange manner it feels as though we are both bound to this house, and in that we are now kindred spirits.

I am eternally grateful to Michael for the gardens. As stifled as I feel inside the house, there is something freeing about the outdoors. I wake early in the morning, often heading outside as the sun is rising. I pass the time by puttering with the flowers and shrubs, letting myself fill in when I am not in the gardeners' way. I have little real skill, but what I lack in expertise I more than make up for in enthusiasm, and over the weeks that pass by, as the house sheds her treasures, the gardens come to life.

"You've a gift."

I rise slowly from my crouched position, turning to face Michael.

For a moment, neither one of us speaks.

My cheeks heat as I remember the last time we saw each other, when he drove me home from that fateful party weeks ago. As I remember that he knows my deepest secret, the source of shame that lingers in my marriage.

He must read embarrassment on my face, because he ducks his head as though to spare me further pain.

"I didn't mean to startle you," Michael says. "I'm sorry."

"You didn't startle me. I just wasn't expecting company. I haven't seen you around the estate of late."

He nods. "I've been working up in Palm Beach on a project for a friend."

"How is it coming?"

"Well, I think. Despite being a friend, he's an exacting customer, but then again, they all are." He flushes. "I didn't mean to give offense."

"I think we're far past that point. After all, you now know all my secrets."

It stings to acknowledge it, but there seems to be no point in pretending.

"You decided to stay." He hesitates. "I wasn't sure if you would."

I lift my chin, meeting his gaze and holding it.

"Yes, I did. For now."

Something flickers in his eyes, some thought I can't read, and even if I could, I'm not sure I want to hear his opinion on the matter. It's easy to judge when it isn't your marriage, your memories, your future, your heart on the line.

"Your husband is a lucky man."

Now it's my turn to be embarrassed, to look away.

"I heard about your recent financial troubles," he adds, his voice earnest. "I'm sorry."

"Did they approach you about the project as well?"

"They did. I declined. You were right—the offers are coming in faster than I can keep up with."

"That seems like a good problem to have."

"It is. Of course. And I am grateful for it. But I've realized that if I say yes to everything with the hopes of turning a profit, the homes I design will suffer."

"How so?"

He looks away from me, his gaze sweeping over the estate, to the bay beyond.

"I fell in love with this piece of property the first moment I saw it. I knew I wanted to design a house here. This place gripped me in a way that I've only felt one other time in my life. It won't always be like that. The projects won't always be Marbrisa. But still, I want to be selective in what I do take on to make sure that I can do them justice. What good is it to build something if I don't put everything I have into it?"

I open my mouth to speak, but the words don't come; instead, I can do little more than stare at him.

"I wish everyone had your conviction," I say finally, unable to meet his gaze as the words leave my mouth.

I feel restless in his presence, uncomfortably vulnerable in the aftermath of our discussion of Robert's affair. At the time, I was so shocked and in pain that I didn't consider the ramifications of confiding in someone who would prove to be a constant reminder of one of my lowest moments.

"I can leave you if you like. I truly didn't mean to disturb your work. I came to drop off some papers for Robert, and I saw you from the back doors."

"Robert isn't here. He's traveling on business."

"Ah. I'll leave them in the study for him, then."

"Did he—" I take a deep breath, inwardly cringing. "Did he pay you for your services at Marbrisa?"

Wives are not meant to question their husband's business, are not supposed to get involved in financial matters between men, but it seems patently unfair for those who worked so hard to see the home built to not be paid for their labor.

"He did. You should have no worries on my account. We settled our affairs before the construction of the home was completed."

He was one of the lucky ones, then, to not have to be paid in my earrings or the fur stole Robert bought me when we were in Paris years ago.

"Are things as bad as they say?" Michael asks.

His voice is low, barely louder than a whisper, and I must take a step forward to hear him.

"I'm not sure. Robert doesn't want me to worry. He says he's doing everything he can to straighten out our finances. We've sold off what we could. He's determined to keep the house at all costs."

There's no point in hiding it, and considering all the gossip flowing around Miami, I'd rather the truth come from my lips than a fiction from someone else's.

"I'm sorry for the part I played in all of this. For encouraging him to make Marbrisa bigger, grander. When I think about what you're going through now—I regret that things turned out this way, that you're struggling."

He looks so miserable when he says it that I reach out and lay my hand on his shoulder to give him comfort.

It appears to have the opposite effect.

His arm goes rigid beneath my palm, his jaw tightening, his entire body still.

I jerk back, pulling my hand away immediately, feeling as though I have committed a grave error, somehow overstepped the bounds of our acquaintance, taken the intimacies of a friendship when none was offered.

"I'm sorry—I didn't mean to make you uncomfortable, I . . ."

I trail off, the words lost somewhere in the wind around us, in the breeze rolling off the water. For an instant, the space of a breath, his guard is down, and when I look into Michael Harrison's eyes I see a passion, a devotion, a yearning I previously only saw when he talked about Marbrisa.

Except this time those emotions aren't directed at the house, but are reflected back at me.

"Oh."

The word slips out of my lips on the tail end of a whisper, my heart suddenly thumping madly in my chest, adopting its own erratic and utterly unfamiliar beat.

I'm no green girl in the throes of a first attraction. I know exactly what it means when a man looks at you like that.

I take a step back, and then another, my hand dropping helplessly to my side.

He looks utterly miserable.

"I didn't know," I whisper.

"No, I never meant for you to. That was sort of the point. It would have been . . ." He appears to be searching for the right word. "Unprofessional."

A laugh escapes before I can help it, the absurdity of the situation hitting me full force. He must be a decade younger than me if he is a day, and he's our architect. I set out to loathe him the moment I met him, considering the role he played in this house being constructed, but now that I've gotten to know him, I must admit that I respect him, even like him.

"Since when?" I ask him, my voice barely audible over the thundering in my ears.

"Since the first."

I gape at him. I remember the day we met; there was nothing remarkable in our interaction, no tension I picked up on, no special interest in me.

"I can't explain it," he adds.

I can't help but laugh at how insulting that sounds even though I know he didn't mean it that way. To be honest, I can't imagine how this happened in the first place.

He looks away. "I'm sure it will pass."

I don't know what to say in response. What a strange morning this has been.

"I should go," he says, giving me a little bow before he's gone, leaving me staring after his retreating back wondering what the hell just happened.

∽

ROBERT'S TRIP TO New York is extended a few more days, leaving me alone longer than anticipated. While part of me admires his attempts to save our fortune, I can't help but wonder how much time we have before the creditors close in on us to the point where none of Robert's efforts matter anymore. If he succeeds and saves our finances and Marbrisa, there's still the matter of our marriage, which I'm not sure is so easily repaired.

"Mr. Harrison is here," Mrs. Morrison announces one morning when I am finishing my breakfast in the dining room.

I always feel more than a little ridiculous sitting at the immense table on my own, more food than one person can eat before me. Despite our need to economize, Robert is insistent that everything must be done on a grand scale as befitting the house, even breakfast when there is no one to see it but me.

Michael stands behind the housekeeper, a set of papers in his hands. "I apologize for intruding on your time. I didn't know Robert was still away. I thought he would be back by now."

We're both silent for a beat while Mrs. Morrison takes her leave, and then it's just the two of us alone in the dining room.

"His trip was extended. Some railroad deal he's working on up north."

"Ah. I see. I'll leave these for him."

Michael turns on his heel, and suddenly, I can't take the awkward tension between us.

"Don't apologize. And please don't leave."

He stills.

Michael turns slowly, his expression inscrutable.

I take a deep breath, trying to tamper down my own embarrassment.

"This will never do. Our paths will continue to cross from time to time. After all, you're living on our property. What you told me the other day—I—you shouldn't feel embarrassed about it."

"If only it were that easy," he mutters.

"Well, maybe it can be. We were on our way to being friends, which, considering how we started out, was an impressive feat," I joke. "There's no reason why you can't join me for breakfast." I gesture toward the food on the sideboard behind me. "There's plenty here. And I promise you, the more time we spend together, any infatuation you have will surely wear off."

His lips quirk in a little half smile. "Very well, then."

He takes a seat opposite mine, and I arrange for a plate to be brought to him, occupying myself with pushing the food around on my own plate.

The truth is, ever since Michael confessed that he had feelings for me, I've thought about his pronouncement at the most inconvenient times. I'll be sitting in the library reading a book when suddenly it comes crashing into me—*Michael Harrison cares for you*—and I'll realize I've been staring at the same page for five minutes, reading the same sentence over and over again.

It is the strangest thing to think you know someone, have formed a picture of their nature and character, understand your relationship with them, only to discover that nothing is as you perceived. Considering the frequency this has happened to me of late, I'm beginning to question my own judgment to a degree that is truly troubling.

We pass the meal making small talk, and as I predicted, with each minute that passes, I feel a bit more comfortable in his presence, can tell that he is loosening up as well.

When breakfast is over, I set my napkin aside next to my plate, preparing to rise from the table, and then Michael is there, pulling my chair out for me.

Our arms brush against each other.

I still.

Ever since he told me how he felt, ever since it entered my thoughts, I've felt an awareness, an anticipation, like that moment before a storm rolls in when everything hangs in the balance.

I take a deep breath.

"I would like to paint you. Here. In the gardens."

Michael says it swiftly, his voice low, the words both a question and a vow, and something tumbles between us as my answer comes quickly, unbidden.

"Yes."

CHAPTER EIGHTEEN

Carmen

"Did Asher kill Carolina?" I ask, bursting into Detective Pierce's office, my heart pounding, feeling more than a little out of breath. "Mrs. Morrison told me that you arrested him. Did you find the weapon? Is there new evidence?"

Detective Pierce rises from his desk, a frown on his face. "Hello Miss Acosta, please do see yourself in," he replies, his voice dry. "I see word travels fast at Marbrisa. I was told you weren't at home when we stopped by to collect Mr. Wyatt."

"I was out for a walk. I saw Mrs. Morrison when I returned, and she told me that you had taken Asher away."

"Believe it or not, Miss Acosta, I'm not typically in the habit of including young ladies in my police investigations. I'm doing you a courtesy by keeping you informed because I realize that you lost your sister, but there are some things in the investigation that I cannot and will not share with you." His gaze turns speculative. "Although your concern for your brother-in-law's well-being is certainly noted."

"In a manner of speaking, he's the only family I have left," I snap. "Not to mention, if I've been living in a house with a killer these past several days, I have a vested interest in knowing about it."

"The best I can tell you is that nine times out of ten, when a murder happens, the killer is the person who has the most to gain from the victim's death. In that case, it is unmistakably true that Asher benefitted from his wife's demise. He had the means, the motive, and the opportunity. Moreover, he was there with her in the maze. *You* found him with the body."

"So that's it, then. You've decided Asher is guilty."

"I think the facts speak for themselves."

"Do you still believe that I colluded with him?"

"You'll be relieved to know that Asher has made it quite clear that you are innocent. On that matter, he was happy to talk."

"So, he hasn't confessed yet?"

"It's only a matter of time."

I suppose I should feel relieved that the police have momentarily shifted their focus off me, but I can't fight the sneaking suspicion that there's something wrong about this.

"I think Nathaniel Hayes was Carolina's lover," I blurt out. "I saw her meeting a man in the greenhouse. I'm almost certain it was him. The head gardener at Marbrisa saw her meeting someone as well. He thinks it was Nathaniel."

"The investigator?"

I nod.

Detective Pierce frowns. "Even if he was involved with your

sister, that doesn't give him a motive for murder. If anything, it only strengthens your brother-in-law's motive. After all, he hired a man to work for him, paid him to investigate, only for the man to carry on with his wife?" Detective Pierce whistles. "That's a strong motive right there. Your sister was stabbed. I'd say that's a crime of passion. The sort of thing you see from a husband."

"And the weapon? How would Asher have been able to dispose of it in such a hasty manner? I'm telling you, there was hardly any time at all between Carolina's scream and when I reached them."

"And yet, you didn't come in here advocating for Asher's innocence. So, there must be some doubt in your mind."

"He's planning on turning over my inheritance to me."

"Sure he is. Or is that just what he wants you to think? I'll believe it when I see it."

"Why do you hate him so much?"

I want to say "us," since I hardly think I'm exempt from his disdain, but I don't because at the moment, trying to make him see me as an ally is the best plan I have.

"I don't hate Asher Wyatt. But I know men of his ilk. They come down here flush with cash and think they can do as they please, that the rules don't apply to them. They don't care that there are people already living in Miami, good people working hard just to make it while men like Asher Wyatt and Robert Barnes flaunt everything they have."

"Do you think this could all be tied to what happened at Marbrisa before? It feels personal, doesn't it?"

It certainly seems personal to you.

"All of the key players who were alive back then are dead. Except for the architect Michael Harrison. He disappeared after all the nasty business."

"And Mrs. Morrison."

He nods, acknowledging my point.

"And that didn't seem suspicious to you? That Michael Harrison disappeared?"

"No. We questioned him, of course, but he was never a suspect. Not with Lenora and not with Anna."

"What happened to Lenora Watson? You said that she drowned, that you didn't believe that it was an accident, that you didn't believe the story the Barneses told you. You must have had a theory."

"I had more than a theory. I just couldn't prove it."

While he'll hardly share anything about Carolina's death with me, at least with Lenora Watson's death he's marginally more cooperative.

"You can't go up against a man like Robert Barnes without proof. Even with the rumors that he was in a bad way financially, he still had plenty of connections and influence to cause me problems."

"You think Robert killed Lenora?"

"I'd bet my life on the fact that he did it. There were rumors about him cheating on his wife with other women. She denied it when I questioned her after the accident, seemed angry that I would even suggest such a thing. But the rumors didn't lie. And some of Lenora's friends knew that she was seeing some rich man. He bought her fancy things. But no one had ever met him or knew his name, just that he was married, and unfortunately, there's more than a few married men in Miami keeping something on the side."

Mrs. Morrison intimated that Robert cheated on Anna with other women, recalled his mistress was someone named Julie. Why didn't she mention that he'd had an affair with Lenora?

I glance down at Detective Pierce's hand, a thick gold band on his ring finger. I'd stake everything I have on the belief that Detective Pierce has never strayed outside of the bounds of his marriage, likely never even considered it. In a town where nearly everyone seems to be on the make, I doubt he's as much as stolen a pencil.

"It just seems like an unlikely coincidence that there would be this many unrelated tragedies at one house," I say. "Why Marbrisa?"

"Next you're going to suggest it's a ghost that's been haunting the house these twentysomething years."

I flush. "No, not a ghost. I don't subscribe to the theory that Marbrisa is cursed. But I will say having spent some time there that something *is* going on."

I hesitate, knowing he's likely going to mock me and dismiss what I say, but still feeling like it needs to be said just the same. He doesn't understand what it's like in that house, the energy that it gives off.

"There's something weird about it. Strange noises at night."

He looks like he's about to roll his eyes.

"Laugh all you want, but I've heard them. I'm not saying that it's a ghost, but there's something going on. One day, I went up to my room and found a necklace lying on my bed. Then it disappeared like it was never there at all."

"A ghost that brings jewelry. How convenient." His gaze turns skeptical. "Are you sure you didn't just imagine it? That it wasn't something you dreamed of, and thought was real? Perhaps you misplaced some diamonds."

"If I was going to dream of a necklace, Detective, I assure you, it wouldn't be of two coiled snakes," I reply, ignoring the thinly veiled insult.

"Wait, what did you say?"

"That if I was going to—"

"You said the necklace was designed to look like snakes."

"Yes. There were jewels on it. Made to look like snakeskin. They had rubies for eyes. I'm no jewelry connoisseur, but it appeared expensive. Unique."

"Would you recognize it if you saw it again?"

"I suppose I would. It was distinct. I picked it up, held it for a bit. It was the strangest thing—it felt damp. It smelled like the sea."

Detective Pierce jumps up from his desk, walking over to the file cabinet nearest to him, his back to me as he flips through the items there, before turning to face me, a piece of paper in hand.

He slides it across the desk to me.

"Was this the necklace you found in your room at Marbrisa?"

I glance down at the paper he's placed in front of me. There's a drawing of a necklace on the page, done in black ink. It's a crude rendering, one clearly sketched by an amateur, but the image is unmistakable.

"Yes, this is the necklace. Where did you get this? *How* did you get this?"

"That's the necklace Lenora Watson was wearing when she drowned. It disappeared. Someone took it off her body after she died—likely her killer. Anna Barnes saw the necklace on Lenora the night of the party, and during one of our meetings, I asked her to draw a sketch of what it looked like. She remembered it vividly because it was so unusual. I took this sketch to just about every jeweler in Miami trying to discover who made the necklace, but I could never find them. I always thought that Lenora's lover bought the necklace for her and then stole it off her body because he didn't want to risk it being traced back to him."

"You think Robert Barnes gave this to Lenora?"

"Yes, I do."

"How did a dead woman's necklace end up in my bedroom at Marbrisa?"

"I don't know."

"Maybe I should believe in ghosts."

"Believe me, the living are capable of plenty of terrible things without having to scapegoat ghosts. If this is tied to the murders that happened at Marbrisa, then it will be a flesh-and-blood man at the other end."

"But you just said that everyone who was involved back then is dead now, besides Mrs. Morrison. I assume you've questioned her?"

"We have. I don't think she's involved in this. To what end? She has no motive, nothing to gain from these deaths." Detective Pierce grimaces. "Michael Harrison is still alive, though. It sounds like it's time for me to see what the architect has been up to all these years."

CHAPTER NINETEEN

Anna

In the mornings, Michael paints me in the gardens. There's an intimacy to the process that I hadn't expected, although I suppose I should have anticipated it given the amount of time we spend together now with me posing for him while he captures every angle of me, Marbrisa looming in the background.

Robert has returned from his business trip, more determined than ever to reverse our fortunes. With each day that passes, I find myself wondering what it would be like if rather than desperately fighting what seems to be inevitable, we simply sold Marbrisa and bought a little cottage somewhere by the water. Perhaps in Coconut Grove or farther north. Truth be told, Florida has grown on me, and despite the heat and the lizards and all the other strange tidings that seem to go hand in hand with this state, I think I could be happy here under different circumstances.

The only problem is that when I see my future, when I

imagine that cottage by the water in the Grove, I no longer see Robert living there with me.

It feels as though I am at an impasse—I can't stay in my marriage, and I cannot leave. I am stuck now, this house and twenty-three years of marriage an albatross around my neck.

Sometimes during our sittings, I worry that my face will betray me, that all the emotions at war inside me are bubbling to the surface, ready to be captured by Michael and his painter's brush. If he can tell that I feel like a caged animal, he says nothing, our sessions for the most part devoid of conversation. He watches me, and I watch him watching me, and I plan, and I dream for what my future will look like, for how I can escape the situation I have found myself in.

A divorce, perhaps, although despite his infidelity, I doubt that is something Robert would ever agree to. He has converted himself into an ideal husband since his return, and I wish that I could say that it is enough to undo all the hurt, all the pain, but the gulf that has formed between us only seems to grow deeper and wider each day.

And sometimes, only when I allow my thoughts to wander, I wonder what my life would have been like if I had met a man like Michael first.

"I've finished."

I drift back to the present, Michael's voice tearing me away from all my thoughts and worries.

"Would you like to see it?" he calls out, gesturing to the canvas and easel in front of me.

"I would," I reply, surprised by the nerves that flutter in my stomach at the prospect of finally viewing the portrait he has created. When we started this process, I didn't realize how vulnerable it would make me feel, and now I'm hesitant to see what version of me will stare back from the canvas.

I walk over to where Michael stands stiffly, looking nearly as nervous as I feel.

I glance down at the painting.

My breath hitches.

I don't recognize the woman in the painting, standing in front of Marbrisa. She looks nothing like the reflection I see when I look at myself in the mirror, nothing like what I've grown accustomed to.

I look free in a way that I haven't felt in a long time.

And in that moment, I know exactly what I must do.

I smile at him, emotions clogging my throat, making it difficult for me to get the words out, for me to show my appreciation properly.

"Thank you. It's more than I ever expected. Thank you for being such a good friend," I say, the praise far too light for the good he has done me, but he seems to understand the emotion behind my words, because he nods, his gaze solemn.

I carry the painting with me into the house once he says his goodbyes, feeling as though it is a secret I would like to hide away, a side of myself I'm not ready to share with Robert. Instead, I take it to one of the guest rooms, knowing he'll never see it there, before heading back downstairs to his study.

I rummage through Robert's desk, searching for a pad of paper to leave him a note, to let him know that I have gone out for a bit.

I have many plans to make.

I find a pen with ease, a notepad proving to be a touch more difficult. I pull open a drawer, feeling around, my fingers closing around something metallic, cold, and slightly damp.

I pull it out of the drawer.

It smells faintly of the sea.

I blink, staring at the object in my hand, confusion filling me.

The necklace is a long piece of coiled gold in the shape of two snakes, their eyes represented by rubies, their skin a coat of dappled diamonds. It's a unique item, custom by the look of it. It's certainly not something I would ever see myself wearing, but beautiful in its own way nonetheless.

The police searched Marbrisa and never found it. Where has it been hiding until now?

My fingers tremble, and then the tremor slides through my whole body, pieces suddenly shifting into place.

"Anna, I—"

I glance up.

Robert stands in the entryway of the study.

He stops mid-breath, freezing, his gaze dropping to the necklace before drifting up to my face.

"Why do you have this?" I ask.

Where has Robert been hiding it until now?

My voice sounds broken to my own ears, and I suppose in a way that's exactly what's happening—there's a crack forming between the life I have cleaved to for so long and the inescapable reality of the situation.

I should have known.

I should have seen.

Even worse—perhaps part of me knew and saw, and still I did nothing.

Robert opens his mouth, and I can see plain as day all the excuses that are forming in his head, the lies he is preparing to trot out before me, the web he has been spinning for how long now?

"What have you done?" I ask.

"Anna."

"This necklace. I saw it that night. The night of the party. Lenora Watson was wearing this necklace."

"Anna, you're mistaken. I can understand given all we've been through how you would be suspicious, but this isn't what it looks like."

"Don't." My voice shakes. "Don't lie to me. It was this necklace. It was on her body when they pulled her out of the water. I saw it. I saw her. I'm not mistaken. I know this necklace well—Detective Pierce even made me sketch it. He had a theory, you see. That Lenora Watson had a lover who gave her this necklace. A wealthy lover. He was convinced that if he just showed the sketch to some jewelers, they might recognize it and remember the man who bought it for her. After all, it is such a dear, unique piece. My guess is that he is never going to have success with that plan, though, because the necklace didn't come from a jeweler in Miami. You bought it in New York, didn't you?"

It's just a guess, but I can see the confirmation, the truth of it in his eyes.

All those times he traveled from New York to Miami, I thought it was because he was devoted to the construction of the house, but now I see that there were other incentives bringing him here. Their affair must have started quite some time ago.

It wasn't just the woman I saw him with at the party—Julie—and it wasn't just Lenora, either. A man who will cheat once will cheat twice, and after he's cheated twice, what's to stop him from cheating again?

Now I remember the moment in which we made eye contact at the party, how Lenora's gaze lingered over me. At the time, I thought it was curiosity over Marbrisa's owners, but now that I think back on the interaction, I see the frank interest in her eyes, the hint of a secret. No one invited her to the party; I can't believe even Robert would have been bold or foolish enough to have his mistress in his home with his wife. She must have come because she wanted a look at his wife, at the life she probably hoped would be hers one day.

I have been such a fool.

"The two of you were involved. For quite some time. Did you make her promises? Tell her you were going to leave me for her?"

He must have. I can't blame her for believing him considering how long he deceived me.

Robert closes his eyes. "Anna."

"No. No. You don't get to sweep this under the rug." I dig deep now, mustering a strength I never knew I possessed to keep from crumpling to my knees under the weight of my husband's betrayal. "Look at me. Enough with the lies. She was your lover."

He doesn't deny it, and his silence emboldens me to press

the matter further. Robert has captained our marriage for so long now that it's a heady feeling to assume control, to have caught him off guard.

I take a deep breath, adrenaline coursing through my veins. "When Detective Pierce questioned me, he mentioned that a witness saw the two of you fighting. At the time, I dismissed it because I didn't understand what you would have had to argue about, but the witness wasn't mistaken, were they? They saw Lenora arguing with you in her final moments alive."

"Anna."

"What did you do?"

I can see it all playing out before me. Now that the pieces line up, I don't understand how I didn't see it before, how I didn't realize all the betrayals that were playing out before my very eyes.

He opens his mouth to defend himself, but he must identify something in my expression that makes him change his mind, because suddenly his body sags, collapsing under the weight of his lies, and I realize that I am finally going to get an approximation of the truth—or the closest to the truth that Robert is capable of.

"It was an accident," he whispers, something that might be sorrow threading through his voice.

I can't tell if he feels sorry for himself or for Lenora.

"She's dead. How was that an accident?"

"She was upset. It was dark. She'd had too much to drink. That all was true. She was so angry, so out of control. She kept threatening to tell you about us if I didn't tell you myself. She wanted me to leave you for her and no matter how many times

I told her that would never happen, that I loved you, she didn't listen to me. She kept pushing for more.

"I was worried she was going to cause a scene at the party, so I tried my best to get her out of there, to avoid her ruining our night. I thought that if I could just talk to her, if I could placate her, then she would leave, and I could go back to the party and to our guests. To you. But she wouldn't listen to reason, wouldn't make sense. We were walking by the water and her heel slipped. The next thing I knew, she went in."

I've envisioned Lenora's final moments more times than I can count since that night she drowned, but hearing it in Robert's own words, knowing that she died in the presence of a man she likely cared for, a man she thought she could trust, makes it unspeakably horrible. No one deserves to be discarded like that, to only be seen as an inconvenience, a means to an end.

"Did you try to save her? You saw her go into the water. Did you go in after her? Did you call for help? Could she swim?"

"It happened so quickly. I was in shock."

Disbelief fills me. The amount of remorse and sorrow he's displaying hardly seems proportionate to the situation at hand. A woman died. A woman he was apparently involved with. How can he stand here making excuses for what happened? Doesn't he care? How can he view her life as so expendable?

"She wasn't even supposed to be here," he explodes. "She knew she wasn't allowed to come to parties at Marbrisa. I told her not to come."

"Why? Because you didn't want your mistress and your wife crossing paths? How considerate of you."

"I never wanted to hurt you."

It such a ludicrous, insulting statement considering the depth of what he has done that it momentarily steals my breath. How can he be so inconsiderate? How can he be so cruel?

"And her?" I ask. "Did you want to hurt her? She's dead."

"It was an accident." His voice rises to a loud boom now, and I take a step back, and then another, fear pricking me. This is a side of my husband that I've never seen before, one that was apparently always lurking beneath the surface. "Do you really think I'm capable of murder?"

If he'd asked me that question the day he proposed, I would have said a resounding no. If he asked me throughout our marriage, I would have said the same. But now, looking down this strange path we have traveled, the truth is that I don't know who he is anymore or what he is capable of. I never imagined any of this when I said my vows.

"I did it for you."

My head snaps up. "Excuse me?"

"I told you—she wanted me to leave you for her."

"Were you planning on it? Something must have given her the idea that it was a possibility."

It hardly matters, given the scope of what we're discussing, but I can't help but be curious as to what his answer is.

"Of course not. I wouldn't risk the life we have together."

But he did risk it. He took the life we'd built together and destroyed it.

"She was a distraction," Robert adds. "Nothing more. It was the same thing with Julie."

How many others were there? And for how long? Was there

always an unseen presence hovering on the edges of my marriage? A specter I never saw?

"You have no idea the kind of pressure I was under," Robert continues. "With them, I could forget about my worries. I had no responsibilities to them, no obligations."

I think about the way he describes their relationships through the frame of his own foibles, but I can't help but wonder what it was like for Lenora. Did she love Robert? Did she dream as so many of us have of a happy ending for what must have been a difficult life? And despite his protests, his assertions to the contrary, I can't help but wonder what he told her to entice her into a relationship, what lies he spun to give her hope, to make her think that there was the possibility of something more between them. I now know exactly how it feels to have a man tell you what he thinks you want to hear rather than the truth to protect his own interests.

"Why did you take the necklace?"

"Anna. Please. Stop doing this. Why do you insist on dragging all of this up? The woman is dead. She drowned. The police have let it go. You need to as well."

"Have they? I didn't get the impression that Detective Pierce was the sort of man to let things go. In fact, the opposite. He seems like a tenacious adversary when his mind is made up. Do you really think the truth won't come out? That in a town like Miami where everyone talks, people won't realize that you were involved with her? Do you really think this is just going to go away?"

"It's going to go away because I say it will. My lawyers will bury the police department if they continue to harass me."

He's probably right. He will throw whatever remaining money and influence we have behind the weight of this to save his own skin. No wonder he's been working so hard to regain his fortune. It isn't just Marbrisa that's at stake; it's his freedom. As a wealthy and powerful man, he may find himself above the law, but as soon as he loses those protections, he'll be as vulnerable as the rest of us.

"You took the necklace because you knew it would be traced to you, because you realized that as soon as the police discovered you were having an affair, you would be their prime suspect. You say that this was all an accident—I don't believe you."

His eyes widen, his face reddening with anger.

"I think you were angry with her," I continue. "Angry that she had the audacity to come here, angry that she backed you into a corner. Maybe you were tired of her, too. Perhaps you'd already met Julie and lost interest in Lenora. It doesn't even matter.

"A man drowned in the bay when the house was being built. I remember you telling me that the first day we came here. Is that where you got the idea? In the middle of your fight, did you realize that if you just pushed her a little bit, if her heels slipped in the muck, you could write the whole thing off as an accident? Did you hope that people would believe you? That you could fool the police?'

"Shut up," Robert hisses. "Mrs. Morrison was in the hallway earlier dusting. Do you want the servants to hear you? For the whole household to find out?"

"Honestly, I don't care anymore. You murdered that poor girl. I went to her house. I saw her mother," I shout at him. "I saw the grief in her eyes, saw the pain that you caused her. You can never make amends for that."

"Are you threatening me?"

His tone has grown progressively calmer the angrier mine has become, and it's that shift in temperament that has me backing up.

I thought I knew all of Robert's faces, thought that I understood my husband better than anyone on this earth, but the man who stands before me now is a complete and utter stranger, capable of things I never fathomed.

And suddenly, I realize that a man who is willing to kill his mistress to keep her from outing their affair is likely just as willing to kill his wife to keep her from threatening his freedom.

My interior thoughts have long been the bedrock of my marriage, self-possession the singularly most effective tool in my arsenal. I retreat into myself, struggling to transform my face into a blank mask, to guard my innermost feelings from Robert with the experience of decades of marriage. Never have the stakes been so high.

Now he is to play the fool.

I take a deep breath. "No, of course not."

⌇

THAT NIGHT, WHEN the house is abed, I hurry toward the forest on the estate's edges, the soles of my shoes slipping against the spindly tree roots in my path. It's too dark to see more than a few feet in front of me, the moon shrouded by the clouds.

I try not to think of all the nocturnal creatures that call

Marbrisa home, their vision much better than mine, hunting for their prey.

My legs ache as I run away from the grand house, my lungs burning from the effort. Around me, the wind howls, another Florida storm building in the distance. I only pray the rain will wait until after I've reached my destination.

I glance over my shoulder, hoping I'm not being followed.

My gaze drifts up, higher now, to the immense mansion off in the distance. The house's windows are dark, but my breath hitches all the same.

Leaving was the hardest part. Rising from my bed with Robert sleeping beside me, the steady sound of his breathing achingly familiar to me. When we went to bed, I laid there on my side, my back to my husband, my heart pounding so loudly that I feared he would realize what I intended, that he would pick up that something was amiss between us. All through dinner after that terrible fight in his study, I was careful to keep my expression neutral, to resist recoiling each time Robert turned his attention to me. I played the dutiful wife so that I could get to the moment when I was convinced Robert was sleeping, when I could climb out of bed, terror filling me. Those first steps were the hardest—willing myself to move, to leave the comfort of my bed, of my marriage, and venture out into the unknown.

I walked away with nothing but the clothes on my back. For this to work, I could take nothing with me.

My nightgown whips around me, the wind kicking up once more and I turn away from the mansion, my gaze set to my future.

It feels like the house watches my every step.

I throw myself deeper into the night, into the protection it provides. If Robert looked out the windows of the main house this evening, he'd see little more than the darkness that envelops me now.

I've left my husband. I can scarcely believe it.

I slow down as the cottage comes into view. Its windows are dark.

Please be home.

I lift my fist and rap on the door, once, twice.

Silence greets me.

In the distance, a bird screeches. Then a howl of sorts.

I grab the door handle, checking to see if by chance Michael has left it unlocked.

It doesn't turn.

Damnit.

The door swings open.

For a moment, neither one of us says anything as we stare at each other, the threshold yawning between us. And then he speaks—

"Anna?"

Michael looks as though he's been sleeping and I've woken him from his slumber, his hair mussed, robe rumpled.

"I'm sorry to come here. I'm sorry to disturb you at this late hour." My heart pounds. "I need your help."

CHAPTER TWENTY

Carmen

As soon as I leave the police station, the rain comes down in thick sheets, pelting Asher's car, the wind swaying the trees in the distance. I'm grateful at least that the top was up on his convertible when I took it.

I lean forward, struggling to see out of the windshield through the water pouring down the glass, my knuckles white as my fingers grip the steering wheel. In Havana, my parents employed a driver, so even though I know how to drive, it's a skill I've had little chance to perfect. When I borrowed Asher's car, the weather was placid. I should have known it could all turn on a dime.

I ease my foot off the gas, the sporty vehicle fishtailing along the road. I pull back against the wheel, narrowly avoiding Asher's car careening into the ditch on the roadside.

My heart pounds.

Is it possible—is Michael Harrison somehow involved in all of this? Lenora's necklace changes things—linking the past and the present—but I just don't see how she could be connected to Carolina's death. It feels like I'm missing some important piece of information, some part of the history that has remained hidden all this time.

The convertible hits a flooded patch of road, sliding for a few yards before I'm able to regain control, terror filling me.

I glance to the left, looking for the entrance to Marbrisa, searching for the iron gates. It's nearly impossible to see anything in this rain, the unfamiliar area compounding the difficulty.

For a moment, I consider just pulling over to the side of the road and waiting out the weather, but in my time here I've learned that storms can last minutes or hours with no predictability between them.

There it is.

In the distance, I can see the entrance's reflection bouncing off the car's headlights.

Relief fills me.

I maneuver the car off the roadway, wishing Asher had purchased something sturdier than this flighty vehicle that skitters over the various bumps in the road.

I pass through the estate's iron gates, the rain coming down harder now, the visibility so poor that I can barely see the house looming ahead.

The palm trees bend on either side of me, their shadows in the moonlight looking a bit like towering monsters.

Lightning flashes ahead, the house coming into view at the end of the long driveway.

Nathaniel's green convertible is still parked in front.

Thunder rolls, the loud booms shaking Asher's car and chattering my teeth.

There's a light on in one of the downstairs windows; at least we haven't lost power. Hopefully, it'll stay on long enough for me to pack a bag to take to the Biltmore, although at the moment, I can't imagine going back out into this night.

Something darts in front of the car, so quickly that there's no time for me to slam on the brakes.

I turn the wheel abruptly, the car lurching forward and veering to the side. I try to recover, to keep the car from spinning out of control, but it's too late, and I lose my grip on the steering wheel, the convertible careening toward a tree.

I slam on the brakes.

I'm thrown forward, my head bashing the steering wheel as the convertible's front bumper slams into one of the mighty palms.

A sharp pain stabs me in the forehead.

For a moment, I pause, struggling to catch my breath, my heart pounding. My neck is sore, and my back aches. Thankfully, I wasn't going fast; I hate to think what would have happened to me if I had been.

The hood of the car is smashed up against the base of the palm tree, smoke coming out of the engine. There's a huge vertical crack in the windshield.

Asher is going to kill me.

I feel something sticky on my forehead and I reach up, touching my forehead, staring down at my fingers that are wet with blood.

Sure enough, when I look at my reflection in the rearview mirror, there's a gash from where I hit my head on the steering wheel. I gingerly probe it, relieved to see that it doesn't look too deep.

I lean forward, reaching for the glove box, looking for a handkerchief or something I can use to stanch the bleeding.

My hands close around something heavy, metal—

A flashlight.

Thank God Asher is prepared.

There's a first aid kit as well, and I grab it—

My hands brush against something else.

Cold metal.

I pull it out by the hilt.

There's a knife in Asher's glove box.

I study the blade dispassionately, as though it's perfectly innocuous, as if there's a wholly logical reason that there's a knife in my brother-in-law's car.

There's dried blood on the blade.

The knife begins shaking, and it isn't until I blink a few times, clearing the tears from my eyes, that I realize it isn't the knife shaking, but the hand that's holding it.

I know with a terrible certainty that rattles my bones that this is the knife that killed my sister.

The police arrested Asher. They've been searching Marbrisa for days now without any sign of the weapon. There's no possibility Detective Pierce wouldn't have searched Asher's car.

It couldn't have been here when the police searched the property, which means either Asher moved the knife after they searched Marbrisa or someone is framing him.

I slip the knife and the flashlight into my purse, using the contents of the first aid kit to patch the wound on my forehead.

I need to tell Detective Pierce what I've found.

I wrench open the car door, the rain pelting me as I step out. The front of Asher's car is completely crumpled, the tree the clear victor in the scuffle. There's no hope of me driving the rest of the driveway to the house. I'll have to make a run for it. At least I'm on the property and not back there on the road. On a night like this, I doubt many people are out for a drive.

I walk around to see what I swerved to avoid hitting.

An alligator stares back at me, its scaly, ridged body illuminated by the car's one working headlight.

The alligator is still for a moment, a standoff between us, and I imagine it's contemplating its next move, deciding whether it's going to have me for dinner.

I pray it has already eaten.

If I had to outrun it, would I be faster?

I glance back at the main house, judging the distance I still must go, the rain showing no signs of lightening. I take a deep breath—

The alligator turns away, scampering toward the forest.

I don't wait for it to change its mind as I head toward the house, my legs pumping as fast as they can carry me, the rain beating down on my back, soaking my dress so that the wet fabric sticks to my legs.

I hurry past Nathaniel's parked car, wincing at the pain in my head.

The front door is unlocked, and I head inside, shutting it behind me swiftly.

I close my eyes as I lean back against the front door for a moment, out of breath from my dash down the long driveway, adrenaline flooding my body.

There's a stillness to the house that makes me feel very alone. The household staff don't live here, which is probably the only thing that kept them from quitting. I don't think there's enough money in the world to convince them to stay overnight, considering everything that has happened in this house.

Despite Nathaniel's car parked outside, when I strain to hear sounds of life—footsteps or voices—I am greeted by silence instead. I open my mouth to announce my presence, but something catches my voice, some warning in the recesses of my mind telling me it's safer to keep myself hidden.

I push my wet hair off my face, shivering slightly as I walk toward the library. I remember seeing a phone on Asher's desk the night we spoke.

I turn on the light, grateful that we still have power.

The grandfather clock chimes eight o'clock in the evening.

I rush over to the desk and set my bag down. I pull the knife out, staring at the weapon. It's unremarkable as far as knives go—it's neither ornately fine nor roughly hewn. The blade is eight inches give or take. I place it next to the phone, my fingers trembling with the motion. I can't look away from the spots of Carolina's blood on the blade.

I feel like I'm going to be sick.

Outside, the storm rages.

I pick up the phone—

"What happened to your face?"

I glance up.

Nathaniel stands near the library door, his gaze on my forehead.

"Were you attacked?" he asks, rushing toward the desk.

"No. I was driving. The car—I was in an accident."

Halfway through my answer, I realize he's no longer paying any attention to me at all. Instead, he's staring down at the desk.

"Where did you find that? Is that . . . ?"

I swallow. "Yes. I think so."

My fingers itch to pick up the blade, to offer me some protection. I don't know who I can trust anymore.

"How did you get that?" Nathaniel asks me.

"I drove Asher's car earlier. After the accident, I was looking for a first aid kit in his glove box. I found this instead."

He moves closer, his body crowding me, only a few feet between us.

"May I?" he asks, gesturing toward the knife.

I pick it up.

I don't hand it to him.

Instead, I grip the handle, my knuckles white, the blade pointed toward Nathaniel.

He freezes mid-step.

"Asher told me he let you go," I say. "What are you still doing here?"

"I was worried. About you. About Asher. It didn't feel right leaving both of you with Carolina's murderer at large. Especially after Asher was arrested. I didn't want you to be by yourself at the house."

It's plausible enough, but I still don't lower the knife.

"The day I arrived at Marbrisa, I saw Carolina meeting a man in the greenhouse from my bedroom window."

He makes an impatient noise. "She was with me, Nancy Drew."

My heart pounds. "Were you having an affair with Carolina?"

"No. Of course not. One, it would be unspeakably unprofessional, and you can believe whatever you want about me, but I take my job very seriously. Not to mention, your sister never showed the slightest interest in me. If anything, she always seemed annoyed by my presence. And as lovely as she was, I wasn't interested either. Besides I never would have done that to Asher. Not only was he my employer, but I like him well enough. He doesn't deserve to be cuckolded in his own house—not that the opportunity ever presented itself."

As far as denials go, it's about as sweeping as they get.

"Why don't you trust me?" he asks me.

There's a thread of annoyance in his voice, as though his professional integrity is piqued by the fact that I won't accept the veracity of his words.

"You tried to be charming when I met you."

"Asher told me Carolina's little sister was coming to Marbrisa. Of course I tried to be charming. I thought that if I was charming, you would like me, and if you liked me, you might be more inclined to cooperate with me, to feed me information. I had a job to do."

"I didn't find you to be charming. I figured you were being dishonest."

"Thank you for the tip. I'll work on my acting skills next time."

"Why were you meeting my sister at the greenhouse?"

"I wasn't meeting her, per se. I was talking to some of the gardening staff. Two weeks before the peacock, Asher found a dead alligator in the front driveway. I was investigating. Carolina and I just happened to cross paths. She wanted to talk to me. I think she had figured out what I was really doing at Marbrisa. She didn't come out and say it as such—she was never as direct as you—but she heavily intimated it."

"What did she want to talk to you about? The alligator? Asher?"

He takes a deep breath. "Do you ever give a person a moment to breathe? It's hard to think around you." He glances back up at my forehead. "You really should get that looked at."

"I tried cleaning it up with the first aid kit in the car. It was dark. I couldn't see."

This time he does move, coming around the desk until we're inches away from each other.

I don't let go of the knife, but I don't stab him with it, either.

He pulls a handkerchief from his pocket, dabbing at the blood on my forehead, his touch surprisingly gentle.

"Carolina had questions about Anna Barnes. And Lenora Watson."

"Why didn't you tell me this before?"

"Because Asher told me to keep you safe. Because you're what, eighteen, nineteen years old?"

I flush. "Almost nineteen."

"This is serious." Nathaniel removes the handkerchief from my forehead, staring at the wound before he takes a step back, putting some distance between us, seemingly satisfied with his handiwork. "Your sister was murdered. I don't want you getting more involved in this. I promised Asher I would keep you safe."

"Carolina and I were the last Acostas. Our parents are gone. We have no family save for distant cousins that frankly never wanted much to do with us. I feel a responsibility to see my sister's murder avenged, and right now, I'm not sure the police are following the right leads. They've arrested Asher, and now, somehow, conveniently, this knife shows up in his glove box even though the police likely searched it."

"I agree with you. Asher isn't dumb."

"No, he isn't. Help me. Help me understand why my sister was asking about the past."

"I don't know. Honestly. I wish I could tell you more. She wanted to know if I thought that Lenora's and Anna's deaths were connected." He hesitates. "She was worried about you. About you coming here with everything that was happening. She asked me to investigate a possible connection between the two women."

"Did you?"

"I put in some calls, trying to learn more about Lenora Watson. I didn't get very far before Carolina was killed."

His expression is filled with regret.

It feels as though I'm meeting him anew, the character he was pretending to be in the dining room the night we first crossed paths giving way to something more sincere.

I'm in too deep.

I need someone I can trust.

I set the knife down.

Nathaniel leans over it, studying it. "That certainly looks like the murder weapon. Have you ever seen it before this evening?"

I shake my head.

"You aren't the first person to tell me that Carolina was asking about Anna's and Lenora's deaths." I fill him in on my conversation with Detective Pierce and what I learned about the necklace. "I think what was happening at Marbrisa in the past is connected to what's happening now. And I think Carolina figured it out before anyone else. I think that's why she was killed."

"We need to tell Detective Pierce about the knife," Nathaniel says.

"I was just about to call him when you burst in."

I pick up the phone, holding the receiver between us so we can both hear the call. I ask the operator to put me in contact with the police department, with Detective Pierce.

We wait for Detective Pierce to come on the line, my hands wrapped tight around the phone. My mind is racing.

I keep thinking about what Detective Pierce said to me, about how the murderer is likely the person who has the most to gain.

What am I missing?

What did Carolina figure out that I haven't yet?

My sister was incredibly clever, and I wish she could speak to me now, could help me see what I can't.

"Hello?" Detective Pierce asks, coming onto the line.

The connection is terrible, no doubt because of the storm, but I can just make out his voice.

"I found the murder weapon."

Static fills the line.

"Detective Pierce?"

There's silence and then—

"How? Where?"

I fill him in on the accident, on the knife in the glove box, Nathaniel interjecting beside me occasionally, with a question or statement of his own.

Static fills the line once more.

". . . Marbrisa."

I can hear the urgency in Detective Pierce's voice, but it's too difficult to understand what he's saying, bits and pieces of our conversation snatched away by the poor connection.

"What did you say?" I ask.

"Sit tight. I'm coming—"

Silence fills the line.

"Detective Pierce?"

The sky explodes in a bright light followed by a sharp crack of thunder that makes my bones shake.

Marbrisa plunges into darkness.

CHAPTER TWENTY-ONE

I scream.

Nathaniel is there in an instant, his hand at the small of my back. "It's alright. It's just the storm. Power losses happen all the time."

I take a deep breath, feeling more than a little silly for my reaction. Of course it's the storm. I could hear the effects of it on my phone call with Detective Pierce.

"How long before the power normally returns?" I ask Nathaniel.

"It's hard to tell. It could be back in a few hours; it could be days."

"Wonderful."

Marbrisa is creepy under the best of circumstances without adding power loss into the mix.

"It looks like both of us will be staying at the Biltmore tonight," Nathaniel says.

"What if we can't get out—or Detective Pierce can't get to

us? How do the roads typically fare in weather like this? Earlier, the conditions were bad."

He doesn't answer me, but then again, I suppose his silence is an answer itself. There's a good chance we may be trapped here until the conditions improve.

I reach into my bag and grab the flashlight I took from Asher's car, grateful I thought to bring it with me.

I turn it on, a small beam of light illuminating the library.

"What do we do now?" I ask Nathaniel.

"Why don't you go up to your room and pack a bag for the hotel?"

I hesitate. "Will you come up with me? I don't want to be alone when the house is like this."

"Of course."

I slip the knife back into my purse and sling it over my shoulder, the flashlight clutched in my other hand.

"Is Mrs. Morrison here?" I ask Nathaniel. "She was at the house when I left to go to the police station."

"I'm not sure. I haven't seen her for a few hours."

"We should find her. If she is here, I don't want to leave her alone."

"I agree."

We move slowly through the house, calling out for Mrs. Morrison, raising our voices to be heard over the sound of the roaring storm. I feel a little braver now that there's two of us. Even with the assistance of the flashlight, it's too dark to see more than a few feet in front of us, the inky blackness surrounding us.

Nathaniel keeps a tight hold on my arm.

We stop at the base of the stairs.

There's a creak, the sound of floorboards shifting above us.

"Let me go first," Nathaniel whispers. He releases me, reaching into his jacket pocket and pulling out a revolver. "Stay behind me."

My heart pounds. It's probably just Mrs. Morrison moving around upstairs, but given all that has happened, I can't blame him for taking precautions. I certainly feel more comfortable knowing that he has a weapon.

We walk up the stairs slowly, with me at his back.

"If there's someone else up there, you go to the nearest room and barricade yourself in there until help comes," Nathaniel instructs.

"I will."

I hold on to the railing, taking each step gently, remembering how I almost slipped and fell that last day with Carolina.

Lightning flashes in the sky once more, illuminating the staircase before the house goes pitch-black again.

The sound grows louder; then, there's the unmistakable thud of footsteps.

We reach the top of the landing.

I notice Nathaniel isn't calling out for Mrs. Morrison anymore.

Neither am I.

We're both likely keenly aware that the storm has isolated us from the rest of the world.

The noise has stopped.

We walk down the hallway, and Nathaniel quietly motions

for me to give him the flashlight. I hand it to him, my body shaking like a leaf.

Thunder rolls.

Then silence.

A moan fills the air.

"Did you hear that?" I hiss.

Nathaniel nods, the flashlight illuminating his profile. His jaw is clenched.

We walk down the hallway, the steps familiar to me. We're nearing a set of guest bedrooms now, mine just two doors down.

I can barely see ahead of me, Nathaniel's body blocking the flashlight's beam, and I regret that I gave him the light, that I—

A curse escapes Nathaniel's lips.

He crosses the threshold to my bedroom and crouches down.

Beyond him, I can just make out a figure, dark skirts crumpled on the ground.

The flashlight's beam skates over the body, the hand holding its base no longer steady.

My breath catches as I recognize her.

Horror fills me.

Mrs. Morrison.

"Is she—?"

I can't say the rest of the sentence aloud.

Nathaniel leans over her, pointing the flashlight at her body, at a nasty gash on her head. His fingers move to her neck, searching for a pulse.

"She's alive," he replies, relief flooding his voice. "Barely, but she's alive."

He reaches out, handing me the flashlight. "Take this. I'm going to see if I can lift her."

I grab the flashlight from him with my free hand, my purse clutched tightly in my other one.

A flash of lightning explodes, illuminating the room, and then I see it—the dark, cavernous space yawning before me.

The door to the passageway in my room, the one I had kept barricaded since the night Asher walked through it—is wide open. The furniture I had used to block it is gone.

"Nathaniel—"

A figure steps out of the dark, a black boot crossing into the beam of the flashlight.

"Look out!" I scream at Nathaniel.

I'm a moment too late. He barely seems to register that I've spoken at all when the intruder reaches out, swinging, a large mallet in their hands.

Nathaniel crumples to the floor.

I shine the light up, up—

Until it rests on George's face.

Confusion sets in for an instant, thoughts rapid firing inside me.

Did George think Nathaniel was trying to hurt me? Was George protecting me? Did he make a mistake?

Was George ever really my friend at all?

I glance down at where Nathaniel's body lies prone near Mrs. Morrison's. Nathaniel's not moving, but he's face down and I can't tell if he's breathing or not, if George killed him or he's merely unconscious.

I can't see Nathaniel's gun. He must have lost control over it when George hit him.

I don't want to risk moving the flashlight to see if I can find it, don't want to draw attention to it while George is standing before me, while I'm still sorting everything out in my mind.

I swallow, stalling for time. George doesn't know that we called Detective Pierce. It's been nearly thirty minutes. Detective Pierce should be here soon if the roads were passable.

"It was you, wasn't it?"

I didn't intend to come out and ask him in such a forthright manner, but I suppose Nathaniel was right all along. Maybe I am too direct.

I keep thinking about what Detective Pierce said to me, about how the murderer is likely the person who has the most to gain.

What am I missing?

What did Carolina figure out that I haven't yet?

George doesn't answer me.

"Why?" I ask again, taking his silence as an admission. "Why did you kill my sister? Why the animals? Why all of it?"

"Haven't you figured it out yet? Carolina did."

My heart pounds. How could I have so misjudged him?

"What did Carolina figure out?" I ask.

"That Marbrisa should be mine, not Asher's."

"What are you talking about?"

Thunder booms through the night sky.

I jump, the flashlight's beam wobbling with the motion.

Out of the corner of my eye, past Nathaniel's body, I spy the gun resting on the ground near my bed.

I jerk my gaze back up to George's face, praying he didn't notice my lapse in attention, that he doesn't turn his attention to the gun's location.

"Robert Barnes was my father," George announces.

It takes a moment for me to place the name, to tie the past to the present. I was so focused on Anna and Lenora, that truthfully I thought little of Robert himself.

I remember what Detective Pierce told me in his office earlier—his suspicions about Robert Barnes's involvement in Lenora Watson's death, his hunch that Robert was the one who gave Lenora the snake necklace. Mrs. Morrison told me there were other women. Now I see. Now I understand.

"Lenora Watson was your mother."

It's the piece of the puzzle I never had, the one that tied everything together, past and present. When I spoke with Mrs. Morrison days ago, I got the sense that she was holding something back from me. Was this the secret she kept?

"They had an affair," I say.

Something flashes in George's eyes. "They did. And Robert Barnes killed her, used his wealth and power to cover it all up. All of this was meant to be mine. Instead, I was raised by my grandmother in a house not much bigger than this bedroom. For most of my life, she lied to people. Said that my father died in the war. That he was married to my mother. She was afraid of the scandal, ashamed that her daughter had carried on with a married man. Right before my grandmother died a year ago, she told me who my father really was, and I came here to see my birthright in person.

"Asher hired me. Can you imagine that? This house should by birth be mine, but instead he wanted me tending his gardens, toiling in the muck and dirt for him. I grew up in a shack compared to this place, miles away, and I never knew who I really was."

"How did Carolina find out?"

"Once she learned about my mother's death, she became convinced that her death was tied to Anna's. She started asking questions of everyone who was involved back then. When she reached out to my mother's family and learned she had a son, well, I think she started putting the pieces together. In the end, I don't know what she knew, just that she suspected enough to be a threat."

"So you killed her. And then you framed Asher by placing the knife in the glove box of his convertible."

"It didn't have to end like this. I had a plan. I knew Asher's finances were tight—there were rumors that he had extended himself buying this place. The more problems I caused for him, the greater the chance that he would have to give up this place. You can't maintain a home of this magnitude if no one will work here."

"How did you get my sister to meet you in the maze that night?"

"She wasn't meeting me. She had been up north earlier in the day talking to my family. One of my cousins works at Marbrisa. He let me know some rich lady was asking about me. I kept an eye out, watching the house, waiting for an opportunity. I learned about the passageways from my cousin when he was involved in the remodeling. I was planning on sneaking into the house that way, but then it wasn't necessary—she was just there, heading toward the maze. So I improvised. She was looking for Asher, probably to tell him her suspicions about me. I just got there first."

He advances toward me, and something flashes in my mind, and I see him not as he is now, but standing outside the maze, looming over my sister. I can feel Carolina with me, as surely as if she stood beside me, linking her fingers with mine, giving me strength.

This was the face she saw right before she died.

It's the last one I'll see, too.

It can't end like this.

I won't let it.

I glance over at where the gun is once more, stalling for time, trying to figure out how to get past him.

"And the necklace? Your mother's necklace? Did you place that in my room, too?"

His gaze darts toward my dresser and back to me, surprise in his eyes—

"What necklace?"

For an instant, he's confused, distracted, and it's all I need.

I lunge forward, scrambling to the floor and reaching for the gun. My fingers graze the handle—

George's hand clamps down on my ankle, yanking me away.

The gun skitters out of my grasp.

At once, he's on top of me, knocking the flashlight out of my hand. It drops to the floor with a crash.

Lightning skates across the night sky.

George's hands wrap around my throat.

I kick my legs, struggling to push him off, screaming for help.

His fingers press into my skin, cutting off my air.

It's too dark to see anything, and I feel as though I am drowning, the weight of George on top of me, the pressure of his fingers on my throat dragging me under.

I'm going to die.

Just like my parents. Just like my sister. It ends here.

Not like this.

There's a voice in my head now, insistent, pulling me back.

My purse is still in my hands.

The knife.

I shove my fingers inside, brushing up against my wallet, makeup bag.

Relief surges through me. My hand closes around the hilt.

I pull the knife out and plunge it into his heart.

CHAPTER TWENTY-TWO

D oes this mean I'm going to make it?" Nathaniel croaks.

I rise from the chair in the corner of his room and walk over to the hospital bed, relief filling me. I was worried he would never regain consciousness, that the damage he suffered at George's hands would prove to be fatal.

"How long have I been unconscious?" he asks when I reach his bedside.

I glance back at the clock in the hospital room. "About twelve hours now."

"What happened?"

"You were knocked out. He snuck up on us when we found Mrs. Morrison lying on the floor of my bedroom. He tried to kill me, too. I stabbed him with the knife I found in Asher's glove box."

The knife that killed my sister.

Somehow, there's poetic justice in that.

Nathaniel doesn't ask me if I'm alright, or say anything at all. Instead, he reaches out, offering his hand.

I hesitate for a moment, and then I fit my palm against his, our fingers linking.

It's strange to share such intimacy with someone I couldn't stand in the beginning, but now that we've been through something so terrifying together, there's an understanding of sorts between us. I doubt either one of us will ever forget what happened last night.

"And Mrs. Morrison?" Nathaniel asks.

"She's in the room next to you. She's awake. The police are talking to her. I haven't had a chance to."

He winces. "Who was it?"

"The head gardener. George."

"I didn't see that one," he mutters.

"Neither did I."

Nathaniel's hospital room opens, and Asher walks through. His gaze drifts from Nathaniel lying in bed, to me, and then he rushes toward me.

"Are you alright?" Asher asks me.

I nod, releasing Nathaniel's hand.

Asher embraces me, and I allow myself to relax into his hug, to fully accept what I never could before when I was plagued with doubts. He may just be my family by marriage, but he's the only family I have left, the brother I never had.

"When they told me what happened . . . I'm so sorry you were alone. I can't imagine how terrifying that must have been," Asher says.

"Are you free now?" I ask.

He nods. "They took a few final statements, wanted to clear some things up about George, but they released me for good. I came here as soon as I could." He walks away from me, toward Nathaniel.

The door opens again and Detective Pierce ducks his head in the room.

"Miss Acosta, we're done speaking with Mrs. Morrison. She'd like to see you now. You can go to her room."

"Thank you."

True to his word, Detective Pierce arrived at the house just after I stabbed George. He was quick to take over the situation, and I'm grateful he was there considering I was in no shape to handle much of anything.

He shakes his head. "Seems like I should be thanking you. Mrs. Morrison helped fill in the missing pieces about what happened to Lenora and Carolina. I never thought I'd see justice for Lenora Watson in my lifetime."

"In truth, I did little. It was mostly Carolina."

I turn toward the door to leave the hospital room.

"Nancy Drew?"

I whirl around.

A ghost of a smile plays at Nathaniel's lips. "Thank you for saving my life."

〜

"I SHOULD HAVE said something," Mrs. Morrison says from her hospital bed.

"You knew George was Lenora and Robert's son?"

"Yes, I did."

"How? When did you find out?"

She sighs. "I overheard a conversation one day between Robert and his attorney. Back when he and Anna lived at Marbrisa. I didn't mean to eavesdrop, you understand. I was cleaning, and I'm sure he thought the house was empty."

"Did you tell Anna?"

"I did not. I thought about it. But back then—well, he wasn't the first man I worked for who fathered a child with his mistress. I wasn't sure what she knew. It didn't feel like my place to tell her. Besides, I was newly widowed, and I needed the job. I couldn't afford the possibility of Mr. Barnes firing me. I've regretted that since."

She takes a deep breath. "I knew of Lenora's family. Not well, but by reputation and some acquaintances in common. I kept an eye on the boy because I felt for him. He came to me when his grandmother told him who he really was. I helped him get a job at Marbrisa. I thought I was righting a wrong that had been done to him. I regret that more than you'll ever know."

Anger fills me, anger and so much regret. Would my sister still be alive if things had happened differently?

"How did Carolina figure into all of this?" I ask.

"She became obsessed with Anna. And then when she learned about Lenora, well, she started digging into the past. I never realized she would put it all together. Or that George would kill your sister. I never thought he could be a killer. He was a good boy. When he came home to care for his grandmother we were all so impressed by how much he loved her—"

She swallows. "I guess you never know about people. They have good and bad in them, and it's hard to know which one will win out."

I should be surprised Carolina put everything together, but somehow, I'm not. Carolina always was capable of anything she put her mind to.

"Carolina was smart. People always forgot that. *I* forgot that."

"She was. Your sister was a complicated young woman."

Sometimes I wonder if Carolina's greatest tragedy was being a complicated woman in a time when women are supposed to be anything but.

My heart aches for Carolina, knowing that she never found peace. It seems supremely unfair that her life was so cruelly cut short, that she was made to suffer so much in her final hours.

Tears spill down Mrs. Morrison's cheeks. "When she died, I thought Asher killed her. They were so unhappy in their marriage. It seemed like it was history repeating itself again. But after the police arrested Asher, I saw George messing around with Mr. Wyatt's car. It didn't look right. I confronted him—I asked him what he was doing, and there was this look in his eyes—

"I saw what he was capable of. I saw what he had done."

I know what she means. I saw the same expression in George's face last night—like a mask had slipped.

"Do you believe in spirits?" Mrs. Morrison asks me.

I hesitate. Had she posed this question to me a week ago, I might have given a different answer. Now, I'm not so sure. Belief is a complicated thing. Does it require you to be all in?

Do you have to engage in unwavering certainty? Or is uncertainty enough? Is the absence of knowing akin to belief?

"I might."

"I think there were spirits in that house. Spirits that couldn't be at peace. You've felt them, haven't you?"

Maybe I was wrong all along. Maybe there were spirits haunting Marbrisa. Did I imagine the necklace on my bedspread that night? Was the smell of the sea on the jewels some invention of mine or was it real? Maybe I'll never know for sure. But I do know this—

"I felt Carolina with me last night. When I was defending myself against George, it didn't feel like I was alone. It felt like I had protection. For a moment, it was as though I saw what her final moments were like for her. I think I felt my parents, too."

"I'm sorry. So sorry. I tried to do the right thing last night when I went to your room to tell you my suspicions and fears, but George followed me."

It feels as though she's asking for absolution for the role she played in all of this, but the truth is, it isn't mine to give.

I can only pray that the women who suffered so much at Marbrisa, who lost their lives, have somehow found peace.

"It's a sobering thing to come to the end of your life and realize you dedicated the majority of it to caring for a house, to guarding its secrets, and know that you did more harm than good." Mrs. Morrison takes a deep breath. "That day we spoke in the gazebo, I didn't tell you everything. Not about Lenora and George, and not about Anna and Robert. I was scared that the truth would come out. That what I did back then—what I helped cover up—would come to light."

"What do you mean?"

"I felt for Anna Barnes. As a woman, as a wife. I lied to you when I told you they didn't fight. Well, not entirely. They didn't fight—except for one night. They had a terrible row. She learned the truth—that he had been involved with Lenora. That Lenora's death likely wasn't an accident. She was terrified. Back then, well, the police weren't always inclined to believe a woman, and a man like Robert had all means of escaping justice."

My heart pounds. "What happened?"

Mrs. Morrison leans forward, her voice lowering, her words for me alone.

"I helped her escape. When the police came to me, I corroborated Michael's story about her drowning in the bay, helped make it look like Robert was responsible for his wife's death."

"You mean—"

"Anna Barnes is still alive."

EPILOGUE

Anna

The taxi driver pauses in front of the enormous iron gates.

"Is this the right place?"

There's a bronze plaque on the stone post connected to the gate—I remember all too clearly the day that Robert stood outside and watched as the workers affixed it. He popped a bottle of champagne, offering me some, and even though decades have passed, I still recall the sensation of the bubbles exploding in my mouth as it slid down my throat.

The effervescence of the bubbles mixed with the bitter taste of fear and nerves, my stomach rolling and pitching at the thought of what we were embarking upon. The house was—is—too big, too demanding, like we were Icarus flying just a bit too close to the sun.

I open the car door and climb out, my heels sinking into the familiar swampy muck. Some things never change. I walk toward the gate and stop in front of the sign, tracing the letters there.

Marbrisa

I shiver.

A memory fills me, of the day I met Michael, almost thirty years ago, when he showed me the plans for the house, when I traced over the name he had scrawled there.

It seems fitting that his legacy would be left on the house, that he would be the one to name his creation.

"It's the right place," I call back over my shoulder.

When we received the creamy invitation to commemorate the hospital's opening, my first instinct was to burn the thing, and then throw its ashes in the trash. But I didn't. Instead, it sat on the entry table in our home in Rhode Island for a week, then two, before I broached the subject with Michael.

"We'll walk the rest of the way," I say impulsively, wanting this moment alone with the house, eager to have the privacy of my memories. I glance over to see that Michael has gotten out of the car as well, his gaze like mine affixed on the name of the house that he dedicated the best part of his career to. We each have our own peace to be made.

The taxi driver gives me a dubious look.

"I can manage the distance," I say, my voice wry. "I'm not that old. Sixty-seven isn't dead." In fact, I walk the cliffs at Newport when the weather isn't overly blustery. It's one of my favorite parts of the day. "We'll meet you back here."

We paid the driver the full fare in advance, and I can only hope he'll be waiting for us when we return. I have no desire to be stuck here any longer than necessary.

"Fine with me. They tell stories about this place. Say it's haunted. Some real scary things have happened here. Now the War Department is turning it into a hospital for the soldiers coming back home from serving overseas. Can you imagine?"

It has been over three years since the United States entered the war, since Pearl Harbor was bombed, life as we know it changing so quickly. It's strange to think that the first time I saw this house was at the end of one world war, and now I'm back and we're in the thick of another one.

This time, at least, I wore more sensible shoes.

I can tell the taxi driver is curious about us, wondering why a woman in her sixties and her husband would hire a taxi to bring us out here. From what I gather from the one-sided conversation he engaged in on the way to Marbrisa, the locals mainly stay clear of this place.

Maybe he thinks we're ghost hunters.

"Can't think why the War Department wanted this place," the driver says. "Now, the owner, he was desperate to unload. I suppose it's big enough to be a hospital. They say it has one hundred rooms. Can you imagine?"

"It has sixty-one," Michael replies, the figure coming to him as swiftly as my birthday might.

I squeeze his hand.

I've never asked my husband what it feels like to create something, to pour so much of yourself into a project but never to enjoy it for yourself, never to live in the rooms you designed, but instead to watch as others move in and inhabit the life you drew. I never asked him what it must feel like to see your masterpiece become the source of so much grief. There are some things we simply do not speak of, some silent, mutual agreement to put the past behind us and move forward with our lives when we ran off together.

Except for today.

Michael takes my hand, and we set off toward the main house, neither one of us speaking, the taxi driver's inquisitive gaze burning a hole in our backs.

It's a longer path than I remember, and I almost regret the decision to not have the taxi driver take us to the front as the other guests are doing, cars whizzing past us, but I sense that my husband needed this, that each step is a memory for him, each piece of gravel beneath our feet part of the vision he brought to life.

Michael catches sight of the house a moment before I do, his body stiffening, the hand holding mine going slack.

I stop in my tracks.

The entryway is as grand as ever, the intimidatingly long driveway flanked with palm trees. They've grown in the years since I fled this place, towering even further into the sky than they used to. In an instant, I am transported back to the first time Robert showed me the house, to the men hauling palms around, to Robert's snappy little roadster, the peacocks with their elaborate plumes.

Tears fill my eyes.

I can see it all now, as though I'm watching a movie. I wish I could interrupt the scene and offer some sort of warning, that somehow if we had taken more care with each other, if things had gone differently, perhaps so much destruction wouldn't have been wrought.

I see us hurtling toward an inevitable tragedy.

I glance over at Michael.

He wears an equally stunned expression on his face.

I squeeze his hand. "It's still beautiful."

And it is.

The house looks like a phoenix rising from the ashes, whatever scandals Robert and I laid at its feet, whatever tragedies happened after us not diminishing the work of art Michael created. We were Marbrisa's custodians for a moment, but its legacy will far outlast us.

I hope that in its new iteration, in offering people a chance to heal, there is peace in Marbrisa's future.

We walk toward the house together.

The house is locked up for today's event, no doubt readying itself for necessary remodeling to turn this grand home into a working hospital. Truthfully, I don't think I could bear going inside, anyway. There are too many difficult memories there, too much fear, too much pain.

It feels a bit like visiting my own grave.

The grounds are a far cry from how I remembered them, and I can tell by looking at Michael that it pains him to see the estate in such disarray. The taxi driver told us no one has lived here since the deaths four years ago, and it shows.

We walk around the main house to the back.

The once perfectly manicured lawn is overgrown and patchy in places. I shudder to think what lingers in the grass, fully expecting to see a snake or an alligator slither by. The peacocks seem to have multiplied in our absence, and the estate is overrun with them, their loud cries echoing in the silence.

Vines crawl up the sides of the mansion, bushes growing out of control. The maze that was once flawlessly symmetrical now looks particularly ominous—a cavernous, overgrown space threatening to swallow you whole.

The War Department certainly has a project on its hands.

Perhaps that's the magic of the estate—its ability to shape-shift, to be paradise for some and a source of damnation for others. The night of our party, the night Lenora Watson died, it was the envy of Miami society.

Now it lies in ruin.

I walk to the water's edge and look out at Biscayne Bay, at the spot where Lenora was killed, where everything changed. Michael leaves me be, his focus on the house, and I take a deep breath saying my own goodbyes.

As I turn away from the water, I glance down at the ground. There are two stone markers lying side by side, names etched on each—

Lenora Watson. Carolina Acosta.

"It didn't seem right to put your name out here," a voice says quietly.

I whirl around, my heart pounding.

A young woman stands a few feet away. There's no one else around us, no one watching this tableau. I knew that coming here was risky, knew there was a chance I would be recognized, but when Michael received the invitation with his name on it, I had to come. Who knows how many years I have left? This was a peace I needed to make.

"I'm sorry. I should start over. I should explain." Her lips curve. "My husband says I can be too direct. I'm Carmen

Hayes. Carolina was my sister. I sent Michael Harrison the invitation."

Awareness dawns. When the incident happened four years ago, it made national news. After all, it had all the makings of a good story—secrets, betrayal, wealth, murder. The press loved it. I followed the events, clipping the newspapers, wondering what role Robert and I had to play in all of it, if things could have ended differently if I had known he had fathered a child, if he had never met Lenora Watson, if he'd never pushed her into the bay.

"When my brother-in-law and I decided to offer Marbrisa as a hospital, we thought it needed an event like this," Carmen continues. "A chance to reconcile the past and present before it became something new. I wondered if you would come. I hoped you would. I recognized you from your painting. Would you like to see it?"

Surprise fills me. "Is it in the house?"

She nods.

I hesitate, not sure I'm ready to face the house, not sure I'll ever be.

Carmen must read the fear in my eyes, the hesitation, because she reaches out her hand to me.

"I can go with you if you like," she offers.

I take her hand.

～

I WALK OUT of Marbrisa into the sunlight, tears dried on my cheeks.

Michael is standing near the entrance steps, looking up at the house. I've known and loved this man for nearly three decades, and still, I struggle to read the expression in his gaze. If he's surprised I went inside, he doesn't show it.

"The former owner's sister-in-law wanted to show me the painting," I say. "The one you did of me in the garden. It's hanging in one of the guest rooms."

"Ah."

"It's beautiful." And sad. "She offered it to me, but I couldn't see it fitting into our house in Newport. Into the life we've built together."

"Better for it to stay here," he agrees. "To remain a part of the house's history."

"My thoughts exactly."

When I left Robert that night, I knew that for people to believe I had drowned in the bay, I couldn't take anything with me, couldn't risk anything showing up as missing. And there was also a part of me that wanted the fresh start, not to carry anything over from my old life at Marbrisa to my new one.

"How do you feel?" I ask Michael.

He sighs. "I'm not sure how to put it into words. It's hard not to wonder if these deaths could have been prevented if I'd never built the place." He reaches out, brushing a stray strand of hair from my face. "And at the same time, how can I regret the thing that brought me to you?"

"Are you ready?" I ask him. "I've said my goodbyes."

It's not the truth, not completely, but there are some things that are too difficult to explain.

He nods. "I have, too."

We walk away from the house together, and when we reach the end of the driveway, I turn and glance back at the house, knowing with certainty that I will never see it again in my lifetime.

That first day that we met, Michael spoke of houses as having a life of their own, and it's extraordinary how much of an impact this one has had on mine. It has been both my destruction and my salvation, and now it's time for me to move on.

I close my eyes, the ocean breeze on my face, and I say the goodbye I didn't dare allow myself to voice out loud.

We were happy once. Even now, I can look back and say with certainty that there were moments in my marriage to Robert when I was the happiest I have ever been in all my life, just as I can say with certainty that I am in a far better place now than I ever was as his wife. I don't know exactly when it was that we went wrong or if our end was always fated and we simply played the roles the stars had dealt us, but I feel both deep, unending regret and eternal gratitude for where I am now. It's funny how a body can contain so many emotions, how a house can hold so many memories.

Michael and I walk hand in hand, leaving Marbrisa behind us.

When we reach the entrance to the estate, the grand house no longer in view, I'm gratified to see that the taxi driver did indeed wait for us like he promised.

"Glad y'all survived. You had me worried for a minute. Wouldn't be the first people who disappeared in that house."

Michael puts his arm around me, tucking me against the

curve of his body, and I wonder if he's remembering that night like I am—

The night I disappeared.

"It's a shame," the driver says as we climb back into the car. "People say they used to give some real fancy parties here."

"Just one," I reply softly.

I wait for him to bring up Lenora Watson's death, but he doesn't say anything, merely starts the car, Lenora's life relegated to a footnote in Marbrisa's history given the more recent, salacious events.

We drive on, and with each bit of distance we put between us and the past, it feels as though the tightness that has resided in my chest for so long unspools.

"I'm glad we came," I whisper to Michael.

"Me, too," he replies.

"Where are you all visiting from?" the taxi driver asks.

"Rhode Island. Newport," Michael replies.

"Newport. Now that's a fine city. The wife and I came down here six months ago from New York, and I'll tell you, we're ready to leave. Between the bugs and the humidity, the lizards and the alligators, the hurricanes, the people—I can't for the life of me understand why anyone would want to live in Florida."

I can't help but laugh. "You'd be surprised. Strangely, it grows on you."

There's potential in Miami, a dream that everyone chases. Not necessarily what it *is*, but what it could be. And I suppose for some—many—that dream is worth a thousand alligators and lizards the size of dinosaurs.

Michael reaches out and threads his fingers through mine so that our linked hands rest on the leather seat between us. I close my eyes, the breeze off Biscayne Bay wafting in through the open car windows, the warmth of the sun heating our skin.

On a day like this, it's easy to see how you could mistake Miami for paradise. On a day like this, it's easy to see how anything can be possible here.

The taxi hurtles down Cutler Road, carrying us north, and I stare out the window at the thick canopy of trees that frames our drive, their intricate trunks forming their own unique history of all that has happened and all that is to come.

The driver slams on the brakes, a curse exploding from his lips.

An alligator slithers by.

AUTHOR'S NOTE

While Marbrisa is a fictional home, as are the characters in the novel, in writing *The House on Biscayne Bay*, I was inspired by Florida's natural landscape and animals, and by many of the grand homes—some of which are mentioned in the novel—that were built in South Florida during the twentieth century. I wanted to convey the spirit of the art and architecture that graced these estates as well as the promise of Miami that drew so many down south. If you've read *The Last Train to Key West*, you probably recognized the infamous railroad Anna references in the novel. The Florida East Coast Railway that plays such a pivotal role in that story also plays an important role in this one—ferrying Anna and her husband down to Miami.

The beginning of the twentieth century was a time of expansion in South Florida's history, culminating in the land boom of the 1920s. The bubble later burst under a myriad of factors including the impact of the 1926 Miami Hurricane. The Great Depression took its toll on South Florida, and on my fictional home of Marbrisa and its denizens. When we "meet" the house again in the later timeline, we see it through Carolina Acosta's eyes in 1941 as much of the world is at war, the U.S. on the precipice of entering the conflict.

Given the tragic events that occur in the novel at Marbrisa, I thought it fitting for the house to have a future that offered healing, and here I found inspiration in a piece of South Florida history—the fact that the famous Biltmore Hotel in Coral Gables was converted to a military hospital during World War II. Giving Marbrisa such a legacy felt appropriate considering the events of the times and provided a hopeful future for the estate and its remaining residents—the infamous peacocks and enormous lizards who are very much a staple of past and present Miami life.

ACKNOWLEDGMENTS

The book community is such a welcoming and passionate group to be part of, and I am so grateful to the wonderful readers who have supported my books throughout the years. Thank you for reading my novels and for your enthusiasm for the characters and stories. It means the world to me. Thank you to all the librarians and booksellers whose advocacy and dedication bring the love of books to so many. To my wonderful writing colleagues—thank you for your friendship and support.

To my agent Kevan Lyon and editor Kate Seaver—thank you so much for your encouragement, wisdom, and guidance. I'm so grateful to both of you for championing my work. Thank you to the team at Penguin Random House and Berkley: Tara O'Connor, Stephanie Felty, Jessica Mangicaro, and Hillary Tacuri, for working so hard to launch my books. Thank you to Madeline McIntosh, Allison Dobson, Ivan Held, Christine

Ball, Claire Zion, Jeanne-Marie Hudson, Craig Burke, Erin Galloway, Tawanna Sullivan, Amanda Maurer, the sales department, subrights department, and art department for bringing my books to life and into readers' hands.

Thank you to my family and friends. I love you dearly.

THE HOUSE ON

BISCAYNE
BAY

CHANEL CLEETON

READERS GUIDE

QUESTIONS FOR DISCUSSION

1. *The House on Biscayne Bay* alternates between Anna's life in 1918 and Carmen's life in 1941. Which heroine did you identify with more—Anna or Carmen? What characteristics in their personalities did you relate to? What differences? How do they grow and change throughout the novel?

2. The novel focuses on Anna's marriage to her husband, Robert. The reader sees both the joy and heartbreak in their relationship. How does their marriage evolve throughout the story? What do you think about the decisions they made? How do Anna's views on her marriage change throughout the book?

3. Both Carolina and Anna are heavily influenced by their marriages. What parallels do you see between their experiences? What differences?

4. Carmen and her sister, Carolina, have a fraught relationship. Which sister did you identify with more? How did

their past family dynamics influence their present interactions? Did you relate to their struggles?

5. When Anna first arrives at Marbrisa, she's a fish out of
water in an unfamiliar setting. Can you relate to her
experience? If you experienced something similar, how
did it affect you?

6. The book begins with Anna's sentiment, "I cannot for
the life of me imagine why anyone would want to live in
Florida." Have you been to Florida before or have you
lived there? What are your impressions of the state?

7. The construction of Marbrisa harkens back to a time
when grand houses were being built in Florida. Have
you ever toured such estates? What did you think of
them? How did you envision the lives of people who
lived there?

8. Marbrisa's architect, Michael Harrison, states: "I like to
think of the houses I build as having their own personalities." Do you agree with him? Why or why not? How
do you think Marbrisa's personality shines through in
the novel?

9. How does the novel's setting influence the book? What
examples of this do you see?

10. *The House on Biscayne Bay* features many of the hallmarks of a Gothic novel. What are some of your favorite
Gothic novels? What do you enjoy about the genre?

11. Some of the characters suggest that Marbrisa might be
haunted. Do you believe in ghosts? Have you had any
experiences that influenced your belief?

Photo by Chris Malpass

Chanel Cleeton is the *New York Times* and *USA Today* bestselling author of *The Cuban Heiress, Our Last Days in Barcelona, The Most Beautiful Girl in Cuba, The Last Train to Key West, When We Left Cuba,* and Reese's Book Club pick *Next Year in Havana.* Originally from Florida, she grew up on stories of her family's exodus from Cuba following the events of the Cuban Revolution. Her passion for politics and history continued during her years spent studying in England, where she earned a bachelor's degree in international relations from Richmond, the American International University in London, and a master's degree in global politics from the London School of Economics and Political Science. Cleeton also received her Juris Doctor from the University of South Carolina School of Law.

LEARN MORE ABOUT THIS BOOK
AND OTHER TITLES FROM
NEW YORK TIMES
BESTSELLING AUTHOR

CHANEL CLEETON

SCAN ME
or visit
prh.com/chanelcleeton